MW01670503

NOBODY'S BUSINESS

The Butterfly Memoirs

Book Four

By

M.J. KANE

5Prince Publishing
Denver, CO

This is a fictional work. The names, characters, incidents, places, and locations are solely the concepts and products of the author's imagination or are used to create a fictitious story and should not be construed as real.

5 PRINCE PUBLISHING AND BOOKS, LLC
PO Box 16507
Denver, CO 80216
www.5PrinceBooks.com

ISBN 978-1-63112-120-3

Nobody's Business
M. J. Kane

Published by 5 Prince Publishing

Front Cover Viola Estrella
Author Photo: Jada Caine

First Edition/First Printing July 2015 Printed U.S.A.

5 PRINCE PUBLISHING AND BOOKS, LLC.

Acknowledgements:

As always, thank you to my wonderful family who continue to support me even when I get on their nerves! You know who you are! LOVE YOU!!!

To the librarians of the Clayton County Library System…when I began my journey as an author, you all were there to point in the 'write' direction to find the books that taught me how to write. Many of you have shown great support in purchasing my stories, asking questions, and sharing them with one another. There's no better reader to have in your corner than a librarian! Because of you, the library became a scene in this story, inspired by the wonderful enthusiasm and love for reading and sharing that love with the community. Thank you for welcoming me into the fold!

Dedications:

In loving memory of my father, Chief Warren Kelly, Spaulding County Fire Department, 1983-1985.

In appreciation and memory of the fallen men and women of the fire departments across the country who have given their lives to save countless numbers of victims they didn't know…thank you!

NOBODY'S BUSINESS

Prologue

"Yo, Tre, what are you doing outside? The party is in there, man." The groom stumbled, caught himself against the doorjamb.

I chuckled. "Shaun, you're drunk."

"So what? It's my party." He raised his beer bottle and gulped the remaining liquid. "Tomorrow, I'll be a married man." He grinned like an idiot.

I tilted my head, raised an eyebrow. "Are you happy about that…or sad? Right now it could be a toss-up."

"Happy!" He grinned, then spied the empty lawn chair beside me, stumbled his way over and plopped down. His butt nearly hit the ground. "Whew!"

I shook my head and watched my fraternity brother as he got comfortable. Shaun's hair was disheveled from the stripper who'd worked her magic in his lap. The frat brothers decided to give him a proper send off by hiring a few girls for the night. Everyone knew his fiancé wouldn't approve, so we went out of our way to keep it a secret. The look on his face when the women showed up an hour into what appeared to be a humble bachelor party was priceless.

Happy…

Seeing this brother's enthusiasm for the arrangement was intriguing.

The idea of marriage was something I avoided. The opportunity had presented itself once, and I gladly declined. The consequences that followed had been…well…the word itself didn't have a positive connotation.

"Shaun, if you're happy, why in the hell are you drunk right now?"

He struggled to sit up and faced me. "Honestly? To keep myself out of trouble. If I'm drunk, I won't be tempted. I can't start my marriage with a guilty conscience." He grinned as if his idea was a no brainer.

I guess in some twisted way, his logic made sense.

He burped, then fell back in the chair and closed his eyes. "So when are you gonna bite the bullet and find Mrs. Campbell?"

I barked out a laugh. "Mrs. Campbell? I have yet to find a woman to fill that position." I tilted my bottle up, and drank deep.

"Can I tell you a secret?"

I glanced at Shaun; his eyes were still closed and his words had begun to slur.

"Sure."

He turned his head in my direction and forced his eyes open. "She's not going to be perfect," he said in a drunken whisper. "If that's what you're waiting for, you'll be alone for life. You gotta remember…you're not perfect either. Accept her faults like you want her to accept yours." He winked and then closed his eyes. Seconds later, he was snoring.

Perfection.

That wasn't new. I knew from the get go that no woman would be perfect. God knows I had my own faults.

The real question was what was I looking for? Would I know when I found her?

My chest tightened at the memory I fought to ignore the memory of the exotic beauty of the woman who stole my heart the moment our eyes had connected.

We spent one night together, and then she was gone.

When our paths crossed again, she broke my heart.

Not only had she lied about her name, she forgot to mention a small detail about her life.

She was engaged.

To make matters worse, she was engaged to my best friend's brother.

Chapter 1

If my heart beat any faster, it would fly out of my chest.

Sweat poured over my brow, down my chest and back.

My arms trembled, my body seized in what had to be the best orgasm a man could ever have.

I collapsed, fighting to catch my breath, and inhaled the sweetest scent. Sultry, seductive, exotic. Just like the woman who lay beneath me.

Unable to hold myself up, I rolled off her to the other side of my king sized bed. My legs hung off. I looked around and realized we had used every inch of the mattress. Sheets and covers lay on the floor, victims of the hot and heavy sex we had had.

I studied the beautiful complexion of the naked woman next to me. Trying to describe the exact color of her skin would take time. It was hard to place, just as her nationality was. I knew for a fact she wasn't black or white. Hispanic? Asian? A fusion of all four?

At this point, I couldn't care less. Whatever she was, it all came down to one thing: Sexy. As. Hell.

"Ready for more?" Her sultry voice drew the blood from my brain, causing it to regroup down below.

"More?" I chuckled. "The question is, are you?"

The woman of my dreams climbed on top of me. I got lost in the deep, dark wells of eyes so brown they were nearly black. Long, midnight hair, hung straight down, nearly covering the swells of the most beautiful breasts I had ever had the pleasure of tasting.

My attention was diverted to her hands as she reached up to pull the long strands behind her neck, the peaks of her breasts stood high and proud as she arched. One hand held her hair in place, while the other traveled slowly down her neck, down the middle of her cleavage, then over to one breast, caressing it. My attention went immediately to her fingers.

"So…you like to watch…" Her smile was seductive.

"Always."

She laughed then proceeded to give me a show.

When I stopped off at the bar for a celebratory drink on my way home, ending the evening like this was not what I expected. One look down the bar at this alluring woman and I was hooked. She didn't make striking up a conversation with her easy, but once I got her to loosen up, we connected on a level I least expected.

A love of reading.

Despite my efforts to learn her name, she refused, suggesting I earn it first. Yet, she had no problem coming home with me. One-night stands were nothing new, but not knowing her name was driving me insane.

I slid my hands up the soft flesh of her thighs, and stopped at her hips. "Now are you going to tell me?"

She tilted her head to the side, bit her lip as if contemplating whether my performance earned me that precious gift.

"Why do you need to know my name?"

"Because this time I want to be able to say it…"

Her sexy slanted eyes lowered before she looked me in the eye. "My name is…Devon."

****

Beep…beep…beep…

I slapped the alarm off and tried my best to ignore the hard on…again.

Eight months later and the chance encounter with the perfect woman had yet to be forgotten. I searched for her, not knowing anything but her first name, which of course made it damn near impossible to do on social networking sites.

Facebook, Twitter, Google +, LinkedIn…

Inputting her first name and searching the list of pictures yielded no results.

For the life of me, I couldn't understand what captivated me. It had been just sex.

Hot, heavy, mind-blowing….sex.

A one-night stand shouldn't leave me feeling desperate.

And then I found her the moment I stopped looking. To make matters worse, the perfect image I'd built up in my mind proved to be a lie. Her name wasn't real. Her profession wasn't real. Yet deep in my heart I knew the connection we'd made that night had been real.

Not that it mattered. She was spoken for and my future now lay elsewhere. The decisions of my past now dictated my future. And my future expected me to arrive in two hours and go to a birthday party.

I pulled myself out of bed and headed for the shower.

****

"You did *what*?"

"I sold my condo."

"Why? I thought you loved that place!" Trina walked over to the side of the living room where our two-year-old-son, Justin, played with the plastic Tonka truck I gave him. "Come on, time for lunch." She removed the toy from his fingers, swooped him up, and headed for the kitchen.

I watched the mother of my child get him settled in the high chair. "I did. It served its use, but it's time to move on."

Though he didn't make a sound, Justin's bottom lip poked out, making it obvious he didn't like the fact his new toy had been taken from him. I picked it up, joined them in the kitchen, and set it just out of his reach on the kitchen table.

"My!" He struggled to get out of the high chair restraints.

"No, play time is over. You can have it back after you eat." Trina shot me look of disapproval. "Tre, you can't do stuff like that. He knows he can't have toys at the table when it's time to eat."

"Come on, it's not like he's playing with it."

Justin whined and kicked the high chair in protest.

"That's beside the point." She turned to him, "Stop, you know what mommy says, no toys at lunch time."

"Miiieeee…," he whined again, this time he looked at me as if his mother hadn't spoken a word.

"Listen to mommy," I said, and then I moved the truck to the seat of the empty chair beside me. That only made matters worse.

"Stop it, Justin!" Trina smacked his leg when he kicked again. Justin went from whining to full blown crying.

"Trina, you didn't have to do that." I reached over to console my son.

"Yes, I did." She shook her head in disapproval. "Look, Tre, you can't come over here and try and change the way I discipline my son. He has to learn the rules and he can't learn by sweet talking him all the time. He was fine when I took the toy from him because he knows the rules. You screwed that up by bringing it in here. Now I'm the bad guy!" She spun on her heel and went to the counter to make a peanut butter and jelly sandwich.

I wiped the tears from my son's eyes and watered down my irritation. "Look, Justin, see? It's right here. Your truck isn't going anywhere. Eat your food like mommy says and then you can get it back. Right, mommy?" I glanced in Trina's direction.

She rolled her eyes at me. "Right, as soon as you eat."

That seemed to calm him down a bit. I poked him in the tummy while making crazy noises in order to distract him until his sandwich arrived. When it did, he happily accepted it with greedy fingers.

Once he was settled, my attention went back to Trina as she moved around the kitchen and washed the few dishes left in the sink.

Justin was a perfect mix of both of us. While he was a spitting image of me when I was his age, he still had features like his mother, caramel colored skin and eyes a shade lighter than my dark brown ones.

My attention went back to her. Trina and I met when we both attended Georgia Tech. We were both Business Majors, though I was there on a basketball scholarship. My dream had been to play pro basketball; hers had been to get a good job working in corporate America.

A basketball injury forced me to make use of my degree.

She, on the other hand, was sidetracked and postponed her career after graduation due to motherhood.

That was after we parted ways and she moved out of the apartment we shared.

If I had known that she was pregnant before I facilitated our breakup, life would have been different for both of us. The house I bought would have been done a long time ago.

I would have been around to watch my son grow in her belly.

We would have been married and living a good life.

"You never answered the question. What did you mean by moving on?" Finished washing dishes, Trina dried her hands on a towel then settled in a chair across from me, curiosity on her face.

I glanced at my son for a moment and then faced her. "Moving on to us."

Her eyebrows shot up as she sat back. "Us?"

I placed my elbows on the table, giving her my full attention. "Yes, us. I want you and Justin to move in with me." Trina's head dropped an inch; she stared at me as if I had sprouted some abnormality on my forehead. "I don't want it to be a live-in situation. I think we should get back together."

The laughter that exploded from her side of the table was a slap in the face. Her hand went to her mouth, but it was too late for her to hide the fact she thought my suggestion was absurd.

"Trevon." She used my full name, something done only when she was serious. "You and me," she waved a finger between us. "That ship sailed years ago. The only reason you and I are dealing with each other now is because of this little man right here." She reached over to wipe a spot of fallen jelly from his crisp blue shirt.

"If you had told me from the get go you were pregnant instead of hiding it from me, things would be different."

Exactly how different, I had no idea. But at least I would have known about my son's existence and been there. Instead, she kept him a secret, not bothering to tell me she was pregnant when we broke up.

Then one day she showed up at the restaurant I managed.

It had been my off day, but a phone call from the manager on duty stating that a customer demanded to speak to me by name, forced me to drop what I was doing and come in to handle what I thought was a volatile situation. Thinking it was a customer about to complain about bad service, I prepared to use my good looks and charm to win them over.

Instead, I got a bomb dropped in my lap.

My ex-girlfriend, whom I hadn't seen, nor spoken to in two years, flashed a picture of a little boy and said he was mine.

The revelation came because Justin was diagnosed with sickle cell anemia and needed a bone marrow transplant. Neither of us was eligible to be donors because we both carried the trait. There was risk involved in the procedure. Knowing this, Trina decided I needed the chance to know my son…just in case.

After recovering from the shock of having a child and the severity of his illness, getting to know him took precedence in my life. Thankfully, he pulled through the procedure. That was eight months ago and he was nearing his third birthday.

Nothing could get back the two years Trina took from me. I didn't doubt for a moment that if he hadn't gotten ill, she would have continued on with the secret. But I owed it to her, and especially my son, to correct the situation and give them what they both deserved, a chance to put our family back together again.

"Different how? You would have decided to take our relationship seriously and stop chasing other women?" A thin eyebrow lifted.

That was a definite slap in the face. One I deserved.

"Hmm, speechless. That's what I thought." She stood from the table, retrieved a sippy cup from the cabinet, and poured Justin a cup of milk.

I had been unfaithful during the last months of our relationship.

In the end, so had she. When it was obvious her attempt to retaliate didn't inspire me to work things out, she packed up and left.

"I wasn't the only one who messed up, Trina, so don't pin it all on me."

"Oh, I beg to differ. My actions were a direct result of yours. The only problem was you couldn't handle it. I was supposed to be the faithful woman sitting around while you did what you wanted. I can't believe you expected me to take it sitting down." She stopped, held up a hand, closed her eyes for a moment, and took a deep breath. "But you know what, that's neither here nor there. What's in the past is just that. The only thing I need or want from you is help raising our son. So, if selling your condo to buy a house is what you expected would make me want to come back," she smirked, "you screwed up."

I sat back in my chair and held my tongue. When Trina got all worked up, there was no way to make a point. But that was fine. I let her believe what she needed to believe. Telling her my true reasons for cheating on her would only make the situation worse. The past was just that, the past. I knew from the beginning that convincing her that getting back together would be what was best for the sake of our son would take time.

That I had a lot of.

After all, I wasn't interested in any other women right now.

Well, except for the one who broke my heart before knowing it belonged to her.

Chapter 2

"Kai, girl, you need to dress it up if you want to get his attention."

"It's a children's birthday party, Ricky. I can't be overdressed; it'll make me look desperate."

My cousin rolled his eyes, grabbed a makeup kit from his duffel bag, and directed me to sit on the corner of my bed. "Girlfriend, you ex-fiancé is the baby's uncle. You left him a year ago and you're still single. By all accounts, you are desperate. He don't need to know that." He sucked his teeth. "So like I said, you need to sex it up so the bastard knows what he's missing."

It was my turn to roll my eyes at my drag queen cousin. I hated when he was right. I did need to throw it in Malik's face. He gave up a good thing.

Cheating bastard.

I plopped down in a chair and faced Ricky. "Fine, but let's set the record straight. It's been less than a year since I broke up with him, and I am by no means desperate."

Ricky laughed. "You know that, but…" He pulled out a small bottle of liquid makeup, held it against my skin and grimaced before putting it back in his bag. "…in the eyes of that man, showing up alone and looking homely will have 'desperate' written all over it."

I scowled. "Fine, give it to me." He laughed and selected another shade, then smiled. "But," I put my hand on his bicep, stopping him in mid movement. "None of that over the top stuff. I still want to look like myself when you're done."

"Girl, please, that artistic shit is for me alone. I know how to do normal," he punctuated with air quotation marks. "Hell, I can do your makeup better than you can."

I laughed. He was telling the truth.

My profession didn't require me to spend a lot of time in the mirror every morning. As a firefighter, the last thing I had time to worry about was makeup when at work. Twenty-four hour on/forty-eight hour off shifts weren't conducive to precision makeup application and good hair days.

A clean face and my hair in a ponytail was all I needed. Simple and efficient. None of the guys wanted to see me walking around the station reminding them of their girlfriends and wives.

Being the only female at the station was enough to make my job challenging.

Before long, Ricky stepped back to examine his work before making a minor adjustment here and there. He held up a mirror. "Okay, what do you think?"

I angled my head to look at all views. "I think you should be working at the makeup counter at Macy's instead of my mother's floral shop."

He laughed. "Hey, I don't perform magic on just anybody. Besides…pucker your lips, doll." He dotted on lip gloss. "Those rich heifers wouldn't know how to deal with me."

I laughed, then got up from the seat and pulled my hair loose from the rubber band. I ran my fingers through the long locks, settling them on my shoulders. I took another look in the mirror. After hours of being twisted in a top knot on my head, the ends managed to maintain a hint of a curl. Not bad at all.

"Do you know what you're going to say to him?" Ricky closed up the makeup kit he had used and stuffed it back into his bag.

"To who?"

He rolled his eyes. "Malik."

I shook my head. "Cheating Bastard. He doesn't get to go by his birth name anymore."

Ricky chuckled.

"Honestly? I have nothing to say. We were together for too long. If he wanted to end our relationship, he should have manned up and said so. I don't know why he thought I'd be cool with him cheating on me."

Ricky shot me a sideways glance. "Uh, probably because you let it go on for so long?" he supplied.

I sighed. He was right. I did let it go on. And on. And on. For some stupid reason I thought he'd get tired of it all and stay with me.

Nope. Didn't happen.

So what did I do?

Repaid the 'favor' and had a fling of my own. Well, it was more of a one-night-affair. And to be honest, it couldn't be called cheating. After promising to meet me so we could discuss our relationship and work things out, Malik conveniently became 'unavailable' at the last moment. Fed up with his lies, I called everything off. The wedding, that had yet to be planned, and our relationship in general. I didn't want anything else to do with him.

Since I was already dressed up and too angry to sit alone at home and get depressed, I went to a bar to celebrate my decision. While I gave off all kinds of signals that said to any man in the vicinity, 'leave me the hell alone,' one man managed to talk to me. And what did I do? Gave him hell, fussed, cussed, and damn near accused him of being the one who broke my heart.

And he let me.

When my tantrum was over, he bought me a drink and we managed to have a decent conversation. He was tall, had the sexiest shade of dark brown eyes, and a smile that made it impossible not to stare at his mouth.

After a few hours it was obvious we were attracted to one another. So, I took advantage of the situation and decided that a few hours spent in bed with a man I would never see again would be the perfect way to take my mind off my broken heart.

After all, Atlanta was a big town. What were the odds of crossing paths with him again?

Apparently in my world, they were one hundred percent.

Pushing the thought aside, I stood and adjusted my shirt so it sat at my waist. Even though my hair looked nice down, I decided to put it back up in a bun to keep the length from my shoulders. Georgia humidity jacked up my hair. I spent enough time keeping the loose spiraled locks tangle free, much less bone straight. I wish my hair was like my mother's.

Satisfied with my appearance, I walked across my bedroom to get a pair of sandals.

"Hold up. Tell me you are *not* wearing that outfit." Ricky looked at me, disapproval all over his face.

I looked down at my attire. A tie-dyed tank top stopped just above the top of my ripped jeans, which hugged every curve of my body. Contrary to what Ricky thought, while my fingernails weren't painted, my toes did sport a hint of color and would look nice in my open-toed sandals.

"What's wrong with what I have on?"

His eyebrows shot up. "You look like somebody's momma."

"It's a birthday party for a one-year-old. I look like an aunt whose about to go have fun at my nephew's party."

A hand went to his hip. "Do you have a kid?"

I glared. "No."

"So don't waste my talent with makeup for a mommy-and-me get up." Ricky went to my closet and sifted through my wardrobe. "Here. Strip and put this on while I find some shoes. I know you've got some sex-me shoes in this closet somewhere." Items of various kinds were tossed out of my closet and onto the floor as he went on the hunt.

I picked up the baby blue skinny jeans and the black halter top. "You've got to be kidding me."

His reply was muffled before he pulled his head out of the closet. "Heffa, put it on."

Fighting with him when he was on a mission was pointless.

My clothes changed, I turned around to see him dangling a pair of black open toed heels.

"Don't argue," he said the moment my mouth opened.

I pursed my lips. "Fine."

"And sweetie, that hair is coming back down."

****

There was a difference between being fashionably late and ghetto late. A glance at my watch showed I'd crossed both of those lines.

I climbed out of my car and adjusted my top, making sure my breasts weren't about to show up to the party before the rest of me did. This was ridiculous. I decided on the drive over that my excuse of being overdressed would be because of plans to go out on the town after this was over.

Yeah, right.

The chances of Sharice or my sister believing me were slim to none.

From the moment I got out of the car, the screams and yells of happy kids could be heard throughout the neighborhood. It was obvious there were fun and games going on in the backyard. Fun and games was what I was looking forward to. I glanced down at my attire; oh well.

The smell of grilled hot dogs and hamburgers greeted me as I made my way past the line of parked cars. Halfway up the walkway, a flying insect crossed my path; I nearly dropped my gift from the surprise. My attention followed the erratic flight of a butterfly like none I'd seen before. It held my attention as it landed on a bush near the front porch.

I rang the doorbell, but my gaze went back to the butterfly that now sat with folded wings. It was beautiful, unique, and unlike any of the butterflies I saw outside my apartment. Wide black wings were decorated with yellow circles along the tips, while a hint of blue and a dot of orange complimented the color. I pulled my cell phone out of my purse, my movements slow so as not to disturb it, and captured a picture with my phone. The minute the door opened, it got spooked and flew away.

"It's about time." Sharice put a hand on her hip while scanning my outfit. "Uh, girls' night out is next weekend. Tonight is about the kids…Auntie Kai."

"What? I've got plans when this is over. It didn't make sense to drive all the way back home and change." I looked around for the gift table and then sashayed over to put my present with the others.

Her laugh was sarcastic. "You must have forgotten who you're talking to. You dressed like that to make Malik jealous." The door shut behind me.

I shot her a flirty look over my shoulder. "What if I did?"

Sharice whistled. "Then that get up will definitely do the trick."

I followed her to the kitchen, cringing at the clacking noise of my heels as I made my way across the hardwood floor. I attempted to walk on my tiptoes, but the stacked height of the heels I lovingly referred to as stripper shoes, made it impossible. The first chance I got, I was taking them off and going barefoot.

A table filled with cookies, cupcakes, and candy, along with various other finger foods, sat next to the centerpiece of the celebration; a Mickey Mouse themed birthday cake.

"Oh, that is adorable!" I went over for closer examination. The trademarked black ears stood up on the top, while the famous red shorts with yellow buttons decorated the bottom layer.

"Junior loves him some Mickey." Sharice studied the table with pride.

I strutted to the sliding glass door off the kitchen and searched the backyard. "Where is the birthday boy?"

"Somewhere out there with the rest of the kids. Andre bought a wading pool for the occasion. They are having a field day out there."

"So I hear. Is my sister out there? I haven't seen my niece in a few weeks. She said she would be here early, but I didn't see her car outside."

A funny look came over Sharice's face. "Yeah, they're here. Alonso dropped them off though."

My eyebrows creased. "He didn't stay? This is a family event."

"You know that and I know that, hell, Kelli knows that. But apparently, he's got a deadline or something at work and could only hang around for a few minutes." She shot me a sideways glance.

"What kind of work needs to be done on a Saturday? He's an architect for crying out loud."

Sharice shrugged. "Your guess is as good as mine."

Shrieks from the backyard drew my attention. Kids were everywhere, along with their parents. Water was flung back and forth by all parties as kids ran around trying their best to shoot miniature water guns at their parents, mainly their dads, who had Super Soakers. The activity was perfect for this time of the year. The heat and humidity would normally run people indoors, but add a bit of water and you had the perfect excuse to be outside. Talk about unfair.

I smiled at the sight, and again regretted listening to Ricky's advice of wearing skintight jeans and heels. Roughhousing was my element.

And then I saw Malik.

All six-foot-two of sexy. He was soaked from head to toe, his thick, light brown curly hair glistening as if he'd just gotten out of a pool. His white t-shirt clung to his chest, highlighting every ounce of chiseled muscle. He chased his nephew around for a moment, but stopped to wipe water out of his eye. And wouldn't you know, he glanced toward the patio door, saw me looking at him, then smiled that halfcocked smile I used to love.

And here I stood, dressed to kill and ogling his sexy frame.

Damn.

"He's been here for a while." Sharice peered over my shoulder. "Can't say I blame you for the late arrival. I wouldn't be in a hurry to see my ex either."

I kept my groan internal, then turned and walked back into the kitchen. Times like this made me wish Sharice had someone else as a brother-in-law. No matter how much I tried, I would never be able to avoid him. Serves me right for dating someone in my close circle of friends and family.

"Is there something I can do to help out? I'm not in a rush to go outside." I looked down and realized my hands were shaking. I don't know why. It wasn't like Malik Lafitte was God's gift to women.

If he was, it was a cruel joke on us all.

"Sure. You can put ice in the cups. They'll be wrapping up soon, and then coming inside to eat." Her hand went to my shoulder. "Take your time. I'll let Kelli know you're here."

I nodded my thanks and went to work. The plastic cups sat in a row on a tray. I scooped ice with an empty one and tried my best to focus on the work and not the man outside the door.

It wasn't long after Sharice left that I heard the sliding glass door open and prayed it wasn't Malik coming inside.

"Where's the bag?"

I knew that voice. Though it was only one night, the smooth and sexy cadence had been burned into my memory. My body tingled as I bit my lip and forced myself to look over my shoulder. Damn, he still looked good.

"Trevon?" Somehow, I managed to be the one to speak first. I cursed on the inside.

A pair of eyes so brown that they drew me in every time I saw him turned in my direction.

"Kai?" His gaze ran over me before meeting mine again. "Hi…you look…um…good."

Unable to look away, I swallowed hard. "Thanks. You, too."

That was an understatement. Like Malik, Trevon was soaked from head to toe as well. The only difference was his sexy body brought on memories of our time spent in bed.

Back before we realized we ran in the same circles. It seemed I was a magnet for disastrous relationships.

He glanced down at his attire and chuckled. "Uh, thanks."

Despite of our past encounters, I decided this time I would be the bigger person. I plastered on a smile and ignored the memory of his fingertips sliding over my bare shoulders.

"Let me guess, Junior did that."

Laughter left his face, his attention going back to the door leading to the festivities. "No, it was my—"

"Tre?" A new voice entered the kitchen, and with it, a woman wearing a bathing suit and shorts. She carried an adorable little boy on her hip. She wiped water from his face. "Where is your daddy?"

It was a struggle to close my mouth.

The little boy was a spitting image of his father.

I looked back at Trevon, who now looked away as if he'd been caught in a lie.

"Tre, where's the bag? Justin is getting cold."

"Right, the bag. I think we left it in the car. I'll be right back." He disappeared down the hall, leaving me and the unnamed woman alone in the kitchen.

She sat her son on the empty space of the counter and ran her hands over his shoulders. "It's okay. Mommy is going to get you warm as soon as daddy gets a towel."

Daddy.

Trevon had a son *and* a wife?

I swallowed my disappointment and went back to putting ice in cups.

'I don't lie'...his words echoed in my mind from the conversation we had the night we met. The night we slept together and played his five-question game.

'Do you have kids?'

His response, 'No, but I want some.'

Our encounter had been less than a year ago. Judging by the age of the little boy, he'd been lying.

After all that crap he talked that night, he managed to prove my point. The existence of any good man was a fantasy.

Wasn't that exactly what my night in Trevon's bed had been? A fantasy? The 'idea' of a man who listened, talked, and treated me like his queen? A man who made love like...

What we'd done sure as hell wasn't love because we'd only met hours before. Yet, he treated me as a precious object.

A woman to be cherished.

And all the while, he had a wife and child.

Damn him!

"Here, Trina."

Unable to resist, I looked up from my task and watched as the little cutie reached for him. Trevon laughed and took his wet son, who wrapped his arms around his neck, and kissed him.

"Hey, little man. Thanks, I love you, too." He kissed him back and tickled his tummy. "Alright, time to go with mommy so you can get on some dry clothes, okay?" Trevon handed his son to his mother and pointed down the hall towards the bathroom. He watched them leave. The minute the door clicked closed, he said, "It's not what you think." The playful tone he had with his son was gone.

I shrugged, trying to keep my irritation hidden. "Does it matter what I think?"

Trevon's eyes shot to the bathroom door, then around the kitchen as if looking to see if there were any other people in earshot. "Keep your voice down!"

"Like I want anyone to know I slept with you!" I hissed, all self-control gone. "It's not my fault our paths crossed that night." I slammed a cup on the counter; little ice chips slid off the surface before sliding to the floor. I used the excuse to squat down and away from his eyes.

It didn't keep him from walking around the counter.

"A fact I still don't understand, but it doesn't change the fact that I owe you—"

"Nothing!" I shot up and threw the fallen ice into the sink before going back to the cups. Why the hell did the fact that he lied to me piss me off so much?

"Kai—"

"Well, well…look who's here. How you doin', love?"

I cringed at the sound of Malik's voice then forced myself to look him in the eye. "Malik."

"Damn, you're as sexy as ever." He made no attempt to hide the fact that he was looking me over. "I remember that outfit. Hell, I remember taking it off, too." He licked his lips.

In the corner of my eye, I saw Trevon's hand ball into a fist.

Malik's attention diverted as if realizing we weren't the only two people in the room. "Yo, player, what up?"

"Nothin' much, man." He no longer looked at me, nor did he look in Malik's direction.

"That's a cute kid you got there. I'm surprised you kept him a secret. And his momma…" Malik whistled. "She's a ten, no doubt."

Trevon's jaw clinched. "Malik…"

His hands went up. "No offense, bruh, but as fine as she is, I don't want to go anywhere you've been, dog."

I shut my eyes and turned away. Even though he knew nothing about my night with Trevon, why did his comment make me feel like crap?

Enough was enough. I couldn't stand being in the presence of either man. I found a tray, layered it with cups, and headed for the back door, leaving the men from my past behind.

The minute I got away from here, I was going to go out for a drink.

Chapter 3

"Tre, Justin said I love you and good night."

"Tell him I said good night and give him a big kiss from daddy. I'll talk to you tomorrow, Trina." I disconnected the call then slipped the phone into my pocket as the Applebee's hostess looked my way.

"Sir, how many are in your party?"

"Just me."

"Would you like a seat at the bar?"

"No thanks. A booth in the back will be fine."

A brief look of annoyance crossed her face. She probably had plans to split tips with the bartender tonight.

Can't say I blamed her; hostesses were barely paid more than the wait staff who made a majority of their money in tips.

I followed her to the rear of the restaurant, taking in the scenery along the way. While the aroma of great food permeated the air, the place was empty for a Saturday night. The location where I worked was always packed. People sat around the hostess area and at times, stood outside along the walkway until their number was called and they were seated. But here…there had to be at least twenty spots that were empty. This wasn't good at all.

Once seated, I accepted the menu, read her nametag, and thanked her.

"Someone will be here to take your order shortly." And with that, she turned and walked away.

"Judith," I murmured, then pulled my iPad from beneath my arm. I selected the note app, typed it in, and made comments about her customer service.

Tonight's undercover assignment, per the Applebee's Regional Manager, was to test the staff at store number #652. The customer feedback about this location had not been stellar. Apparently, the manager of this location did not take his job seriously. I'd been assigned by the corporate office to come in as a customer, evaluate the situation, and then submit my recommendation on how to fix it.

I hadn't been looking forward to the covert activity, but after today's run in with Kai and Malik at the birthday party, I needed the distraction.

A time check showed five minutes had passed and my server had yet to make an appearance. It wasn't like she was tied up with a ton of patrons in her section. The only occupied tables were mine and two others. She hadn't been over to check on them either.

I studied the menu to see what dish I hadn't eaten before. I ate at the location I managed nearly five days a week. I had my favorite dishes, but with a new seasonal menu available, there were different meals to sample.

While I'd had my fill of birthday cake, ice cream, and hamburgers at the party, it didn't last that long. I was hungry.

Not to mention, I really wanted a beer.

"Hi, sir, can I take you order?"

I glanced at my watch. Eight minutes.

I smiled after reading her nametag. "Andrea, I have a ravenous appetite. What do you suggest?"

In a blink of an eye, her stance changed as she jutted a hip to the side at a suggestive angle. As it was, her blouse was already unbuttoned too far, exposing the swell of her cleavage. An obvious attempt to garner more in the tip department. "What do you have a taste for?"

"Something thick and juicy." I placed my menu on the table and sat back.

Her eyes lowered before she made a show of leaning down to point out the rib eye steak I had already decided on.

And what do you know; I got an eyeful of Andrea.

I hid my disappointment. That trick may work at Hooters, but this was a family establishment. Maneuvers like this could offend a customer, or even worse, infuriate a woman if she were on a date.

"Can I get you anything else?" This time her tone was beyond suggestive.

"Bud Ice, please. Thanks." I folded the menu and gave it back to her. Her disappointment was obvious.

I made notes about our encounter the minute she left. When done, my attention went to the restaurants décor. The location still had the layout of the older floor plans. The lighting was dim, seats worn, and decorations meant to be conversation pieces were dated. At the bar, older versions of flat screens three sizes smaller than what could be found in most restaurants hung above the liquor display shelf.

How had this location missed the renovations? My boss would not be pleased.

I was in the middle of making notes when a flash of baby blue caught my attention.

I looked up, sat back in the booth, and shook my head. "You've got to be kidding me."

Kai had entered the restaurant. I watched as she looked around the place while being escorted to the bar by the hostess. She was alone.

Talk about déjà vu. I watched as she slid onto a barstool. Unlike the last time we'd met, she wasn't dressed up as if going on a date, but she still looked good. I wondered why she was here. Was she waiting for someone? Maybe that was the reason why she'd come dressed to attract the opposite sex at a one-year-old's birthday party. She had other plans.

Plans that were none of my business.

I forced myself to stop watching her and focused on the work at hand. Where was I? Okay, the floors. They were outdated just like the wallpaper. The lighting needed to be revamped as well. I looked around. The wait staff uniforms were also behind. And as far as electronics…my attention went to the bar, but instead of guessing the age of the TV monitors, my eyes settled on Kai. She was still alone.

"Here's your beer, sir. Can I get you anything else?"

The flirty waitress stepped in the way, blocked my line of sight to Kai, and flashed another smile. And what do you know, she'd undone another button.

Annoyed, I looked past her to the bar. Kai nursed her drink and looked down at empty hands. She held no phone, so checking in on social networking or messaging someone wasn't what she was here for. She had something on her mind.

I'm pretty sure I had a clue what it was.

"You know what, yeah. I think I'd rather eat at the bar. Looks like there's a good game on."

Andrea's eyes narrowed. Her whole flirt for a fat tip routine went out the window.

"Here." I dug in my pocket for a few bucks. No need to leave her hanging.

"Thanks." Her smile brightened a bit. "You can go grab a seat. I'll make sure your dinner finds you at the bar."

My iPad and beer in hand, I headed for what was sure to be an unwelcome intrusion.

I must be crazy. Kai's attention was still on her hands so she didn't see me when I placed my drink and iPad on the bar beside her.

"Mind if I sit here?"

Kai looked up, her eyes narrowing. "You've got to be kidding. Did you follow me here?"

"No. I was here first, sitting in a booth in the back. Are you following me?"

She rolled her eyes then flagged the bartender to get his attention. "Can I get an extra shot, please?"

"Sure thing, Miss." He grabbed a fresh shot glass from beneath the bar, filled it with clear alcohol, vodka, no doubt, and slid it her way.

She dumped it into her drink, stirred with her finger then threw it back, emptying the glass. "Can I get another one, please? This time with two shots? Thanks."

My eyebrows rose. "Bad night?"

She shot me a look of irritation. "Trevon, what do you want?"

"To clear the air between us." I settled in on the barstool next to her. The look in her eye made me wonder if placing an empty seat between us would have been wiser.

She turned those fiery dark brown eyes on me. "Ha! Why? I told you already, you don't owe me anything, just like I don't owe you, either. It was a one-night fling. Period. We both lied about something. We're adults. Move on." Her attention went to the TV, tuning me out as if I didn't exist.

My jaw clenched, grinding my molars. How could she pretend she hadn't felt anything that night? God knows I did. No matter how hard I tried, I couldn't forget about it either.

"I didn't lie to you."

"Thanks," she told the bartender sweetly when he set the fresh drink in front of her. She paid him before turning a hard gaze on me. "You told me you weren't married and had no kids. I just saw you hours ago with a wife and son. I know how to do math, Trevon. That kid was at least two years old. We were together a few months ago. What does that equal? You had a son and lied about it."

"You're wrong." It was her turn to raise an eyebrow. "Trina is not my wife; she's the mother of my son." I raised a finger to stop her as she opened her mouth to speak. "I didn't know about him until after you and I…met. So no, I didn't lie."

She sat back and huffed. "You didn't know you had a son? What kind of father are you?"

"The kind who's living up to his responsibility now that I do know." Disbelief was in her eyes. "Look, Trina didn't tell me she was pregnant when we she left me, okay?" I drank my beer. "It wasn't a good break up."

"Are they ever?" She sipped her drink. "What did you do?"

I shot a glance in her direction before focusing on the television. "Cheated on her."

"Seriously?"

I nodded then took a long draw on my beer.

Kai laughed, paused, then laughed some more.

Irritated, I looked at her. "And this is funny because?"

"Your girlfriend broke up with you because you cheated, yet you want to be pissed at me because you think I lied about Malik." She pointed at me. "Pot. Black. Enough said."

I conceded. "You're right. I was wrong. Honestly, I was pissed more because of who you were engaged to than anything else. Malik?" I scoffed. "I've known him long enough to know that he has a serious issue committing to one woman."

Her laughter stopped abruptly.

I glanced over and saw an expression of pain on her face.

"Sorry…I didn't mean to—"

"No apologies needed. He's an asshole. I had my reasons for staying with him. I honestly thought he would change. I was stupid."

Unsure of what to say to that, I drank; so did she.

"Your ex decided to tell you about your son. Why? She wants to get back together and do the family thing?"

I stared into the nearly empty bottle, swirled it around a bit then finished the contents. "Nope. He was sick…is sick. He has sickle cell anemia. At the time he needed a bone marrow transplant. He was two years old." Beside me, Kai gasped. "There was a chance that he wouldn't survive the procedure. Her conscience got the better of her and she decided to tell me in case he didn't make it."

The revelation still stung, eight months later. Not a day went by that I didn't wonder if I'd have ever known about him if it hadn't been for the illness.

"That's messed up. How is he? He looked well."

"Great, actually. That's the beauty of kids. They're resilient. Don't get me wrong, we still have to keep an eye on him. The transplant is holding, but he still has his good and bad days."

I looked over and noticed Kai studying me, a small smile on her face. "He looks just like you."

"Yeah, he does."

I forced myself not to stare and realized that I was sitting next to the woman I dreamt about last night. A woman who was unattainable because neither one of us were in the same place we were when we met. Yet for me, our encounter meant something.

Apparently that night meant nothing to her.

I forced myself to focus on that fact and let it be. I had a plan that dealt with providing the right kind of environment for my son to grow up in. Convincing Trina to give me a second chance was more important than the surge of hormones I felt from being in the presence of Kai. My goal in coming over to the bar was to break the tension between us. Our initial run-in at Andre's house months ago didn't give either of us much time to explain ourselves.

Now that we had cleared the air, maybe we could be friends, or at the very least, be in the same room without being pissed.

"Are you guys getting back together?"

I took a moment to process the question. "I don't know."

She sat back in her seat. "You don't know?"

"I want what's best for Justin. If she'll have me then—"

"You'll do what's right for his sake."

"Yes."

And because I still love Trina.

Why did it suddenly feel as if I were repeating a mantra?

Kai cocked her head in my direction. "Good luck with that, seriously. Real love is hard to come by. If you've got someone worth having in your life, do what you can to right the wrongs and move on. We're only on this merry-go-round once. Make it count."

She stared into her drink, toying with the pink umbrella. She seemed sad. Then I remembered the brief encounter in the kitchen with Malik.

The arrogant son of a bitch.

He'd strolled into the kitchen and treated her as if she were nothing. As if they hadn't had a relationship. To make matters worse, he decided commenting about Trina in her face would be the cherry on top. Why the hell she'd been with him in the first place was something I'd never understand.

"When did you break up with Malik? When we crossed paths a few months ago, it seemed you were together."

"Shortly after we ran into each other at Andre's house."

That had been a memorable encounter for sure.

One minute I was joking with my good friend, Andre; the next, the woman I'd been lusting for appeared out of nowhere sporting an engagement ring on her hand and a completely different name. The woman I had slept with lied about her real name and her profession. How the two of us managed not to let on that we knew each other in front of Malik, much less slept together, was a miracle. The only person who'd figured it out was his brother, Andre. Determined not to get in the middle of any drama, he kept the bit of info to himself.

Her attention diverted, I allowed myself to take one last long sideways look at Kai. Those low cut hip hugging jeans and bare shoulders brought back memories of having her tight body beneath me in bed.

I cleared my vocal cords and forced my attention to anywhere else but her body. "What made you decide to break up with him?"

A long pause forced me to look her way. The intensity of her gaze made my heart stop. "I met someone who made me realize I was worth more than the way Malik made me feel."

Well…

Damn.

Chapter 4

"Kai, you're up."

"Mmhmm."

"Kai, the guys are getting restless."

"Okay, okay. Let me finish…" Annoyed, I sped up my reading to get to the end of the page.

Lopez sighed and walked off.

I hated when someone disturbed me during a good part of a book. But, not wanting to deal with the repercussions of serving a late meal to a room full of restless men, I had to do my job. I shut down my Kindle and headed for the kitchen.

Working out of Firehouse 19 was a dream come true in more ways than one. Having a Malone stationed at the firehouse for the past thirty years was part of my family's history. My being the first female firefighter at the station, or even in my family, made it that more special.

Following in the footsteps of my grandfather and uncle had been my dream. My parents, on the other hand, were not happy about it. Neither was my sister. For the longest time, I stood out as being different in my family. I was even taller than most females in my family.

My father was a career postman, my mother a third generation florist. Kelli had chosen to follow in our mother's footsteps, but branched out to focus on the interior decorator aspect, which went hand in hand with mom's business.

As a teen, I trained at my mother's and grandmother's sides, learning the art of floral design. I was good at it. My mother had dreams of Kelli and me taking over the shop when she retired. So did I.

Until my uncle became a local legend.

Uncle Jeramiah gave his life in an effort to save a family in one of the worst fires in the history of our city. Add the fact that my grandfather was named the first African-American Fire Chief in the state back in the eighties, and well, that sealed the deal for me.

The one thing I was proudest of was not only following in my family's footsteps, it was doing so while creating a legacy of my own. I was the first African-American-Cambodian female firefighter in the state.

Talk about breaking the stereotypical lines of race and gender.

Earning the badge hadn't been easy, though. Gaining the respect of the men at the station was even harder.

After five years, most had gotten over their initial fear and discomfort of having a woman on the team because I carried my own. There were still a few who wouldn't hide their distrust, mainly because no matter how well I performed in the field, I was still a woman. To them, I represented their wives and sisters, the innocent victims we risked our lives to save. I realized long ago there was nothing I could do to change their minds.

So, I did my job in the field and fulfilled my responsibilities at the station. Cooking dinner was part of my rotation duties for this shift.

In the kitchen, I pulled out the ingredients for tonight's meal: restaurant styled hamburgers, or as I liked to call them, Juicy Lucy's. It was a name the guys liked to use in inappropriate ways, of course. Nothing thick skin and a good pair of earbuds couldn't handle.

"How was your weekend, Lopez?"

My friend and confidant at the firehouse joined me in the kitchen and grabbed a can of Coke out of the fridge.

"Had a nice night out with my lady. Dinner and a movie. How about you?"

"I got caught up on sleep then spent Saturday with a house full of kids under three feet tall."

He laughed. "Sounds like fun."

I shrugged and grabbed seasoning out of the cabinet. "It wasn't bad. It was a birthday party for a friend's son. He turned one."

"My lady wants one of those."

I looked up from the skillet I pulled from the cabinet. "A frying pan?"

"No, a kid." He grimaced.

My brow furrowed. "You said that like a kid is an item to be bought from the store."

"What can I say?" He popped the lid on his soda. "I think her clock is ticking."

I emptied the ten-pound tub of ground beef into the mixing bowl and added seasoning. "What about you? Your clock ticking?" The expression on his face made me laugh.

"Men don't have ticking clocks. We get the urge to sow wild oats. Totally different thing."

Leave it to Lopez to have an off the wall explanation of things. "How is that different?"

"Women expect sexual encounters to be full of romance and love. You want to walk away satisfied and knocked up. We just want to get off and go to sleep."

Unable to put my hand over my mouth because my fingers were deep into the ground beef mixture for the patties, I turned my head and put my mouth on my shoulder to keep my outburst from disturbing the guys who watched TV. "Lopez, you are a fool. How does Maria put up with your crazy ass?"

"I could tell you, but then you might get jealous." He wagged his eyebrows and winked.

I shook my head and went back to forming patties.

"Anyway, what about your clock? Your lady parts looking for a sperm donor? I've got a few friends who think a woman that can handle a huge hose is hot. They'd be happy to service you anytime."

I groaned on the inside. I hated when people asked me that question. The reality of my life was simple when it came to my inability to conceive and carry to term. My issues were my business. I dug into my bag of lies and shared my 'truth'.

"Uh, no thanks. I can find one on my own. Besides, I'm not sure having kids is the right thing for me. Don't get me wrong, I love my niece and can't wait for my nephew to be born. I'm the aunt who spoils them and sends them home to momma. But be a full-time mom?" I pointed to the lounge area full of grown men. Some played pool while the others watched CNN. "You guys have been enough work as it is."

Lopez chuckled. "True. But seriously, Malone, you're what, thirty-eight and you don't want to reproduce?" He leaned on the counter and stared at me as if I was an anomaly.

I glared at him. "I'm not thirty-eight, I'm thirty-five and proud of it. I worked too damn hard to get where I am in my career to give it up just yet." I concentrated on forming a hamburger patty. "Besides, if I got pregnant, do you know what a female firefighter has to do in order to keep her job? Under no circumstances would I be allowed near a fire truck or any equipment for fear that I'd have a miscarriage. The county would look at me like a walking law suit waiting to happen."

Lopez's eyebrows knitted together in thought. "You could do community service work. Visit schools and talk about fire safety."

I smirked. "Actually, I'd be doing office work." I shuddered at the notion. "No thanks."

He raised his can. "Ouch." He drank, and then frowned. "Seriously though, no kids?"

"Lopez, for me to consider having a baby, he'll have to be one hell of a guy worth putting my job on the back burner. The chances of that happening are slim to none."

****

"Sugar! How's my girl?" I scratched the underside of my dog's jaw as she licked my hand. Her tail wagged so hard, her bottom shook like a milkshake machine. "Thank you for watching her, Ms. Andrews."

"Anytime, dear. She's such a sweet puppy. Besides, she keeps old Brutus active. With my hurt hip, I don't have the strength to walk him like I used to."

"That's why I don't mind doing it for you. Walking them together is great exercise. In fact, let me go to my apartment and change clothes. I'll be back for Brutus so we can jog off that belly of his." I bent down to rub the underside of the oversized Pug. He yawned and lay down. "I don't buy that tired routine, fella."

I walked across the hall, Sugar on my heels. She sat as I unlocked my door. "After you." I stepped aside so she could jog past. Her nose, eyes, and ears were on alert. I waited as she went about her inspection of the apartment. Having Sugar wasn't just for companionship, it was for safety. Living alone in an area that had break-ins at least once a month meant you stayed on your toes. My firefighter conditioning trained me how to drag a man twice my size across a room. I even had training in the martial arts. That didn't mean I was a fool.

Having a Pit Bull trained to protect was worth every penny. Sugar was all white except for her black nose and dark brown eyes. She was the sweetest thing when it came to dealing with children and people I introduced her to, like Ms. Andrews. But given the correct command, she was a force to be reckoned with.

Sugar returned, tail wagging, and licked my hand. It was her all clear signal.

"Good girl." I went into the kitchen to retrieve her favorite treat. "Sit."

She did, ears facing forward, eyes on me.

"Stay." I lay the carrot down in front of her.

She dipped her head just a little to see where her reward had gone.

"Wait."

She did, maintaining the eye contact. I held up my index finger; Sugar licked her lips. "Eat." I pointed to the carrot and she went for it, carried it into the living room, then settled beside the sofa to enjoy her snack in private.

I went to my closet to change from my work uniform and into workout clothes. This evening would be three laps around the apartment complex. My iPod went in my arm strap and ear buds were in place. I logged into my Audible account and pushed play to resume listening to the current audio book on my list. I hooked Sugar up to her leash then went across the hall for Brutus.

Walking in the evening after a twenty-four hour shift was the perfect way to wind down. While I loved my job, it could be stressful. Between dealing with the male chauvinists at work and the countless tragedies I assisted with on a daily basis, finding peace when off duty was hard.

Correction, living alone after not having the distraction of a relationship to keep me balanced was hard. That is why I bought Sugar the minute I kicked Malik's cheating ass to the curb. She was a great companion, but licks weren't hugs or kisses and they didn't keep you warm at night.

Both dogs were happy to be outside. After relieving themselves, we started on the walk. My attention went to the dogs and my surroundings as I listened to a story that had nothing to do with sappy romance and happily ever after.

It was a typical Georgia evening. After a long day of intense sunshine, humidity hung in the air so thick; you could see the vapors rise from the heated pavement. I could feel my skin cutting through it as we walked. Beads of sweat formed on my arms and legs within seconds, and I hadn't done a thing to cause my body to burn calories yet. With my level of endurance and on a day that wasn't muggy, I could complete a full circuit before moisture formed and my heart rate accelerated. My residence lay in the middle of the huge complex. With my average pace, it would take twenty minutes to loop back to my starting point…if the dogs weren't too distracted.

Halfway around, we neared the playground. Children chased one another around the swings and jungle gym under the supervision of doting parents. My heart warmed at the sight of a toddler who appeared to be excited about discovering a rock. She ran as fast as her little legs could take her over to her mother. The smile on my face came naturally.

'Is your biological clock ticking?'

Lopez's words came back to me.

The honest answer to the question was yes. Not only was it ticking, it had been sending out that message for years. I wanted to have a family, had even come close to becoming a mother more than once.

The results had been disastrous.

Sometimes, the things we wanted most in life could be out of our control.

Chapter 5

"Trevon, this is some good work. I like the way you pay attention to detail."

"Thanks, Steve."

The clock on the wall in my boss's office moved slowly. How long did it take to go through a report? I had been sitting here for nearly thirty minutes as he read through it, periodically stopping to ask questions. The report was sent to him a week ago. Why the delay?

He cleared his throat. "I'll be honest with you. The prospects for that location aren't good. I have no idea how that GM got put in charge, but he's damn near run that place into the ground. He'll be fired this week."

I nodded. Sucked to be that guy.

Steve sat back in his chair, steepled his fingers, and held them to his lips. "I have two options. One, close the location and sell the property in hopes of regaining a profit. The employees will have the option of working at other locations, if room is available. Or," he sat up in the chair. "Keep it open with a new GM in place and a chance to get things back on track." His attention went to me. "What do you think?"

My hand went to my chin in thought. "I'll be honest…do you mind?"

"Certainly."

I shifted in my seat. "Closing that location wouldn't be good for the community. As of now, it's one of the few places left in the area for people to go celebrate, have a good meal at affordable prices, or just hang out. From what I've seen, they are trying to rehab the shopping centers in that part of town. The community needs jobs. What better way to help build Applebee's good name than sticking around, fixing up the place, and getting involved in the community?" Steve's eyebrows went up in interest. I dug in as my creativity took over. "Gift cards and giveaways could be donated to charities, sponsorships to local schools and community sports programs…"

Steve shook a finger in my direction. "I see where you're going and I like it!"

"Thanks. I grew up in a community where businesses doing their part brought everyone together. As a kid, I joined a basketball team sponsored by a local restaurant. Their business grew as a result."

"Where was that?"

"Charlotte, North Carolina."

"Do you have any ideas on what charities or organizations to go after in the area?"

I shook my head and sat back. "No. I don't live in that part of town. I have friends who do, though. I can put some feelers out and get back to you with the information."

Steve laughed. "I won't need it."

"Okay. Let me know who to forward it to and—"

He shook his head. "Still won't need it." He appraised me before sitting up. "Don't take this the wrong way, but you're young, African-American, good-looking, and male. You fit the profile of what we need in that community in order to run a successful business. If you take the job and pull this off, I will make you the permanent General Manager of the store."

I sat forward a bit to make sure my ears weren't deceiving me. "My own location?"

Steve nodded. "The position will include a pay raise, effective immediately, and will remain in place contingent on your successful completion of the project. Better benefits, of course, and more vacation time are part of the deal. And of course, longer hours. What do you say?"

My eyebrows rose. "Yes?"

Steve stood, and offered his hand to cement the deal. "Someone from corporate human resources will contact you in detail about the pay raise and benefits in the next few days. I'll contact you tomorrow with the plans and details of what we have to offer in the way of location upgrades. You'll have time to put a budget and calendar together. We'll go from there."

****

"Daddy!"

Justin jogged as fast as his little feet could carry him up the walkway to my home the moment Trina released him from the car seat. I bent down to catch him. "Hey, mini me." I tickled him as I swooped him up.

He laughed, wrapped his little arms around my neck, and squeezed.

"Hi, Trina." I tried not to stare too hard at the mother of my child and the tight jeans she had on as she leaned over in the back of her Trailblazer.

She regarded me as she unhooked his car seat. "Hi."

I grabbed his weekend bag she held out to me, tossed it over my free shoulder, and walked towards the house. Trina followed with the car seat.

"You're all dressed up for a Friday night. Got plans?" I fought the urge to look over my shoulder and read her body language.

"None of your business, Tre. We've been over this before."

I decided to ignore her reply and focused on my son instead. "Are you ready for a fun filled man-weekend?"

Justin giggled. "Yes!"

"Make sure you stay on top of his medication, regardless of how much fun you're having."

"I always do. How did his doctor's appointment go?"

"He's doing well. The doctor is pleased with the results. There's still no sign of tissue rejection which means he's on his way to being completely free of the disease."

Inside, I sat the bag and Justin on the sofa. He rolled off and ran for his room, attempting to drag his oversized bag behind him.

Trina watched in awe. "I just can't get over how much more active he is. It's like he's trying to make up for the weeks he spent lying in the hospital bed."

"True, plus I think he likes it here. It's better than living in the confines of an apartment." I wiggled my eyebrows. "Large rooms, no nosey neighbors, huge fenced yard. Perfect for a boy to run around in with his dog."

Trina's arms went across her chest as she sighed. "For the fifteenth time, no."

"Come on. We've lived together before and it wasn't bad. I know things didn't work out last time and it was my fault. I promise it won't be like that this time. We have a reason to try again."

"No, *you* have a reason. We are fine where we live now. Justin has his own room and everything he needs. Quit trying to act as if you're stepping into the picture is doing more for him than I have."

"I'm not saying that at all. What I'm saying is with the two of us together, that will double the income—"

Her hand went up. "No, don't go there. I make enough to pay my own bills. Keep doing what you're doing. You know every bit you give us goes into the bank to care for him. We're good. There's no need to mess up what works."

I shook my head and kept my sigh internal. Trina could be stubborn and hardheaded when she was hell bent on not listening to reason.

She brushed past me to go to Justin's bedroom. I grabbed her arm and pulled her close.

In the eight months since she and Justin had entered my life, we'd made love once. Correction. It was one night fraught with emotion and worry before Justin's procedure. The act itself happened multiple times.

Tears were shed. Hurt feelings revisited.

Resolution reached.

If Justin survived, we'd do our best to make things work between us.

That's where our opinions differed. She wanted split parenting. I wanted them to move in and get back to what we used to have.

I wanted marriage.

Trina's body came to rest against mine, her hand landed on my chest. The fragrance of the sensuous perfume she wore had me inhaling deeply.

"You know, this doesn't have to be just a boy's night. Stay with us," I murmured, looking into her eyes.

Trina looked away and leaned against me for a moment, then met my gaze. "Tre…"

"Yes?" I took a chance and ran a hand over her shoulder and strayed toward her hip.

"That's not a good idea. It'll give Justin the wrong impression." She looked away, though she hadn't broken the physical contact.

My hand came to a rest at the top of her jeans. I leaned lower, letting my lips graze the top of her ear. Her body trembled. "I think the three of us spending time together as a family would be reassuring. Once he goes to sleep, we can spend some time alone, you know, see what it would be like for us to be mom and dad."

"It would be a lie, Tre, and I'm not about to sleep with you out of convenience." She pulled away and walked down the hall, severing the momentary connection.

"Trina, that's not what I meant."

She ignored me and walked towards Justin's bedroom.

I stood in the hall and ran a thumb over my forehead. That didn't go the way I planned. Not that I was planning anything in particular. I just wanted her to see what I saw…what our family could be if she stopped being defensive and gave in.

The walls between us had been breaking down for the past eight months, but the progress was slow. I wanted to move forward. Trina was the type that would stall for as long as possible unless someone took charge.

I may have lost this round, but there would be others.

I watched from the doorway as she kissed our son goodbye. When she turned to leave, the look she gave me told me my suggestion was no longer up for discussion. I stepped out of the way and followed her down the hall towards the front door.

"By the way, jealousy doesn't look good on you." She smirked and dug into the back pocket of those form-fitting jeans for the key to her SUV.

"It's not jealousy."

Disbelief was on her face when she reached the door and looked my way.

Okay, I had to admit, my comment sounded like a lie in my own ears. I had no idea whether Trina was seeing someone or if she was going out for the night to hang out with her sister or friends. Either way, she would bring major attention to her curves and draw men to her side in seconds.

In order for us to get back together, there couldn't be another man vying for her attention.

But, Trina was a grown woman and what she did on her weekends away from Justin was her business. If I pressed the issue, it would only drive a deeper wedge between us. I had to let it go.

"I got a promotion today."

"Congratulations. Why are you telling me?"

"I'll have more money and better benefits. I can put both of you on my insurance. Then you can take Justin off of Peachcare."

She paused. "That's a great idea for Justin. I don't need it; I've got my own health insurance."

I sighed. "Why do you make this so difficult?"

She turned and put a hand on her hip. "I'm not being difficult. I'm being real. You're the one who insists on living out some fantasy of having the perfect family. You don't get it, Trevon. You hurt me." Her hand went to her chest. "You may have moved on, but I…," her voice trailed off as she looked over my shoulder; Justin had come out of his room, brushed past me, and grabbed her leg. "I'm not sure I can."

No matter how many times we had this discussion; it seemed progress was never going to be made.

"Trina, I can't keep apologizing for the past. What's done is done; it's the past. You and I have a chance to do something different this time. I'm willing to give it a try. I can't promise perfection, but I can promise I will never hurt you that way again. You and Justin are my family. Give us a chance, okay? Think about it."

Trina looked down at Justin, ran a hand over his head, then looked back at me. I could see my words had hit a mark somewhere. "I'll think about it."

Chapter 6

"Auntie K, what's that?"

I set my Kindle down and studied the picture my niece held up. "It's a butterfly."

"Is a butterfly a bug?"

I smiled. My niece, Christina, was an inquisitive thing. At the age of five, she was all about asking questions. And like most kids, no topic was out of bounds. Thankfully, this question was an innocent one.

"Yes, it is."

"Do butterflies come from the same place babies come from?"

I stifled a laugh, wondering where this question was about to lead. There was never a dull moment when babysitting my niece. Kelli had already told me she'd been avoiding the 'where do babies come from' question as much as possible. She, of course, told her it was from her tummy, but refused to answer the question of how did it get there. I told my sister she was going to have to answer it someday, like it or not.

"What do you mean?"

"Is momma going to have a butterfly?" Lying on the floor of my apartment with Sugar next to her, Christina closed her book, sat up, then crawled onto the sofa next to me. Her eyes were full of questions.

This was indeed the warm up for something more.

"No, sweetie. Mommy's not having a butterfly; she's having a baby. You're going to have a little brother in a few months."

"He's not going to have wings like a butterfly?" Her disappointment appeared genuine.

To that, I really laughed. "No, silly. Human mommies can't have insects, and a butterfly is an insect."

Her little nose wrinkled in thought. "How does a mommy butterfly have baby butterflies?"

And there it was…the precursor to asking how her little brother got to be inside her mommy's tummy. "Good question, let's find out."

I set the Kindle down and reached for my iPad, pulled up the internet and searched. Christina was fascinated by the pictures and information we found. Her curiosity satisfied, she asked to watch a movie. I let her select tonight's kid flick, then popped a bag of popcorn. Having watched *Despicable Me* plenty of times, I found my thoughts going back to what we learned about butterflies.

The life cycle and symbolic meaning was nothing new. But for some reason today, it resonated with me on a different level.

I settled in on the sofa, kicked my legs up, and did more research. It was amazing what you could find on the internet. Most information, though, had to be taken with a grain of salt, because anybody could post anything on the World Wide Web. There were facts to be found and a grain of truth hidden within the fiction.

One page in particular got my attention.

Someone posted a question regarding the spiritual meanings behind butterflies. I had never thought of a butterfly that way, and wasn't sure I ever would. Yet one person's comment made me think.

'You may have changes going on in your life and are unsure of how things will turn out. Sighting a butterfly over and over again could mean that you will emerge from the situation an unexpected new you.'

Wow. My mind went back to the day of the birthday party.

The moment I got out of my car and walked up the walkway to the front door, a butterfly had crossed my path then landed on the bush next to the front porch. It drew my attention because of its odd color. The body of it was black with matching wings and yellow accents around the edges. I'd never seen anything like it before.

I'd taken a picture of it with my phone, though after my run-ins with Malik and then Trevon at the party and Applebee's, I forgot about it. Phone in hand, I pulled up the pictures, cycling through until I found what I was looking for. Curious, I searched the web for more information about what could be the promise of something new in my life.

After thirty minutes I found my butterfly; a Black Swallowtail. It was beautiful. I saved the image and sent a copy of it to my cell phone. Once it was downloaded, I set the image as the screen saver. Intrigued by the prospect of seeing a butterfly that stood out among the usual small yellow ones I saw around my house, the florist in me decided to research the meanings of its coloring. Black and yellow.

Instead of using the internet, I got off the sofa and went to the bookshelf in the corner of my living room. It took a few minutes to locate my florist books, given to me by my mother when I was younger, hidden behind my favorite paperback and hardback novels. I wiped off the dust and went to the kitchen to grab a cup of peppermint tea. After filling my mug with water, adding a tea bag, and putting it into the microwave, I flipped to the chapter that discussed the meanings of colors.

Black and yellow…black and yellow.

"Wow…"

According to the information, the color black stood for power, adaptability, mystery, and the promise of things unknown.

Yellow represented joy, happiness, and the promise of a happy future.

"The promise of a happy future…I could really use that right about now."

Not that I was exactly upset with my life. I had my dream job, a home I was proud of, and family that loved me. Not to mention, I was blessed with good health.

Christina's laughter brought me out of my thoughts.

Then again, I was home on a Saturday night, babysitting my niece while my sister and her husband went out for a night on the town.

I looked at the picture of the butterfly that now graced the home screen of my phone and focused on the black wings and wondered…

What unknown promise awaited me in my future?

****

"Got it!"

I covered my mouth and looked around the library. My outburst in the quiet building did not go un-noticed by patrons in my vicinity. I mouthed, 'excuse me', and carried my prize in the crook of my arm as if I'd won the lottery.

Finding the fifth book in a series I loved by one of my favorite authors was one of life's little pleasures. I could have easily purchased the title on my Kindle, but some books were best read in the traditional form. The weight of it in my hand and the smell of the ink and paper took me back to days spent lounging in my bedroom as a child. Getting lost between the ink and my imagination always took me to my happy place.

"Hello, Kai. I haven't seen you here in a while."

"Hi, Anna." I handed the librarian my book. "I've been stuck between work and my Kindle." Her expression seemed as if I'd committed a cardinal sin. "But see, I came for this book instead of downloading it." I beamed.

Anna laughed and reached for my library card. "I'll let it pass this time. Are you coming to our book signing event next month?"

"I haven't heard about it. Who's the author?"

She filled me in on the details, making sure I had a flyer with the information so I wouldn't forget. I locked the date in the calendar on my phone.

An outburst of clapping and singing came from the far side of the library. I glanced in the area of the children's department. And I thought I had been loud. "What's going on over there?"

"Miss Becky is doing her weekly kids' program. They read books, sing, dance, and do an art project. It's great for kids who are too young to read. It teaches them to develop a love of books."

"That's great. I'll have to bring my niece one day. Can I get more information about that?"

She handed me another flyer. "That reminds me. My daughter keeps asking when we're going to have the big trucks come back to the library. She had a ball climbing up in the fire truck. In fact, she says she wants to be like you one day."

My heart warmed. "That is so sweet! I'm not sure when we'll be doing another community outreach program like that. I can mention it to the chief and see when we can schedule another visit."

"Sounds good to me."

The alarm on my phone sounded, alerting me that it was time to leave the library. "Speaking of which, it's time for me to head to the station. I'm pulling a double shift. With any luck it will be a quiet night." I held up the book. "Important reading to do! Talk to you soon, Anna."

She laughed. "Stay safe."

****

The first hours on shift were quiet. Not a bad way to start a Monday, especially when pulling a double shift. After performing my duties, joking around with the guys, and equipment check, I settled into my bunk to read. I was on chapter ten when the alarm signaled. I marked the page, jumped up, and raced to my gear locker. The dispatcher rattled off basic information about the call.

"Sounds like a big one," Lopez shouted as he stuffed his legs into his turnout gear beside me.

I did the same, hiked up the suspenders over my shoulders and grabbed my turnout coat. "I hate apartment fires."

It was two in the morning, which meant most people would be asleep. The chances of people being trapped on the top floors increased dramatically. Often times smoke detectors failed and people died in their sleep. Scared children would hide in places that were hard to find in dark, smoked-filled rooms.

Add the chaos of those who escaped and watched in horror as they lost everything they owned…

The scene, if not controlled properly by police, could turn into a mad house, especially when someone tried to sneak back in to save the family photos or beloved pet.

I claimed my seat in the truck and held on as we raced through the night.

"Just got word, this has escalated into a four-alarm fire!" The captain shouted from the front of the truck. "Be ready!"

I said a prayer for those affected and for my team. The minute we arrived on scene, it began to rain.

Could the conditions get any worse? True, rain could aid in putting out the fire, but it made the use of climbing equipment dangerous, especially with the heavy gear we wore.

The truck lurched to a stop. We piled out to assess the situation. The bottom portion of the three-story complex was engulfed in flames. Fumes carrying a mix of unknown toxic chemicals permeated the air. Thick, black smoke wafted out of the lower level where firefighters battled the blaze. Burnt debris accompanied the raindrops and accumulated in the puddles forming at our feet.

Survivors of the disaster huddled together in the parking lot, some nearly naked, others holding tight to what possessions they had managed to grab as they ran for their lives. In the distance, shouts from people trapped in their burning homes drowned out the truck sirens.

"Listen up!" We gathered around the chief. "We've got several scenarios happening simultaneously. According to the chief from Truck #73, the lower level is the source of the fire. They managed to clear it, and he has men on the second floor searching for people who are trapped. To top it all off, we've got several families trapped on the third. He's got a truck working rescue, but we need more men. We've got to get things under control. Now. Captains, get your teams squared away. Let's go, let's go, let's go!"

"Malone, you've got ladder! Lopez, back her up," my captain yelled.

"Yes, sir!"

I tightened my helmet and did a quick double check of my gear.

"Ready, Malone?" Lopez slapped my back.

"Ready!"

We waited impatiently as the truck maneuvered into position as close to the apartment building as it could get, then extended the ladder. The moment it connected with the first window seal, I ran to the base and grabbed hold of the wet railing. While my boots were water resistant and had extra grip to keep me from slipping, that didn't make the task easy. I forced myself to breathe easy and focus on every step I took. I had faith in my equipment, but no matter what measures were taken to make my job safer, human error could always screw things up. Lopez was on the ladder behind me as my back up. We moved systematically from window to window. I used my ax to break the glass and yell inside before we climbed through to make a quick search for anyone who may be unconscious, huddled in a corner, or in a room behind closed doors. So far, it appeared everyone was out.

After what felt like forever, we had two apartments left. I held on and braced myself as the ladder moved to the next window. I broke the glass and yelled before leaning in to repeat my call. I was about to step across the threshold when Lopez grabbed the back of my jacket.

"Malone! We've got one next door!"

"What?" I stepped back onto the ladder, taking extra precautions to keep from slipping.

He pointed to the final set of windows before using his radio to alert the captain of the situation.

The sight made my heart freeze.

A woman covered with soot leaned out of the window with what appeared to be a young child in her arms. A heavy curtain of smoke wafted out the opening behind her while bright red flames silhouetted her frame, meaning the fire had to be in the room she was in.

"Help us, please! He's not breathing!"

Damn.

I held on tight as the ladder moved.

"Ok, ma'am, I've got you. Hold on!"

The minute we got within range, I reached for the child. Fear and relief were evident on the mother's face beneath the soot and grime. "Please, help him, he's not breathing!" she said between heaving gasps and coughing.

I took the child from her; he was limp in my arms. I tried to be as gentle as I could, but unconscious, his limbs flailed around as if he were a rag doll. With my gear on, there was nothing I could do in order to resuscitate him.

Adrenaline pumping in my veins, I turned to my partner and handed him off.

"Lopez, get him to a medic, now!"

He took the young boy in his arms, balancing his weight while taking each step down the ladder as fast as he could under the dangerous conditions.

I turned to the woman who now gagged repeatedly. Her face was streaked with tears that mixed with black soot.

"It's okay, my partner has him. Now it's our turn to go down, okay? It's slippery out here and I know you want to hurry down in order to get to your son, but we have to take our time. Okay?"

She nodded and focused on me.

I held my hand out and encouraged her to step out of the window and onto the ladder.

Her feet were bare and she bore the evidence of someone who had been fast asleep when disaster struck. Though she had stopped crying, it was obvious she was scared. Once on the ladder, she froze.

"I'm scared of heights!" Her fingers seemed to be fused to the wrung and her body was curled up tight.

"It's okay, I promise. I know it feels odd on this ladder, but we aren't that far from the ground, it's all a matter of prospective." That didn't help any because she now whimpered.

Glass broke in the distance, and it wasn't from someone trying to be rescued. It was the sound of something exploding due to the heat. That was not good.

This woman needed a distraction in order to get her to move. While I was trained to carry an unconscious person wherever I needed them to go, trying to carry her under these rain soaked conditions would not be smart. She was conscious and able to move on her own. She just needed motivation to get her feet going.

"What's your name? Mine is Kai."

The scared woman turned her head in my direction. "My…my name is Trina."

Away from the smoke, I got a chance to see her face, and in the back of my mind, she seemed familiar.

"Trina, it's nice to meet you. I wish it was under other circumstances, but that's life, right?" I looked behind me and saw Lopez touch the ground. A team of paramedics were nearby and took the little boy over to a stretcher where they started CPR. His mother couldn't see past me. "Trina, it's our turn to start moving, okay? It looks like the paramedics are working on your son. Tell me about him. What's his name?"

Trina attempted to look past me, but stopped the moment she saw how far up from the ground we were. "Justin…his name is Justin."

Justin?

"And how old is Justin?"

"Two, Justin is two!"

A chill went down my spine as I looked back down at the scene below; the paramedics were still working. Lopez stood nearby watching. He looked back up at me and his head nodded ever so slightly.

Oh God. If my memory served me right, Justin was Trevon's son…and this was his mother. I may have only seen them once, but their faces had been imprinted in my memory. Trina twisted around again to see her son. God…this really was Trevon's family.

"Come on, Trina, let's get to your son, he needs you."

My words got her moving. It wasn't fast enough, though. Between her wracking coughs from smoke inhalation and the slippery equipment, my job was to stay behind her and aid her in the descent.

Halfway down, she slipped and fell into me. I managed to catch myself, but the sudden weight of her body added to the weight of the gear on my back forced me to lose my footing. I grabbed onto the ladder, thankful for the safety clamp I had strapped to the railing, and stopped both of us from falling. Unfortunately, the sudden twist shot a pain up my spine and made me curse. I worked through the pain, guiding her down as fast as I could.

"I've got you," I managed through gritted teeth. "We're almost there, almost there!"

Instead of focusing on the pain, I thought about the little boy waiting at the bottom of the ladder who needed his mother.

The moment my foot touched the ground, I handed her off to another set of paramedics, then started stripping off my gear.

Lopez came over to check on me. "Damn, Malone, what happened?"

I ignored his question. "How's the boy?"

"He's breathing and being transported to Egelston Children's Hospital."

Thank God.

"What about you?" He helped me remove my oxygen tank.

"I'm hurt. I need a medic." I gave up on hiding the pain and sprawled out on the ground. Rain poured on my face, so

I did my best to turn on my side. Lopez aided me in the maneuver then shielded me from the rain with the coat I had ripped off.

Two seconds later, and the paramedics were on scene to check me out. I yelled as they sat me up. My captain walked over to assess the situation.

The paramedics' fingers ran down the length of my spine, poking and prodding. I yelled when he hit my lower back. "Nothing's broken, but you need to go to the hospital and get some x-rays." He signaled for his partner to bring over a backboard and stretcher.

"Take her," my captain said before walking away. He went two steps, stopped and looked in my direction. "Damn good save, Malone."

Chapter 7

"Damn." The pain that shot up my leg as I crawled out of bed and limped to the bathroom was close to unbearable. Old injuries didn't heal well, even after several surgeries.

After relieving myself, I grabbed a bottle of Tylenol PM and prepared to numb myself, and the pain, unconscious. Today had been the first time in months that I had spent the afternoon in the gym playing one-on-one basketball against Andre. While I was only thirty, I still had issues with my old college injury.

I made my way over to the dresser in my bedroom and dug around for the knee brace. I was halfway down the hall to the kitchen for a bottle of water to take the aspirin when my cell phone rang. Who could be calling at 3:53 AM? The ringing ended. Whoever it was could leave a voicemail. Seconds later, the phone vibrated, indicating one had been left.

I was about to pop the pills when the nosy side of me insisted I check the message. When I clicked the screen, I was surprised to see there were five missed calls and three voicemails from an unknown number.

I hit the button above the last message.

'Tre, God, answer your phone!" There was a sigh and pause. 'I'll say it again. Justin and I are at Egelston's. There was a fire, Tre…we barely survived. We've lost everything…clothes, his meds…' Another pause. 'The room number is 1812. Call this number as soon as you get this. I lost my cell phone, too. We need you, Tre. I need you.'

My world stopped.

Trina…Justin…fire…Egelston?

I hit redial, put the phone on speaker, slipped the knee brace on, and searched for a pair of jeans and a shirt. My heart beat a mile a minute.

"Hello?"

I grabbed the phone, took it off of speaker, and sat it on my shoulder as I laced up my tennis shoes. "Trina, how is he? Is everything okay? What happened?"

"Trevon? Thank God…" The line was filled with sniffing. She was crying. "It was horrible! I tried to get us out, but there was fire in the hallway and nowhere to go. The fire department came and we were rescued." She coughed hard. "Justin had stopped breathing…" More coughing. "The firefighters got to us in time. Justin is on forced oxygen, but they say he should be okay in the next day or two."

I breathed a sigh of relief. "What about you? That cough of yours doesn't sound good. Have you been seen?"

"I'm fine. I got checked out in the parking lot before I got in the ambulance with Justin. It's just a bit of irritation from the smoke." Another sniff, another cough. "Just…Trevon, could you—"

My wallet was stuffed in my back pocket and keys were in hand. "I'm on the way."

****

Getting past hospital security and up to the ICU where Justin was being kept under observation was almost as nerve wrecking as the thirty-minute drive from my home to the hospital. It was 5:02 a.m., and no traffic clogged the streets. My hands ached from gripping the steering wheel as I raced along the highway. Thankfully, no police had been around to stop me.

One of the nurses at the Nurses Station directed me to Justin's room. My hand on the knob, I braced myself for what lay behind it.

The room was dark, the only illumination coming from a small lamp in the corner. The consistent beep of machines as they pumped and whined flooded my ears as my eyes adjusted to the light.

The sight of Justin lying in bed connected to wires and tubes made my heart drop.

The day Trina found me and introduced me to my son, he was lying in a hospital bed at this very same hospital. He'd just undergone testing in preparation for a bone marrow transplant.

Then came the months spent by his side after surgery as he underwent therapy in hopes that the procedure was a success.

Now, as soon as Justin had gained a sense of normality in his life, he was back again, stuck in a bed, his young life threatened by something not even the doctors could cure.

His body had been through so much too soon. How could he recover?

My hand went to my mouth and held back the moan that threatened to take over the sound of the equipment. Tears ran down my face and collected on my shirt.

My feet felt like lead as I walked over to the bed. I rested my hands on the railing and studied my son as he slept while holding his mother's hand. His hair appeared damp, as if someone had taken a rag and wiped it clean. It was impossible to see his face due to the oxygen mask that covered the bridge of his nose, cheeks, and mouth.

Trina lay in bed next to him, cradling him as much as she could in her sleep.

Evidence of the fire showed in spots on her face. Apparently she'd splashed water to remove the majority of the black soot, but cared more about Justin's wellbeing than her appearance.

I leaned down, kissed my son's forehead, and placed my hand on hers. "Trina…"

She opened her eyes and grasped my hand. "Tre…thank God you're here. I was so scared." She squeezed my hand before looking at the monitors beside Justin's bed.

"Is he any better?" I checked the machines, trying to make sense of the madness.

"Not really. His oxygen level has increased a little, but he's not out of the woods just yet." She covered her mouth and coughed.

I studied Trina. She wore a green hospital shirt and pants. Someone at the hospital must have given her something to wear once she arrived. Her eyes were bloodshot, the rims heavy and swollen and stood out in skin that did not have its usual brown undertone.

"What about you? Are you sure you're okay? You don't look so good."

"I'm fine, Tre. I'm tired, stressed, and worried about our son." She kissed his forehead. "What are we going to do now? Everything…pictures, birth records, clothes, toys…it's just gone." Her eyes welled.

I reached over Justin to wipe her tears. "Stay with me. I'll take care of everything. You don't worry about it."

She looked up at me. "My parents want us to move in with them. They've got a spare room."

My jaw clenched. Trina's parents and I were not on good terms. They didn't like me when we dated. Now that I was back in her life, they hated me for not being there for Justin from the day he was born. Like that had been my fault.

"They aren't his parents, Trina. We are. We decide what is best. I've been telling you for months that we need to be together. After this tragedy, Justin needs to be somewhere stable. Sleeping in the guest bedroom at grandma's is not stability, not when you've got a better option. I have a house big enough for all of us. He has his own room, toys, and clothes." I looked into her eyes. My voice softened. "You can use the guest room if you want. Or, you can stay with me."

"Tre, I don't know…"

"Yes, you do. The answer is no."

My jaw clenched at the sound of Trina's mother's voice. I stood straight and faced her as she entered the room.

"No disrespect, Mrs. Waters, but this isn't your decision."

"The hell it's not." She placed a small bag and coffee cup on the counter next to the sink then walked to Trina's side of the bed. "You abandoned my daughter and left her to raise my grandson on her own. I've been taking care of her my entire life and my grandbaby since the day he was born."

"Mom—" Trina put a hand on her mother's arm to get her attention. It didn't work.

I put my hands on the bedrail and forced my voice to stay low and remember this situation was stressful for all of us. It made no sense starting an argument with a woman who refused to listen.

"First of all, I didn't abandon Trina; she left me. Second, I've been here since I found out about my son, and believe me, I'm not leaving. Third," I leaned over the bed in an attempt to be heard and not disrupt Justin's slumber. "The last time I checked it was *my* sperm that brought Justin into existence, making *me* his father. Your tiny bit of DNA doesn't give you the right to decide what's best for him. Justin and Trina are moving in with me. That's final."

We locked eyes until Momma Waters' mouth fell open.

I looked down at Trina expecting her to say something in her mother's defense. Instead, she nodded in agreement.

"We're moving in with Trevon as soon as Justin is released."

Her mother's lips thinned in disappointment.

"And you," I said to Trina, "are going to see a doctor immediately. I'm here; I've got this."

Trina reached for my hand, squeezed tight, but shook her head in disagreement. "I'm not leaving him until I know he's fine. I promise you, I'm okay. My throat is just aggravated because of the smoke."

"I don't care. You're not going to do Justin any good if you don't—"

"Wow, this is a full house. This little guy is really loved."

I turned to see a nurse walk in, retrieve Justin's chart. I stepped aside so she could check his arm band.

Trina sat up. "This is Trevon, Justin's father."

"I see the resemblance," the nurse smiled, then walked over to the sink to wash her hands. "I'm Nurse Patricia. I'm on shift until eight a.m. It's time to check Justin's vitals."

I moved out of the way, ignoring Mrs. Waters' fuming stare.

Justin woke as Trina climbed out of the bed so the nurse could do her job.

Nurse Patricia gently poked and prodded his abdomen and listened to his chest. He became restless and was about to cry until he looked around the room and saw me.

His cry was nearly inaudible because of the mask on his face. His eyes were slits as he reached his arms out for me, fingers gripping the air. He wanted me. He wanted the comfort of his father.

Tears wet my eyes.

I walked over and reached for his hands, stilling them.

"Hold on, dad, I'm almost done." Nurse Patricia checked his pulse and placed some sort of clip on his finger. She then put a stethoscope to his chest and listened.

"How is he?" Trina stood beside me, grasped my free hand.

"The same basically, but the chest sounds are a little better. It's going to take time." She put the covers back in place on Justin's bed. "I can tell you this, though. It's a blessing the firefighter made it to you in time. A few minutes more and he would have died."

My head dropped.

"Thank God for that firefighter," Trina added.

"Exactly. I heard the paramedics say she got injured during the rescue."

"Oh no!" Trina's hand went to her mouth.

She?

My brain went numb. "Do you know the name?"

Nurse Patricia stood in thought. "Hmm…Mathews, Miller…it started with an 'M'."

"Malone?" I held my breath.

She snapped her fingers. "That's it! Malone."

"Do you know what type of injury?" I prodded.

She shrugged. "All I know is she's been taken to the hospital."

Chapter 8

"Kai, are you awake?"

My eyelids heavy and in no rush to open my eyes, I pretended to be asleep.

The attempt to ignore the pain was short-lived. I jumped as the blood pressure cuff rattled and squeezed the crap out of my arm.

"Ow!" Movement only made the cuff tighten more.

"So you are awake. How do you feel?" Kelli leaned over the side of my bed and adjusted the sheets.

I squinted at my very pregnant, yet perky sister as she sat down in the chair next to my hospital bed. "I'm on morphine. How do you think I feel?"

Her brow knitted. "Normally I have something smart to say, but you did something good today. You saved a life. Two, if I'm not mistaken. At least that's what your firefighting buddies, co-workers, whatever you guys call yourselves, said; little boy and his mom."

The events of the evening flooded back.

The lifeless body of the little boy hanging out of the window in his mother's arms. The smoke and flames billowing out of what used to be their home. The slip of his mother on the rain-soaked ladder followed by excruciating pain in my lower back.

Uncomfortable, I leaned over, grabbed the bed rail, and sat up a bit. Though I could feel no pain, the nausea had my stomach rolling. "They made it?"

"From what I hear, yes."

I lay my head back on the pillow. "Call Trevon."

Kelli looked at me in confusion. "Call Trevon? Why?"

"It was his son…he's the one I saved."

She gasped and covered her mouth with her hand. "The fire was at his baby momma's apartment?"

I nodded and closed my eyes.

Kelli was quick to pull out her cell phone. I heard the low clicks of keys as she dialed her best friend's number to call Sharice, who was married to Trevon's friend.

She put a hand over the phone. "She's getting Andre to call him now. He said he hadn't heard anything about it."

I nodded, adjusted the bed using the buttons on the railing, and peeked at the clock on the wall. It was nearly six in the morning. The family and friends grapevine usually slowed after midnight.

Then again, life altering news often took a moment to process before you could share.

"Oh my God, you're right! Andre's got him on the phone now." She paused, listened to the conversation on the other end. "He says he's hanging in there and that he's going to be on oxygen for a while, but he has woken up."

I sighed in relief.

"He says the mom is okay, too." She paused. "He wants to what?" She paused. "Give him my number."

I drifted into a state of euphoria from the pain meds. The few minutes of lucidity were leaving. My eyelids were too heavy to open again.

The next thing I knew, Kelli was standing over me, shaking my shoulder.

"Kai, sweetie, wake up."

I forced my eyes open. "Trevon is on the phone. Can you talk?"

The mention of his name was like a shot of adrenaline. I nodded and tried to reach for the handset, but my arms felt as if they'd been weighed down and coordination was not about to happen.

"I'll hold the phone." Kelli placed it front of me. "Trevon? I've got you on speaker. She's heavily sedated so you better make it quick."

"Thanks, Kelli." Trevon's voice rang clear through the line. "Kai? Can you hear me?"

"Yes…" My tongue felt heavy and dry.

"God, Kai…I can't believe you saved my family…" His voice caught with emotion. "Thank you…thank you."

Water gathered in the corners of my eyes as I listened to his voice, imagining his brown eyes filled with tears.

"No need to thank me…doing my job…"

"Yes, there is. And you were hurt? What happened?"

I opened my mouth, but it was hard to articulate a coherent thought.

"Hold on, Trevon. I'm going to give her something to drink. They have her medicine on a timed drip and I think it's kicked in again." Kelli reached for the hospital mug filled with ice water and brought the straw to my mouth. "She's drinking. From what I understand, she was behind Trina when she slipped as they were coming down the ladder. Kai caught her, but between the fall and the gear she wears, it damaged her back."

Water gone, I nodded my head in thanks. "They're….okay? Your son…his mother?"

"Justin is hanging in there. The doctor says he should be okay in a day or two. Trina is…"

A wracking cough came through the line. It had to be Trina. From the sound of it, she was worse than when I pulled her from the burning apartment.

"Trina?" Trevon's voice moved away from the phone. "Trina, what's wrong?" The phone dropped. "Oh, God! Nurse, Nurse! She's not breathing!"

"Trevon, what's happening?" Kelli yelled in the phone.

The panic of Trevon's voice was enough to wake me up. What was going on? No matter how many times Kelli and I yelled his name, Trevon never came back to the line.

We listened as he continued to call for help. When it arrived, multiple voices took over, making it impossible to make out a word that was said.

Then there was silence.

Chapter 9

"Trevon?"

My eyes flew open at the knock on the hospital room door, drawing me out of deep thought. "Andre…"

My best friend walked past Justin's bed and gave me a hug. "How's little man?" His attention went to the bed where Justin slept.

"Better." I wiped my eyes.

His attention turned back to me. "What about Trina?"

I plopped down in the seat next to Justin's bed. "I don't know. One minute she seemed okay. Just a dry cough, you know? She was checked out by the paramedics after the fire and released. By the time I got to the hospital, she had a real bad cough. I told her she needed to be seen again, but she refused to leave Justin's side. Then all of a sudden, it got worse. She started gagging and choking… she stopped breathing." I dug the heel of my palm into my eyes, unable to blot out the memory of Trina's skin as it grew pale, her eyes wide as she struggled to get air. "The doctor and nurses were able to resuscitate her, and then she was rushed to Emory. Her mother was here and went with her. Justin woke from the commotion and started crying, so I stayed here. I keep calling her mom, but it's going to voicemail. I don't have a clue as to what is going on."

"Damn." He sat in the next available chair. "What about you? How are you holding up?"

I let my head rest in my hands. "I don't know. One minute everything was fine. Then the fire. Justin hanging on to life…now Trina. If something happens to her…"

"Hey, don't think like that."

My eyes watered a bit, and I ground my teeth to get rid of the feeling. There was no time for tears.

"I'm trying not to, but what choice do I have? The fire was the last thing I ever imagined happening. But it did. Life can just…" I glanced at my son and the tubes attached to his little body. "Shit happens and it's something we can't control. I nearly lost my son last night. He's not out of the woods yet, but he's going to be okay. But Trina…" I swallowed hard to keep the tears and frustration inside. "I don't know. She didn't have the same medical attention Justin had. For her to be okay one minute and then damn near dead the next…I'm not liking those odds, man."

Andre walked over to where I sat, put his hand on my shoulder, and squeezed. "We're praying for her. Sharice, Kelli, her husband. We're all behind you, no matter how this turns out. We've got you."

"Thanks."

It was a blessing to have friends. And family.

I groaned. In the aftermath of everything that had happened in the past few hours, calling my family to make them aware of what happened with Justin was the last thing on my mind. The minute my parents found out, they'd pack up the car and make the drive down. North Carolina and Georgia weren't that far apart.

No doubt LaShana and her family would come, too.

Ebony couldn't, though. Not only did she live in L.A., she was pregnant. I'd hate to have her get on a plane while in her condition.

"Can you sit with Justin for a few minutes? I need to make some phone calls."

"Sure. I'll find you if he wakes up."

"Thanks. I won't be far."

I checked the monitors before leaving the room. Oxygen levels appeared to be steady and improving. Good, that was good. So was his blood pressure and heart rate.

I kissed his forehead. "I'll be back soon. Daddy loves you."

At the nurses' station, I advised them of my whereabouts and Andre's presence then I walked down the long corridor. My intention had been to go to the family waiting room, but then I realized my stomach was empty. I checked the time on my phone. It was after eight A.M. Maybe the cafeteria would be open.

I punched the down button for the elevator and waited.

Inside, I hit the button marked for the cafeteria, then rested my head against the elevator wall as the cab descended. It felt a lot like my life.

Just a few days ago, I had been offered the opportunity to step up to the corporate level at work, and a raise that would allow me to comfortably take care of a family. All I had to do was convince Trina to let me back in. Hadn't we been through enough over the past few months to earn me the chance to make up for past wrongs?

Dealing with Justin's illness made us a team, two parents who loved their son and wanted only the best healthcare and happiness life had to offer.

Relationship-wise? While I knew what I wanted, Trina was still on the fence. Not that I could blame her. After spending three years of our life as a couple, two of them living together, I was the one who chickened out at the hint of a lifetime commitment. Unable to break it off and walk away, I did the typical male idiotic thing; cheated and made it obvious so she'd find out and break up with me.

What I didn't expect was the backlash that came from a very pissed off woman, my family, and friends. I tried for months to convince everyone that the breakup between

Trina and I was for the best. To keep myself from feeling like an ass for deliberately ending our relationship on a bad note, I decided to play the role of being a player. In the end, it was easier, and to be honest, a lot of fun.

Fun that eventually lead to a decision that affected my friends.

Kai.

Meeting her opened up a side of me I forgot existed. The desire to want more from a woman than just a good time. The desire to start a real relationship again. Two years of waving my player card, turning thirty, and watching my sisters and friend find lasting happiness and comfort in their mates and kids left me longing.

Then the truth came out. She was engaged. Or not engaged.

Neither was relevant once Trina re-entered the picture with Justin.

The chance to reestablish our relationship and give her what she wanted and put our family together became the focus. What we once had was real. It just took me two years to catch up to that fact.

It took us having a son and his illness to bring us back together.

Since Trina reappeared and delivered the news that changed my life, not a day went by that I didn't wonder what would have happened if she'd told me she was pregnant before she left.

Would I have convinced her to stay? Would I have wanted her to?

The elevator dinged and the door opened on the first floor. I followed the aroma of fresh brewed caffeine to the cafeteria. A bagel and large coffee would have to work because I wasn't in the mood for a breakfast platter. I settled in a far corner for privacy and dialed my parents and big sister, LaShana's number, to deliver the news. After tears were shed on both sides of the phone call, they promised to get to Atlanta the next day.

I checked the time and saw that Ebony and her husband, Brian, who lived in California, would be awake.

"Trevon," there was a pause as she yawned. "Sorry, I slept in today. Why are you calling this early in the morning? You're usually rolling over right about now."

"Yeah, well, I wish it were one of those days." I informed her of the situation, ending with the unknown about Trina. "Emory is just down the street; I can literally walk outside and see the hospital, Eb."

"And her mother still hasn't answered? Could it be bad cell phone reception in the hospital?"

I shrugged, even though she couldn't see it. "Maybe."

"Have you called the hospital?"

My sigh was deep. "I thought about it, but I'm scared. What if I call and something has gone wrong? No news is good news, right?"

The line was silent for a moment. "I can call if you want. Tre, you don't need to sit around stressing yourself. Justin needs you."

"Which is why I haven't walked out the door and gone to that hospital. I don't want to be too far away in case he wakes up. Speaking of which, I need to go back upstairs now." I cleaned up the remnants of my half-eaten breakfast and disposed of it.

"Okay. Kiss my nephew and call me when he wakes up. And Trevon…hang in there."

"Thanks. Love you, Eb."

"I love you too, knucklehead."

It didn't take long to get back upstairs. A shift in the sheets made it apparent Justin had moved in his sleep. A monitor check showed nothing had changed.

Andre looked up from his phone. "Sharice sends her love."

"Thanks." I took a moment to run a hand over Justin's head.

My cell phone rang, which caused him to fidget in his sleep. Not wanting him to wake up, I pulled it out of my pocket and hit the accept button. I looked over at Andre. "It's Trina's mother. Hello? Mrs. Waters, how's—"

"Trevon, she's gone…she's gone…"

Chapter 10

One week later…

"Daddy…I wan Daddy!"

Justin squirmed in my father's arms as they approached. I ran the back of my hand across my eyes, catching the moisture that formed.

"I got him. Thanks, Dad." My son's arms wrapped around my neck and held tight. I kissed his cheek and rubbed his back. "What's wrong?"

"I wan Mommy!" Tears began to well up in his eyes as he stared at me, begging for me to take him to her.

My heart broke into a million pieces. I placed my hand on the back of his head and urged him to rest on my shoulder so he couldn't see the anguish on my face.

My father stood beside me, one firm hand on my shoulder in support.

"I know, Justin, I know. I want mommy, too." I rocked him, hoping the movement would encourage him to calm down.

How did you explain to a two-year-old that mommy was never coming back? That she wouldn't be there to tuck him in the bed at night or kiss his cheek when he wasn't feeling well?

She's with the angels?

God called her home?

I hated both of those explanations. In my opinion, telling those stories could cause a child to distrust angels and hate God. I refused to have my son do either.

"Mommy's not coming back, Justin." It was a truth that, of course, brought on more tears.

I walked over to an empty seating area in the lobby of the funeral home. The services for Trina would start soon.

I paid my respects to her family and viewed her body. She looked so peaceful, as if she were taking a nap. Beautiful, just like the day we met.

Guilt for the pain I put her through over the years instead of giving her the happiness she deserved wracked me since learning of her death. In the past week, I had barely slept.

Unable to handle watching her family mourn, and some of them giving me a look of hatred through red eyes filled with tears, I decided it would be best if I stayed away until the service started, and waited in the atrium of the funeral home.

I glanced over at my dad and the sympathetic look in his eye as he sat down next to me. Though he was silent, his presence strengthened me. As promised, they drove down the next day to see Justin and stayed until he was released from the hospital. The advice given from parent-to-parent was priceless.

I don't know how I would have managed to settle Justin into his new home if it weren't for them. Between dealing with Trina's family who wanted to have Justin with them and Mrs. Waters blaming me for her daughter's death, I was about to lose my mind.

While I knew it wasn't my fault, part of me had to wonder if she were right.

If I had married Trina two years ago, she wouldn't have lived in that apartment complex. She and Justin would have been safe at home with me.

How many months had I tried to convince Trina to move in, even if she wasn't ready for the relationship part? I'd taken the steps: sold my condo, bought a three-bedroom house that would be perfect for them. Though we shared custody of Justin, I made sure rebuilding our relationship was a priority, too.

In the end, it took a fire for her to decide to move in.

The fire that had killed her.

If I hadn't been an ass years ago, we would be married. I would have been there to see Justin born.

No amount of sorrow or wishing could change the past. Now all I had was an unknown future.

"Trevon?"

I looked up to see my best friend standing in front of me, holding his wife, Sharice's hand.

"Andre." I was about to stand, but he gestured for me to stay put and shook my hand instead.

Sharice leaned down and kissed my cheek and Justin's, whose cries had calmed to a hiccup and sniff routine.

They stepped aside to reveal Kelli and her husband, Alonso. More hugs, more pats on the back and condolences. I wiped my eyes, grateful for my friends' support.

When I looked up again, I saw the last person I could have imagined.

"Kai?"

She moved slowly with the aid of a cane by her side. Dressed in black, her long dark hair was pulled into a ponytail. She winced as she moved closer, in obvious pain.

I stood with Justin in my arms and met her before she reached me. My throat clogged with tears and the words I desperately needed to say.

I embraced her with my free arm, pulling her as close as possible without hurting her. "Thank you…thank you…thank you…"

"I'm so sorry, Trevon," she sobbed. "I wish there was more that I could have done."

I pulled back and looked into her eyes. "You saved them, Kai. If it weren't for you, Justin would be…" I couldn't bring myself to say the words.

Kai's attention went to Justin, who sat up to see what was going on. His eyes were rimmed in red, his little nose swollen, and his body shook from what remained of his crying jag.

"Hi, Justin."

He lowered his head to my shoulder. His grip around my neck tightened as he stuck his thumb in his mouth.

"I know you don't know me, but I'm a friend of your daddy's. Can you do me a favor? Take care of him for me, okay? He's really sad right now. Can you be a big boy and give him a really big hug and kiss?"

Justin pulled his thumb out of his mouth, kissed me, and laid his head back down on my shoulder.

I kissed him back.

When I looked around, I realized my friends were all standing there, watching the exchange. The women had tears in the eyes while Andre had a slightly different look, recognizing the connection that Kai and I shared.

Then again, he was the only one in our group of friends who knew the truth about my confusing relationship with Kai.

"Trevon."

I turned as my mother joined us. "Edna is asking for Justin. Can I take him?"

I held my son a little tighter by instinct. Trina's family had every right to spend time with him, especially on a day like this. "Justin, do you want to go with Grammy?"

He nodded and kept his thumb in his mouth.

"Come on, baby. Walk with Grammy, okay?" My mother held out a hand.

I sat him down, adjusted the vest and tie of the little suit I picked out for him for the funeral. He gripped my mother's hand and walked back into the room where his mother's body rested. I had mixed feelings about him seeing Trina lying in a casket. Fortunately, so did her family. They made it a priority to keep him away from the front of the room.

My father rubbed my back. "It's going to be okay, son. It's almost over."

"I know. Can you keep an eye on him, please?"

"Of course." My father nodded at my friends, then followed my mother.

My friends did the same. Kai was the only one who remained.

She appeared uncomfortable.

"Sit down." I aided her as she settled on the small sofa then joined her. "How are you?"

"I would complain, but in light of the situation, that would be selfish and stupid."

I took a moment to study her. It was the first time I'd seen her since the night our paths crossed at Applebee's. So much had changed since then.

"Kai, I'm sorry to ask this but, I just can't make sense of it all. You were there. What happened with Trina? How bad was it?"

She grimaced in obvious pain. "It was a bad fire. My partner and I were checking apartments for anyone who needed help when we saw them. It was really bad, Trevon. Trina was in a window with Justin. I handed him off to my partner and helped her out of the window. It was raining and the ladder was slippery. Trina..." she paused and looked away. "She slipped and fell into me. I managed to catch her and stop the fall, but the weight of the equipment did some damage to my lower back." Her eyes shot to me. "I'd do it all again, believe me. I just wish I would have gotten to her sooner. Then maybe…"

I held up a hand to quiet her. "Nobody knows how that would have turned out. The coroner said the damage to her lungs was from smoke inhalation. Adult Respiratory Distress Syndrome. One minute you're okay, the next minute it sneaks up on you. Trina should have seen the doctor and been thoroughly checked out. Instead she stayed with Justin." I looked down at the ground. "Trina was a good mother. She gave Justin everything. She put so much of her life into caring for him alone…leaving me when...," I gulped. "Things didn't end well between us. She had every right to hide her pregnancy from me. She could have hidden his illness and I would never have known about my son. This could have still happened and Justin would have been some bastard kid without a father." I huffed, anger taking the place of mourning. "Her parents hate me. I'm sure finding me would not have been a priority for them." I sighed. "Now I have my son, and he has no mother. Trina's the one who took care of him… managed his illness. I only know some of the things to do. What if I screw up and fail?"

Kai reached over, her hand going to my knee. "Trevon, I can't say I know what you're going through. I'm not a parent so I have no idea what you're facing. I will say this, though…you'll figure it out. Trina had to do the same without you, and from what you're saying, she managed to find what worked. No doubt she had family and friends to assist. So do you."

My eyes rose to meet hers. For some reason I knew she was right. It would be okay. Justin and I would be okay.

"Trevon."

I looked past Kai to Trina's sister. Her expression was one of sadness and a bit of anger. Her attention went to Kai whose hand rested on my leg. "We're about to start the service."

Kai moved her hand and gathered her cane.

"Thanks, Felisha."

I stood, offered Kai a hand as she rose.

It was time to say my final goodbye and begin the next phase of my life.

Fatherhood.

Alone.

Chapter 11

Six Weeks Later…

"Justin, stop playing around. Daddy's got a schedule to keep."

"No, no, no, no, no!" Laughter erupted as water flew across the bathroom. Giving Justin a bath was the equivalent of taking one.

In the past, it hadn't been a problem, mostly because bath time was right before bedtime when he'd spent the weekend with me.

Now that I had full custody, it was every night, or at least when I could wrestle him into the tub. Some nights I was so exhausted we crashed in my room, both in need of cleaning.

How had Trina done it? Six weeks of consistent one-on-one time and I was about to go crazy. I had no idea what I was doing.

My parents were on speed dial. Mom checked in nearly every day to be sure we were okay. God I loved her. If my hands were full with one 'mini me', how had she handled twins? I was a handful by myself. Despite the situation, I'm sure my mom was getting a kick out of watching my payback.

"Come on, Justin. Enough is enough. I said bath time is over."

"No!" More water splashed out of the tub.

The terrible twos. I used to joke with Trina about it when we talked on the phone and I heard her fussing at him or complaining about something he'd done. I claimed to have the magic touch. On Justin's weekend visits, we rarely had a problem. Trina said it was because my visits were all about fun and games. No discipline.

I would say she was jealous of our father/son relationship. She'd roll her eyes.

It took losing her to realize how right she'd been. There was a lot to learn on how to be a good parent and not just a fun dad.

Discipline, how to manage his illness, continue potty training. Nutrition and entertainment.

In the short time of being a single father, I had dealt with tummy aches, diarrhea, a nosebleed, insomnia, and nightmares. And that was just the general health issues of children. Justin's illness was a special case.

Justin was diagnosed with sickle cell anemia when he was nearly a year old. He had issues with his lungs, which lead to respiratory infections such as pneumonia. To keep matters from getting worse, he received blood transfusions once a month. When it became apparent his condition would only get worse as he got older, his doctors suggested Justin was a good candidate for a bone marrow transplant. The risks were significant…everything from possible tissue rejection to death. Yet, the possibility of him never dealing with bouts of pain, life threatening infections, and strokes outweighed deciding against it.

Those were the type of choices Trina had dealt with for months without me. Those were the decisions that made her decide that keeping me out of the picture for the rest of Justin's life was no longer an option.

It had been months since he had had the transplant. For six weeks, he'd been under the constant care and monitoring of the doctors and nurses of the children's hospital. Trina and I, along with her family, had taken turns staying in the room with him, practically moving into the place. The support from the medical community had been overwhelming.

Somehow I managed to adjust from being single to being a father who was taking part in making life-altering decisions for a child I didn't know. But I did it because it was impossible not to fall in love with him.

Once Justin was released from the hospital, Trina took over as the primary caregiver. She saw to it he made it to each doctor's appointment. While the transplant seemed to be holding, he was being monitored to insure his body did not reject the donation. Since neither of us were candidates for the procedure, and he didn't have any siblings to donate healthy bone marrow tissue, the doctors had gone another route. Finding a non-related donor that was a close match through a bone marrow registry program had been a blessing. While the recovery process had been slow, it was amazing to see my son's activity level begin to increase as he grew a little bit stronger every day.

Trina would have loved seeing this.

I took time off of work for bereavement and unused vacation in order to adjust to this new lifestyle. Trina's family stepped in to help, but I was wary about leaning on them too much. They didn't like me. The last thing I wanted was for them to find a reason to turn my son against me, due to their negative opinions.

The stress of the situation was taking its toll.

"That's it; I'm pulling the plug on this party." I flipped the latch for the drain and let the water out.

Justin stomped his feet and yelled. I swatted his naked bottom at the outburst. He looked at me with tear-filled eyes and cried.

He balled his fist and put them to his eyes. "I wan Mommy!"

How many times had he said that?

How many times had I responded, 'Me, too'?

I couldn't keep doing that. In no way did I want to replace Trina or let him forget about her, but we had to move on. He needed to understand I was the one caring for him now.

I took a deep breath, and then exhaled slowly. My frustration would not make the situation any better. "Justin, remember when I said it's time to be a big boy?"

He didn't respond, only continued to cry.

"Now's the time. Daddy's got an important meeting today. As soon as you're dressed, I'm taking you to Aunt Felisha's house, okay?"

The mention of Trina's sister did the trick. The tears ceased. I lifted him out of the tub and stood him on the counter to dry him off. When done, I set him on the floor, and directed him to his bedroom. Watching his attempt to put his clothes on with his underwear on backwards always made me smile.

When he was all dressed, I settled him on his bed and put in a DVD of his favorite movie, then went to get dressed myself.

Regardless of what was going on in my personal life, reality was kicking in. My district manager understood my situation and the need for Justin and me to get settled into our new life. But business was business. Corporate needed the situation with the restaurant resolved ASAP.

It was time to get back to real life.

****

"Yo, Tre, my man, what's up?"

I clasped hands with my best friend from back home. "Derrick, it's good to see you, too." I turned to pop the trunk of my car then stepped aside so he could drop in his duffle bag. "Let's get out of here before airport security decides to come this way."

The pickup lane at Hartsfield-Jackson International Airport was packed. There was no time for reunions.

Derrick slammed the trunk then got in the passenger's seat. "How are you holding up?"

In the car, I merged into traffic, eyes forward, watching for pedestrians. "I'm hanging in there." I blew the horn at the idiot in the SUV who decided to change lanes at the last possible second. "You have no idea how much I need your help. This is going to make my career if I can pull it off right. I can't trust any other contractor but you. Thanks for flying down to check it out."

"And again, thank you. Besides, I need to get out of Charlotte for a few days. Helping a friend was a good excuse as any."

Back on the main street, I shot him a glance. "Is that code for 'I've pissed off another woman who's keyed my car'?"

Derrick laughed. "Hey, I don't piss women off. I please and satisfy. If they get attached, then," he shrugged, "that's their fault. I go in the door up front about what they're going to get. Good sex, fun times, and when it's over, it's over."

I glanced his way. "Maybe you should put that in writing."

"I tried that once. Still didn't work."

I laughed. "With all the women you've been with, it's a wonder you don't have any little Derrick Juniors running around."

"I stay wrapped up, you feel me? I got no time for baby momma drama. Speaking of which," I felt his gaze come my way. "You lucked up, you know. From the few times I was around Trina, she was a good woman. I'm sorry she passed.

After the whole baby thing, I was sure you guys would get back together."

I signaled to change lanes and jumped on the highway. "It wasn't like I had a ring on her finger, and it wasn't for a lack of trying either. We had some serious issues to get over before she would give real thought about moving forward. We were just…feeling things out day by day." I squeezed the wheel.

"Did you love her? Before you answer, I want you to really think about it. I'm not talking about that caring shit because she's the mother of your child. I'm talking about that deep, soul-connection kind of love."

I shot him a side eye. "What do you know about that, player?"

His expression was serious. "I know it exists. I see in the way my stepfather looks at my mother. I haven't found it because I'm not looking for it." He shuddered in mock disgust then glanced at me. "There's a point to the question, so answer it."

I focused on the road ahead. "We had something like that once."

"And in the end?"

My brow creased. "No, but that doesn't mean it wasn't going to happen again."

"Let's be real. You guys were dealing with each other for nearly a year. If it was going to happen, it would have happened a long time ago. If neither one of you were feelin' it, then you were wasting each other's time."

I glared at him.

"Hey, look at me any way you want, you know I'm right. My point is you're not meant to be a single father. You like family, and unlike me, you've got the commitment gene. One day you're going to meet the woman who is meant to be your wife and stepmother to Justin."

I shook my head and exited the highway, merging onto city streets. "My hands are full. I don't have the time to invest in romancing a woman. Besides, Justin just lost his mother. He doesn't need a replacement. Getting caught up with a woman right now would make it seem like I can't do this on my own. I'm not about to ask anyone to put up with my son in order to be with me." I shook my head. "Not about to happen."

A whole lot of quiet came from the passenger seat. I risked a peek over and saw Derrick's head moving side-to-side. "And you expect me to believe you're going to be celibate for the next what, sixteen years?" He laughed hard. "Yeah, right."

"Some things are more important than—"

Derrick threw his hands up, forefingers creating the sign of the cross. "Don't you dare say it!"

"Sex." I burst out laughing as he feigned a heart attack.

"Today is…," he pulled his cell phone off his hip after he recovered, fingers racing over the keys. "I'm marking this down on my calendar as the day my best friend said sex was no longer a priority. This coming from the same guy who got busted doing his girl in the kitchen of his parents' house when they were out of town."

I smiled at the memory. "Hey, I was seventeen and horny. Who knew dad would get sick on the road and they'd cut the trip short? But what does that have to do with what I said?"

Derrick raised a hand and counted off fingers. "First of all, you're a man and we have needs that a personal hand job can only remedy for so long."

I laughed.

"Two, you're a man with a kid out of the blue. You didn't do the 'watch her get fat thing while carrying your seed', or watch it come out," he shuddered, "so you haven't had your mind tarnished with the wonders of a woman's treasure." I made a face while he chuckled. "And three…you're a man, damn it. Enough said!"

My grin spread a mile wide. "I've got needs alright. Needs, as in *needs* to take care of my son; priority number one my friend." I turned on the blinker and slowed down to turn into the Applebee's parking lot. "The next priority is getting this place up to company standards. I need the promotion."

Derrick sat forward in his seat, peering out the window. "Don't worry, I got you. After this walk through, you and I are going out for the night. You may be ready to give up sex, I'm not."

Chapter 12

"Kai, come give your mother a hug."

I made my way past the containers of floral supplies littering the space where my mother worked. She was three inches shorter than me, making leaning down in my condition nearly impossible.

My groan couldn't be contained.

"Sit down, sit down!" She pushed the stool she'd occupied in my direction. "Kelli, your sister is here!"

"Mom, did you have to yell?" I rubbed my ear. She shushed me.

"We talked about you this morning. You see the doctor today?"

I nodded.

"And?"

"And…I haven't been released to go back to work yet."

Talk about depressing. The injury to my lower back was worse than I thought. What should have been cured with a few ice pack sessions, prescription pain medication, and bed-rest turned out to be a serious issue.

"What did he say?" Mom watched me with worried eyes.

"Now that the swelling has gone down, they want me to have another CT scan to see the damage. If it was just a sprain, my back should have stopped hurting a few weeks ago. It's possible I might have torn a ligament. If that's the case, recovery is going to take a lot longer."

Which really sucked. Six weeks of being home alone was driving me crazy. Though Sugar was a great companion, I needed to see people outside of my mother and sister coming over to check on me.

"Hey," Kelli walked over and hugged me from the side.

"You're looking more pregnant than ever. I swear you've gained more weight."

Kelli rolled her eyes and waved off my teasing remark. "How's the invalid today?"

"Hey! That's not fair! Mom!"

Our mother laughed and shook her head.

She laughed. "Neither is calling me fat on the sly." She leaned against the counter and put both hands on her belly. "I walked in on the last part of what you were telling momma. So you've really hurt yourself, huh?"

"Apparently. The CT will let them know how bad the tear is. If it's not that bad then I may be able to do some light work or something."

"No, you're not going back to work!" My mother slapped the counter with her fist. "You should never have taken that job. I told you, this is where you need to be. With family."

I sighed. How many times had we had this argument over the last five years?

"Mom, my job is to save families. I got injured doing my job. I don't regret doing it either."

"That's right, Mom. I've never been happy about Kai risking her life, but she did save Trevon's son. That means a lot."

My mother made a face. "That is good, but what about my daughter? I need her to live, too."

"Mom…"

She wiped her face, refusing to let a tear fall.

"You should make flowers like your tjoniy, m-daay thom. Then you'll avoid this," she pointed at my back. "This job isn't dangerous."

While I knew how to speak my mother's native tongue, it would have been much easier for her to just say grandmother and aunt.

"Don't forget cousin." Ricky emerged from the storage room doors carrying a large box.

Mom rolled her eyes. "And him." She mumbled something akin to a curse word in Cambodian.

"You know you love me, m-daay maa." He gave her a quick hug before she swatted at him, a half-hidden smile on her face.

I looked around the shop. *Silk Expressions* had been for generations. My grandmother, an immigrant from Cambodia, opened the location several years after gaining her citizenship. It was a gift from her husband, a white military officer she'd met and fell in love with overseas. He promised to help bring her parents to the U.S., and after several years, not only had her parents come, but her siblings as well. They integrated into the local Cambodian community. Over time, various relatives reached outside our culture and into others. Our family gatherings were never boring. Mixing customs from various cultures was always fun, but at the heart of it all were our Cambodian grandparents' ways.

My mother's gift to the interracial stew had been to marry a black man.

My genetic makeup consisted of Cambodian, Irish, and African-American. I wouldn't trade it for a thing.

My only issue was the fact my mother wanted me to give up my job and follow in her family's footsteps and become a florist.

I was following the family business…just the black side of my grandfather and uncle.

"Kai, you know mom has a point. You're a trained florist, like me. Why don't you come in and help out a few days a week? It'll get you out of the house for a bit while you recover. All you'll have to do is sit and work with your hands. We'll make Ricky do all the heavy lifting because regardless of what he wears after hours, he's still a man." She shot him a wicked grin.

"Watch it, Kelli, or else I'm gonna let your next outfit make you look like the barge you are."

Kelli shot him a sideways glance. "Bitch."

"And proud of it," he snapped his fingers.

I laughed but thought about the offer. The idea of being around family instead of staring at the four walls of my apartment had its advantages. "It's been a while since I made any arrangements. I might be a bit rusty."

"Once you learn, you never forget. No excuse. Come, come." Mom beckoned me to stand beside her at the table where she worked on a large centerpiece. "You finish."

One look at what she was working on and I froze. "What? Mom, no. This is too expensive for me to screw it up."

She rolled her eyes. "What are you gonna do, screw it up like Kelli?"

My sister groaned. "That was one time, a long time ago."

The image of the misshapen centerpiece that was supposed to be for a wedding came back to mind. There was no balance, no structure or symmetry. Hundreds of dollars of fresh flowers had been ruined.

"You have natural talent." She shoved a red rose into my hand. "Don't think. What did Yoda say?"

I shook my head and smiled. Mom knew how much I loved reading the Star Wars novels. Over the years she referred to it when determined to make a point.

"He said 'there is no try, only do'. Or are you thinking about the Nike slogan, 'Just Do It'?"

Mom swatted my arm. "What's the difference? All the same thing. Do." She grabbed my hand and pointed it in the direction of the arrangement. "Just do."

Arguing would only lead to frustration. In the end, she would still get what she wanted.

Clearing my mind, I studied the arrangement, looking for the pattern she'd laid out to determine the arrangement's design.

"Where is this going?" The planned location of the arrangement mattered as much as what combination of flowers would be used.

"Funeral home entrance. Large table display."

Oh, perfect. Death. Wasn't that a sobering thought?

An image of Trevon holding his son outside the funeral home the day of Trina's burial flooded my memory before I could stop it. That had been the last time I'd seen him. It had taken a great effort to attend the funeral. My doctor had ordered me to stay in bed, but I couldn't.

I forced my attention back to the present and let the calm that came from creativity take over. I inhaled the smell of the fresh flowers of the shop and focused on creating perfection. When I looked up again, my mom had placed another vase on the counter beside me and started the foundation for another arrangement.

Had I done that well?

I stepped back from the counter, wincing a bit at the pain that shot down my leg. Close examination revealed a very pleasing arrangement. Well, what do you know…I did still have it.

"I can give you two days a week to start. I have to work around my rehab schedule."

Mom smiled. "Deal."

Chapter 13

"Kai, I have to finish this order. You'll have to handle Miss Thang over there and her mother."

I looked up at Ricky, then over to the customers who'd entered the shop. Mom and daughter admired bridal bouquets on display in the front window.

"Sure, no problem."

He walked over, leaned down to whisper. "They've been in here three times in the last month. Each time it's to change their order. The wedding is in two months. Trust me, you're about to take a trip into florist hell." He patted my shoulder then put on his best fake smile as the daughter waved in our direction. "The daughter is a brat, the mom's a bitch. Do me a favor…don't call me for assistance. I'll end up cussing them both out."

I laughed. "It can't be that bad."

He huffed. "Find me when you're done and repeat that comment with a straight face and I'll pay for your dinner. If you need their current order, see Kelli; it's in the office."

Ricky disappeared into the back to work out of the customers view. Unable to believe his dramatic comparison of the bride-to-be as a Bridezilla, I went back to dusting the display shelves. They would let me know when they were ready.

Day three of working for my family had proven to be very therapeutic for the mind. Out of the house, I had the opportunity to get my thoughts away from all the negative stuff happening in my life.

Lack of a relationship, unknown job security…

At this point, the only happy anything was having my dog.

At least I wasn't a thirty-five-year-old woman obsessed with cats.

"Excuse me, where is Nary?"

A glance over my shoulder showed the mother sizing me up. I put on my customer service smile. "She isn't here today. How can I help you?"

"She's not here?" Hmm…where's that gay guy? I saw him when we came in."

I gritted my teeth in irritation. No wonder Ricky decided to work in the back.

"*Ricky*," I said with emphasis, "is not available. My name is Kai. I'm Nary's daughter. I can assure you I am more than qualified to handle your needs."

She pursed her lips.

"Mom, come on, let her do it! I don't have all day. We have to get our nails done in an hour."

Did I just listen to a grown woman whine like a twelve-year-old?

The mother plopped a purse that was large enough to carry a small dog on the counter. "Fine. My daughter is getting married in two months. We've been here before and have selected everything we want. Your mother took the order. We want to change it. Instead of fuchsia gowns, we're going with yellow, which means the entire color scheme needs to change."

I fought to keep my brow from rising. What Rickey said about the ladies rang true. "Okay, let me get your order form and see what we can do."

I left them standing at the counter and went to the back office where Kelli sat. She appeared exhausted.

"Are you okay?"

She grimaced as if in pain. "I'm tired and this chair is not helping with my back pain. I have ten more weeks before this alien is born and I can have my body back." She rubbed her belly. "Sorry, sweetie. What mommy means is I can't wait for you to be born."

I cracked up. "I don't think babies know what an alien is, Kelli."

"So? Babies can hear in the womb. It's best to keep everything positive so that when they are born, they are happy."

I smirked. "Which book did that come from again?"

"It worked for Christina."

"I thought all that happy came from her dad."

"Whatever," she grumbled. "We'll see how you feel when you get…" Her eyes shot to me. "Damn, I'm sorry, Kai, I didn't mean to—"

I put up a hand and ignored the brief shot of pain in my chest. "Don't worry about it. I came to get the file for, dang, she didn't give me a name, but it's the mother and daughter team Ricky affectionately called 'the brat and the bitch'."

Kelli grimaced. "Mrs. Thornton. Hold on." She rose from the chair and waddled over to the file cabinet. "Here you go."

"Thanks." I took a minute to watch as she rubbed her lower back. "Are you sure you're okay?"

"Yes, I'm fine. I have a doctor's appointment in two hours. After that, I'm going home."

"Do that." My big sister mode clicked in as I noted the bags under her eyes. She hadn't been sleeping. "Are you sure you don't want to leave sooner? Ricky and I can handle the shop."

She slid a hand over her stomach while her eyes went to the pile of paperwork sitting on her desk. "I wish. I'm behind as it is. Plus, there's planning to be done for Trevon's job."

My curiosity piqued. "Trevon's job?"

"He hired me to do some interior design work at the restaurant he manages. I've done a walk through and have most of the layout completed. I want to get this done before my due date. That contractor he's working with is seriously pissing me off, though."

Curious, I walked around her desk and studied the swatch boards, with their samples of colors and textures, and the floor plan lying on the empty table behind her. She was good, that's for sure. What she lacked in floral design talent she seriously made up for as an interior decorator.

While I bucked the system and went outside of the traditional job my mother wanted, Kelli fell in line, but found a way to silently buck and make it her own. Realizing that customers looking for floral arrangements to decorate their homes could use help in doing more, she went to school and got her degree in interior design. The concept worked well. I was proud of my baby sister.

The customer service bell rang at the front desk. "Crap." Caught up in the designs, I had forgotten about the Thorntons.

"Don't worry, it's not like we haven't been down this path with them before. What's the issue now?"

"Dresses have changed color."

Kelli groaned. "Again?"

I stole a quick glance at the file in my hand. "Apparently."

"This makes the third change. Momma said if they came back to make another change, it would be final. I've got to place the order for them next week. They better be sure about it today or else they are going to have a mismatched wedding."

"Won't be our fault. I'll handle it. You take it easy until your appointment."

File in hand, I walked to the counter and was greeted with a whole lot of attitude.

"Sorry for the delay. You want to change the color of your floral arrangements. Correct?"

"Yes." Mom, or rather, Grouchy Number One, tapped her nails on the counter.

I tried my best to ignore the sound. "No more hot pink and white." I took a moment to read over the file and scratched through notes and made some of my own. An asterisk in red indicated notes written by my mother.

'No more changes after July 15th. Order will be sent in. Deposit of half due. If customer has problem, cancel order.'

Reading the note was like hearing my mother's voice.

"Mother, no! I told you, I want different flowers, too."

Grouchy Number One rolled her eyes. "Give her what she wants."

I looked at the order form. "Okay…"

The amount of scratches and notes taken were beyond ridiculous. Now I knew what Ricky and Kelli were talking about.

"Ma'am, you do realize these are fresh flowers we're working with. That means they are seasonal. I can't guarantee what you want will be available. I also have to tell you that this is the last time you'll be able to make a change. Your order needs to be placed next week, but we can't do that until you make a deposit. And just so you know; it will be non-refundable."

"What? You can't just get them from the Farmers' Market?"

I kept my sigh internal. "No, ma'am. Exotic varieties such as the calla lilies come from growers outside of the state of Georgia and are sent cross country."

The door chime rang, announcing the entrance of another patron. A quick peek showed Trevon walking in, holding Justin's hand. A smile spread on my face before I could stop it.

Our eyes met, he smiled back and waved.

"Talk it over then let me know when you've made a final decision." I excused myself and went to where he stood. "Hi, Trevon." I looked down at the spitting image of him. "Hi, Justin."

The little cutie sucked his thumb and leaned into his father's leg. Big brown eyes stared up at me.

"Kai, it's good to see you. You look…better."

My attention went back to Trevon. "Thanks. I am better." I cocked my head to the side and studied him.

It was obvious he'd been through a lot. While as handsome as the night we met, his eyes no longer held the confident, cocky heat. Weariness and a bit of sorrow had replaced them. Exactly what happened when your world got turned upside down.

"Daddy…" Justin tugged on Trevon's pant leg, arms raised, as if expecting to be picked up. Trevon complied. Satisfied, Justin laid his head on his father's shoulder.

"How is he?"

Trevon rubbed his son's back. "He has his good days and bad days. Today is an in-between day." He kissed Justin's forehead. "Is Kelli here?"

"Yes. She's in her office. I'll get her."

I tried to ignore the disappointment I felt at the abrupt end to our conversation.

"Trevon, hey," Kelli said when she emerged from her office. "I'm sorry, but I haven't completed the sketches yet. Were we supposed to meet today?"

"No, and that's not why I'm here. I'm in a bind and wanted to know if you can do me a favor?"

Kelli rubbed her belly. "What's going on?"

"An emergency at work. Today's my off day, but the manager on duty got sick and had to go home. I have to go in but don't have a babysitter."

"What about his grandparents?"

Trevon shook his head. "Things aren't going well with them. They've been giving me a hard time about how I care for Justin." He sighed. "I don't need to give them any more ammunition."

She shook her head. "I'm sorry, but I can't. I've got a doctor's appointment this afternoon."

"Damn." He rubbed Justin's back as his eyes lowered in thought.

Watching stress overcome his already weary expression pained me.

"I'll do it."

Kelli glanced at me in disbelief while Trevon stared, surprise replacing the stressed expression.

"Are you sure? You don't have to—"

I rolled my eyes. "I'm good with kids, so there's nothing to worry about."

Trevon's eyes shot to Kelli for confirmation.

"It's true, she's great with my daughter," she qualified.

Trevon studied me. "I don't think you're not, it's just…Justin has some special needs and—"

I pulled my cell phone out of my pocket, opened the voice recorder, and held the phone in his direction. "Tell me what I need to know."

His eyes widened, looking from me to the phone. Then he started to talk.

When he was done, I saved it and then replayed the recording. "Satisfied?"

His nod was slow, as if questioning whether he should trust me with the wellbeing of his son.

The urge to remind him it was I who saved him from a burning building and that babysitting would not be a challenge was on the tip of my tongue. Instead, I grabbed a blank sheet of paper and wrote down my cell phone number and address. "We'll leave here when the shop closes. I have no plans tonight, so you can pick him up at any time."

Bewilderment crossed his face, followed by gratefulness. "Thank you, Kai."

"You're welcome."

Chapter 14

"Kai, its Trevon. I'll be leaving work in ten minutes. I should be at your place in say…an hour?"

"There's no need to rush. Justin and I are fine." I ran my fingers over the sleepy boys head. We were lying on my bed watching *The Lion King*.

"How is he?" The worry was evident in his voice.

"Better, I think. I followed the instructions you gave and he seemed to settle pretty quickly. Though," I chuckled, "I think it was Sugar who did most of the work."

"Sugar?"

"My dog. They took to each other in no time. You'd think they'd known each other since she was a puppy."

"Oh, well, that's good. Let me wrap up here. I'll see you soon."

The line disconnected. I glanced down at Trevon's son. "Justin, daddy will be here soon, okay?"

He gave a half-asleep nod, thumb in mouth, and free hand on Sugar's back.

Babysitting Justin had been a bit of a challenge. Unlike playing with my niece, who was a few years older, and could run around doing pretty much anything, Justin needed more. Special attention was given to be sure there weren't things he ate and drank didn't work against the medications he had to take, or that he did anything that could cause him to injure himself. He also needed to drink plenty of fluids and take his medication on time.

When we left the floral shop and came to my house, the first thing we did was take Sugar and my neighbor's dog for a walk. Then we ate a snack. Justin all but jumped for joy when he saw my DVD collection of children's movies I kept for my niece's visits. After that, it had been smooth sailing.

Justin was a very well behaved little boy; his mother had done a very good job. For the most part, he'd been quiet, but observant. If he wanted to know something, he'd ask. 'Wha dat?' seemed to be the standard question said around a thumb in his mouth as he pointed with his free hand.

An hour later, on the dot, the doorbell rang. "Justin, daddy's here." I looked over and realized he'd fallen asleep with one arm wrapped around Sugar. She slept, too.

I climbed off the bed, pulled the edge of the spread over him, and headed for the door.

Trevon stood in the doorway, his head bent down, and hands in the pockets of his dress slacks. When his eyes lifted, I saw the weary expression on his face, like a man who'd had a long day and was about to endure an even longer evening.

"Hey, come in." I stepped aside; letting him pass, then shut the door. He stopped just inside the living room. "Did you have a hard time finding the place?"

"No. GPS worked great. Nice place you have here." His eyes traveled around my apartment. "Where is he?"

There was no mistaking the worry on his face. I would have been offended, if I didn't recognize his concern was about his son's health and not my babysitting skills.

"Thanks. Follow me." I led the way down the short hall of my two-bedroom apartment. Boy and dog lay in the same spot. The only difference was Sugar had lifted her head and begun sniffing the air to catch Trevon's scent. She growled low in her throat.

"It's okay, Sugar. He's a friend." I placed a hand on Trevon's bicep and emphasized the word. "Friend."

Sugar's eyes left Trevon and met mine as if studying my demeanor in order to see if I felt threatened. Sensing I was okay, she looked back at Trevon, growled once more in warning then laid her head down. Though she quieted, her eyes were still trained on him.

"Wow…she's…trained."

"Worth every penny. She won't bother you unless she feels I'm in danger or I give her the command."

Apprehensive, Trevon's attention went to Justin, who rested next to my bodyguard.

"Justin is fine. She took to him the minute he came in the door. She'll protect him like she protects me. He's part of her pack."

One of his eyebrows rose in question. "Her pack? Guess that means leaving will be hard to do."

I angled my head. "No, it won't. Are you in a hurry?"

"I don't want to impose; you've done enough already."

My lips pursed. This time I was offended. "You know, you make it hard for me to like you. I thought we were two adults who'd moved past what happened between us. I would like to think of you as a friend." I turned, walked down the hall and into the galley styled kitchen.

He followed. "A friend?"

"Or at least an acquaintance. Sit down." I pointed to the small table sitting in the equally small dining room.

"Acquaintance?"

I looked up at the ceiling. If he repeated what I said one more time…

Inhaling deeply, I faced him.

Trevon was more than concerned about his son. He was exhausted, but not in the physical sense. It was emotional, as if he carried the weight of the world on his shoulders and had no one to help him along the way. I decided to use a different approach.

"Sit down, please." I smoothed the tone of my voice to be less demanding and more inviting. "Have you eaten today?"

He blinked, then rubbed his face. “Once. This morning when I made Justin pancakes for breakfast.”

It was now eleven PM.

“I’ve got just the thing.” I reached in the fridge and pulled out a tray of leftovers. “Hope you like lasagna; it’s what we had for dinner.”

We both looked down as his stomach growled at the suggestion.

Grinning, I reached for a plate.

“Thanks.” Trevon sat at the table.

Plate in the microwave, I turned to find him rubbing his eyes yet again with the heel of his hand. There was no mistaking the level of stress he was under.

“About this friend thing; I think you need one.” I leaned against the counter.

Trevon’s head shot up. “I’m not the same man you met at the bar, Kai. I’m not looking for—”

I burst out laughing, then quickly covered my mouth. “Not that kind of ‘friend’”. I did air quotation marks. Though truth be told, he looked as if he could use some form of a physical release.

The memory of what it felt like to be with him that night made my body tingle. I turned as the microwave dinged, thankful for the distraction. I retrieved the plate and faced him.

“I meant a real friend. You’ve been through a lot. Losing Justin’s mother and nearly losing…” There was no need to complete the statement.

“Justin.” Our eyes met and I was the first to look away, using the excuse of getting a fork as a reason to break the contact.

“I guess we really are more than aquaintances.” His chuckle sounded sad.

I turned and found Trevon's eyes were no longer on mine. Instead, he watched my body. When he realized he'd been caught, he focused on the plate in my hand instead. His cheeks seemed to turn a slight shade of red. "Thanks." He accepted the plate, studied it. "Um, can I have a fork?"

Caught off guard by the way he'd been watching me, I blinked, realizing it was still in my hand. "Here. Would you like something to drink? The pickings are a bit slim."

"Whatever you have is fine." He accepted the fork and dug in.

At the cabinet, I glanced over my shoulder as I grabbed a cup. Every ounce of his attention was on his plate. He was hungrier than I thought.

I poured us both a glass of soda and then sat in the chair across from him. It didn't appear he wanted to talk, so I gave him a moment to get a few more bites down. Satisfied that he would finish, I decided to instigate the conversation.

My attention went to the engraved decorations on the side of my glass as I ran my fingers over them. "How are things going with Justin?"

He chewed, swallowed, then poked at his food. "I'm not sure how Trina did it alone. Juggling a job, home, his health." His laugh was cynical. "Actually I do; her family, that's how."

Confused, my brow creased. "They're not helping you? That doesn't make sense. I thought they would go out of their way to look after him."

Trevon sat his fork down on a near empty plate and sat back in his seat. "It's a bit more than that. They want to help too much."

"I don't understand."

He sighed and ran a hand over his low cut hair. "They want full custody, Kai. Trina's mother told me last week after I picked him up from a weekend visit. It was more than a comment. I got served custody hearing papers two days ago."

That explained the stressed out expression. My heart ached for him.

"What about your family? They're not helping?" Obvious he was no longer interested in food, I stood to remove the dishes and put them in the sink.

"They want to, but can't. They live in North Carolina."

"Oh." I leaned against the counter.

"I've been blessed with friends who know how to take care of kids and have had my back since day one. Andre and Sharice babysit when they can, your sister, too. That's why I dropped in like that. I could take him to day care, but he needs special attention. Even though he's had the bone marrow transplant, he still has to be monitored. Individualized and private care cost more." He shook his head. "I understand why they want to take him, though. His grandparents are retired, and she's a registered nurse. They've got a crap load of aunts and uncles who have helped with babysitting and doctor's appointments since he was diagnosed with the illness." He huffed. "Then there's me, the inexperienced father who's been in his life for less than a year and his equally inexperienced friends who have no idea how much it takes to manage his illness. What leg do I have to stand on in court?" His eyes red, he looked down at his hands. "I can't lose him, Kai. I just found him. I just can't…"

I walked over to where he sat and put a hand on his shoulder. "Trevon, I'm here. I saved him once. I'm willing to do whatever it takes to help you keep him. He's already lost his mother. He can't lose you, too."

Trevon turned in his seat, wrapped his arms around my waist, and put his head against my stomach. "Thank you, Kai…thank you…"

I wrapped my arms around him, running my hands over his shoulders and the top of his head. Though he made little sound, it was obvious by the shaking of his shoulders that he was crying. It wasn't hard to imagine what type of stress and issues he was going through at a time like this. "Anything you need, I'm here for you."

After a moment, he pulled away and wiped his eyes. "Whoa, didn't expect that to happen." His light brown complexion and dark brown eyes were red, both from crying and what I guessed to be embarrassment, since he wouldn't meet me with eye contact.

"The physical contact or the offer to help?" My laugh was forced as I stepped back, putting space between us.

It was hard to tell who was rocked more by the unexpected hug. While it was apparent he needed emotional support, my body's reaction was one of the physical kind.

"Both." His voice was filled with honesty. So were his eyes. "There's no way to get around the fact we've had sex, Kai…damn good sex. But the truth of the matter is…I'm not that guy anymore."

Our eyes met and held for a moment as the implication of his words sank in. "I understand."

His eyes stayed on me and were hard to read. "What do we do from here?"

I inhaled deeply to calm my still unsettled nerves. "I'm not looking for a relationship. My focus is on healing so I can get back to work. I've already had too much down time. Until then, I've got free time on my hands. Keeping an eye on Justin would be my pleasure. It won't cost you a thing, except maybe an occasional dinner if you haven't eaten. You can't take care of him and yourself if you don't eat. I want to be your friend, Trevon. Friends look out for each other."

He studied me. "I feel the same. Too much is on my plate to think about a relationship, either. Keeping Justin and my job in order to support him is my focus. I could definitely use a friend like you, though."

"So, we're on the same page? Friendship, but no sex?"

His nod was slow. "That sounds about right."

I extended my hand. "Deal?"

After a moment, he accepted. "Deal."

Chapter 15

"Mr. Campbell, Mr. Clark will see you now."

I stood, adjusted my tie, and followed the receptionist down what felt like the longest hallway I'd ever been down in my life.

"Mr. Campbell?" The lawyer stood, hand extended. "My name is Peter. It's nice to meet you. Unfortunately it's under dire circumstances. Please, sit." He directed me to an empty chair across from his desk before sitting himself.

I held the file I brought with me in my lap. It seemed slim and empty compared to the mountainous file he slid in front of him. He flipped it open and scanned a yellow Post It note.

"You are a referral?" He pushed the glasses up on his thin nose before looking at me.

"Yes, sir. A friend of mine, Andre Lafitte, sent me. He told me you were a good lawyer. You assisted him with determining paternity and child support for his daughter."

He repeated Andre's last name several times. "Sorry, I've dealt with so many cases with those types of issues that I would have to see him face-to-face to remember. If he referred you then the results of his case must have been in his favor."

I wasn't sure how to take the comment. Was it that he really did have that many clients or did he not care about the results, only the money earned?

He glanced over the rim of his glasses. "Yes, I really am that busy, Mr. Campbell." He flipped through the first pages of the file.

Were my thoughts transparent? I squirmed in my seat.

"Look, you don't know me, but feel free to check my number of case responses. My career is an open book. I'm not saying that to brag. When I am representing a client, you are my focus, not someone I represented last year, last month, or yesterday. You are paying me hard earned money to keep what is most precious to you, your son. Tell me about him."

Point taken. I cleared my throat.

"Justin is two, but will be three in a few months. His mother and I parted on bad terms when we were dating. I didn't know she was pregnant at the time."

"Bad terms; meaning someone was unfaithful?" He looked up from the file.

I adjusted my tie. "Yeah."

"By your response I take it that was you."

"Does it matter?"

"Mr. Campbell, you are about to take on a case with family members of the deceased who don't feel you're fit to care for your son. Your life and record of decisions made, both good and bad, are going to be public record. We need to address them now. The more I know, the better prepared I will be to protect your rights. I don't want to be blind-sided in court."

I took a deep breath; time to air my dirty laundry.

"Yes, I cheated. Trina and I had been together for a few years. We lived together. She wanted to get married and I wasn't ready. I should have broken up with her. In the end I cheated so she'd break up with me. It was stupid. I was stupid."

"And she was pregnant at the time?"

I shook my head. "No, well, I guess yeah, but I didn't know about it."

"Is there any chance Justin could be someone else's child?"

"No, I'm certain he's mine. When she contacted me and told me I was the father, I knew it when I saw the photos." He looked at me as if I were an imbecile. "After I found out about his illness, a test was done to verify that I carried the sickle cell gene and was not compatible for a bone marrow transplant. A paternity test was done as well." I dug into my file and slipped him the results.

He read the paper and then made notes on a yellow legal pad.

"Justin's illness brought you together. Do you think she would have told you about your son if he wasn't sick?"

I shrugged. "Honestly? I don't know. As it was, it had been two years."

"Since you were made aware of your paternity, what steps have been taken to care for him? Did you pay child support?"

"Yes."

"Was she awarded monthly payments?"

"No, we never went before a judge. I just did it."

Mr. Clark regarded me as if I were an oddity. "Do you have anything in writing about this agreement? Any receipts, cancelled checks?"

"No, should I?"

"A paper trail makes a difference. You can say you paid, but without the mother being alive to testify to the fact, the family can claim you didn't."

I flipped through the papers in my file again until I found the ones I was looking for. "We did open a joint savings account for Justin. I made deposits there. She pulled out money for his medicine, clothes, and toys." I handed him the statements.

He reviewed them. "This will work. You said you both signed up for this account?"

"Yes."

"I'll need a copy of the signature paperwork from your bank."

"Okay." I sat silent as he made more notes.

"Now; visitation. I take it there was a verbal agreement here as well?"

"Yes. Justin lived with her, but spent every other weekend with me. In between times, I'd go over for dinner or we'd meet up at the park or something."

"The shared custody went well?"

"Yes."

"What did the family think?"

"Hers or mine?"

"Both."

I squirmed in my seat. "My family lives outside of Georgia, but they are supportive. My parents have flown in twice to see him and love him to death." I cleared my throat. "Trina's family, well, the fact we're having this conversation pretty much says it all."

"Not necessarily," Mr. Clark stated. "It could be they fear losing touch with their grandson who is now living with his biological father. Or," he shrugged, "They could not like you and feel your lack of being there from the beginning and his illness leaves you inexperienced and unqualified. What do you think?"

"They hate my guts because I broke Trina's heart."

He chuckled a bit and shook his head. "You wouldn't be the first one, that's for sure. So let me ask you this, is there a woman, or significant other in your life?"

"What?" The abrupt change in subject threw me.

Mr. Clark sifted through more papers before pulling out one and reading it. "It says here that you were seen in the arms of another woman with Justin by your side at his mother's funeral." His eyebrows lifted before his gaze shifted to me.

"What?" I sat up in my seat. "In another woman's arms? What kind of bull—"

"I'm just reading the claims set to me by the family's lawyer. Apparently there is concern that while you may have been trying to patch things up with the mother of your son, you were seeing another woman on the side. It says here you were seen with another woman at the funeral." He looked up at me, adjusted his glasses that had slipped down the bridge of his nose again.

I forced myself to think back to that day.

I had been sitting alone in the atrium of the funeral home with Justin in my lap when my friends arrived with Kai in tow. We'd hugged. She spoke to Justin. My mother came, saying Trina's mother wanted Justin. Kai and I sat alone for a few minutes before Trina's sister appeared.

Damn.

It did look as though I had a girlfriend.

"Kai is a friend. A firefighter ...*the* firefighter who saved Justin's and Trina's lives a few days before. What the hell does that have to do with—?"

"I would think it's rather obvious."

I sunk into my seat. Talk about uncomfortable. For the first time, I was sure my chances of being awarded sole custody or custody at all, was dwindling. And if it ever came out that we'd slept together...the consequences could be damning.

Mr. Clark wrote some more notes. "You have been in Justin's life for how long?"

I took a deep breath. "Nine and a half months."

"During this time, what proof do you have that an effort was being made on the part of Justin's mother to get back together?

Proof? The signs had been there towards the end. Especially after the fire. For once, Trina had stood up to her mother and acknowledged the fact she and Justin needed to move in with me. Her mother had witnessed this. What were the chances she would admit that in court before a judge and risk losing her grandson?

"Nothing in writing. Before she died, just after the fire when Justin was in the hospital, I convinced her to move in with me instead of her parents."

Mr. Clark's eyebrows peaked with interest. "Any witnesses?"

"Yes, her mother, who disagreed with her decision. I had the final word and said it would happen."

"Good." He wrote more notes. "This is very good."

"I seriously doubt she'd be willing to admit that."

Mr. Clark looked up with a gleam in his eye. "Probably not, but the fact that she was in the room and witnessed the final wishes of her daughter will be enough to give some credit to your side of the case in the eyes of the judge."

I felt a small weight lift from my chest. "You think I have a chance to win this?"

"Mr. Campbell, as the biological father, you always have a chance. To be honest, unless you are doing something that could endanger the life of the child, there's not much they can say to the judge to prove you are an unfit parent. The stronger your case is and the more people you have on your side, the better your chances will be. All you have to do is keep doing what you're doing with Justin. If there is room for improvement, make it. And though I know this will be hard, you need to keep the communication with his grandparents active. Now is not the time to cut ties or deny them access to their grandson. Their fear is part of the reason they are asking for custody. Allowing them visits will show the court that you are willing to do what's in the best interest of the child. They are who he's known since he was born.

Cutting him off completely could be detrimental. Is that something you are willing to do?"

"If it will help me keep Justin, I'll do whatever it takes."

Chapter 16

"Come on, Kai. You don't have anything else better to do with your night. Join us."

My sister's voice went from its usual cadence of authority to a whine. Just like when we were kids.

My purse in hand, I turned to face her. "Yes, I do, Kelli. I've got a date with a good book and some homemade chocolate chip cookies, straight out of the oven."

"Don't you mean straight out of the bag?" Ricky looked up from his hand and blew dust off the finger nail file.

"From bag, to my oven, to my belly." I rubbed it for emphasis, causing us all to laugh.

"Exactly," Kelli continued. "And if you keep that up, the belly won't go away either. The point is you have no life and need to get one."

"And hanging out with you guys making flower arrangements after hours does what exactly?" I held my hands up, balancing invisible weights in my hands.

"We're taking part in an age old ritual in our family: women, flowers, food, and conversation. It's the perfect way to end a week by sharing the good, bad, and getting rid of the ugly."

"Plus there's alcohol and snacks," Ricky added.

My attention was piqued. "Alcohol? Why didn't you say so?" I put my purse down and rubbed my hands together.

"Uh, slow your roll. In order to participate, you have to do your part. Since this is your first official night with the *Black Lilies*, it's your job to secure snacks and beverages. We'll handle the rest." Kelli dug into her purse, handed me a list and some cash.

I read it and smiled. "Fine by me."

Outside, I unlocked my car, hopped in, and let the windows down to release the built up steam from the day. 'Hotlanta' sure knew how to live up to its name. I turned the air conditioner on to the max. While waiting for the car to cool down, I plugged in my phone and took a second to review my emails. My heart leapt at the one from the fire chief.

I took a moment to gather myself before hitting the open button.

Disappointment. Complete and utter disappointment.

I put my car in reverse and headed to the grocery store.

Nearly a month had passed since I started working for my mother and I was still under the doctor's care. I felt better and expected to be released from the doctor any day. The only problem was now my chief required me to see the county shrink before being allowed back on duty. That sort of action normally went to firefighters who'd witnessed death in the line of duty. I hadn't. Trina had been alive when I pulled her down the ladder. Her death wasn't until hours later.

That didn't prevent me from feeling responsible, though.

At night, I dreamed that she had appeared in her window in need of rescue before we wasted time entering apartments that were empty. Those few precious minutes could have been the reason why she inhaled those damning breaths of poisonous air.

Help would have arrived sooner and she would be alive. Trevon would have his…what? Baby momma back?

I parked in front of the liquor store. Inside, I purchased the alcohol needed for the evening. Vodka, orange juice, a bottle of wine, and sparkling grape juice. That was for Kelli, no doubt. When pregnant, she lived off the stuff. It was the closest thing she could use when pretending to have a glass of real wine.

When I arrived back at the shop, the 'closed' sign had been flipped, yet the door remained unlocked.

The lights were low in the front of the store, and on full blast in the back. A folding table and several folding chairs sat in the usual open floor space. A festive cloth covered the table, while the basics needed to create a floral arrangement sat in front of each empty chair. Ricky walked in, pushing a cart full of baskets. Each one held bunches of silk flowers of a wide variety of color and species.

"Looks like you had a fun trip to *Hobby Lobby*." I sat my purchases on an empty side table where fresh cut fruit and other snacks had been set out.

"Oh yeah. You know I can't let these ladies do anything with the fresh ones."

I laughed. "I thought this was supposed to be a class."

"How in the hell do you teach tipsy women the correct way to cut a fresh stem? That would be a waste of time and money." He pointed to the cart. "Silk flowers aren't real so they can't damage the hell out of them and I don't have a heart attack."

"Makes sense to me. Where's Kelli?"

"In the restroom."

The door chime rang, signaling the arrival of the first member of the *Black Lilies*.

"Hey, Ricky!" A woman who appeared to be of Indian descent entered with a tray of goodies in her hand.

"Miri!" Ricky met her half way and the two of them air kissed each other's cheek.

I fought to keep from rolling my eyes. Ricky loved moments like this when he could be 'one of the girls'. Once the shop had officially closed, he dipped into the bathroom to put his 'face' on. His clothes remained the same, however, tastefully selected as always. Though he loved cross-dressing, he didn't put on the full queen get up except for special occasions.

I studied his artfully applied makeup. Damn. He did a better job than I did. I shook my head, and made a mental note to ask for private lessons…again.

"Miri, this is my cousin, Kai, Nary's oldest daughter. Kai, this is Doctor Miri Patel."

"Doctor." I accepted the handshake. "Wow, that's cool. What field?"

"Pediatrician. Kelli's daughter and Sharice's son are my patients."

"Really? Small world."

"Yes, it is."

"What brings you to this crazy group of people?" We walked over to the snack table.

"Your sister. She kept going on and on about how great these meetings are. She didn't lie. This is the best form of stress relief after a long week of crying babies and stressed out parents." She picked up the bottle of Red Moscato and grinned. "Now that's what I'm talking about."

"You know the rules, Ms. Miri. No poppin' bottles until everyone is here."

"Who's left?" I glanced around at the empty seats.

"Kelli, Sharice, and Aunty." Ricky took his seat.

My eyebrows rose in surprise. "Mom's a part of this group?"

"Yep, and let me tell you, honey," Ricky put a hand on his hip. "Your momma is full of stories. You wouldn't believe she used to be a 'ho' back in the day."

"Ricky! Quit lying!" Kelli joined us at the table. "No, she wasn't. She…," Kelli's brow pulled together in thought. "She got along with men. That's all."

Her attempt to clean up Ricky's revelation was lost once he and Miri burst into uncontrollable laughter.

Curiosity piqued, I was anxious for the last members of the group to arrive. Apparently, there were a lot of things I'd been missing.

****

An hour and a half later, the wine was nearly gone, along with the small bottle of vodka, orange juice, and most of the snacks. Everyone's floral arrangements were nearly complete. I had to admit, somewhere along the line, Sharice and Miri had actually picked up on a few floral design techniques.

"Kai, when are you going to let go of your self-imposed celibacy streak and ride the saddle again?" Sharice accentuated the question by throwing her hand in the air and twirling a make-believe lasso.

Daggers shot out of my eyes at the woman I'd known since she became best friends with my baby sister. A quick glance around showed the question had drawn everyone's attention.

"Wait a minute; I thought this was supposed to be a floral design club. When did we start gossiping and getting into each other's business?"

"First of all, we've been doing it all night, so don't think your business isn't going to be put out there. Second, the *Black Lilies* is a floral design club. It's also a place where we let our hair down and work out the details of what's going on in our life. It's like a sisterhood," Sharice explained.

"Exactly. Our unofficial logo is the Black Calla Lily. Each of us has a flower assigned that represents us as women. It defines our personalities and where we are in life. It's empowering, too. We chose lilies because they represent beauty and femininity. Everyone has a different lily and different color," Kelli added.

Because I learned the symbolic meaning of flowers and their colors under my mother's tutelage, the logic made perfect sense.

"So the black is because it's a combination of all colors, right?" She nodded. "What's your flower?"

"Kelli and I share the same one, Lily of the Valley, because it is the wedding flower and it's symbolic of elegance, calm, and gentleness." Sharice replied, her enthusiasm speaking volumes about how happy she was with her life. "And since we are the happily married women of the group, it's perfect. I love the little white bell shaped flowers. I like to think each one of them stands for my husband and son."

I noticed my sister didn't respond to that comment, and looked away instead.

"Mine is the Easter Lily because it represents life, hope, and virtue, which is pretty much what I do as a doctor, give hope and make life better for those who are sick." Miri beamed. "And white is my favorite color by the way."

I smiled and looked over at Ricky. "What about you? You're not a woman. Where do you fit in?"

He smirked. "My flower is the Stargazer Lily. It symbolizes liberation from life's obstacles and worry. When have you seen me give a damn about what someone has to say about me and my lifestyle?" He rolled his head and snapped his fingers. "Besides, you know I look good in hot pink."

We all laughed.

"What about you, Mom? What's your flower?"

My mother had been silent for the most part of the evening, laughing at our jokes and commenting when she felt the need. It was obvious something was on her mind, though, at least when it came to me. It was hard not to miss the fact she watched me as the evening went on.

She picked up her plastic cup of wine, sipped, then set it down. "My flower is Tiger Lily. It means courage. It means I find balance and happiness in my life. Unlike my daughter." She pointed a finger in my direction. "Answer Sharice's question. Why are you celibate?" As always, her sentences were clipped, reflecting her Cambodian tongue.

My eyes widened in embarrassment, but there was no running away from answering a question once my mother zeroed in on you. I squirmed in my seat and looked at my near empty cup. I swallowed the rest of the Moscato, then scooted my chair back from the table and went for a refill. "I haven't self-imposed anything. I've been rehabbing a back injury. I'm in no mood for that type of physical activity."

Sharice snorted. "Hmm. Then why have you been spending so much time around Trevon?"

Ricky slapped the table. "Honey child, spill the beans!"

I turned to stare at Kelli who'd shrunk back, a look of guilt on her face. Her eyes darted to the arrangement in front of her as if it were suddenly lacking something special.

Beside her, my mother leaned in, shoving her completed vase to the side to get direct access to my facial expression.

Miri sat back in her chair, slightly buzzed and wide-eyed, her gaze bouncing between everyone at the table.

"I'm not spending time with Trevon." I glared at Kelli. My sister had a really big mouth. "I'm babysitting his son. We're nothing but friends," I added, forcing my words to sound genuine.

Miri's hand went up. "Excuse me, but fill me in? Who is Trevon and what's up with his son?"

"It's like this…" Ricky poured out the details. The fire, the rescue, the death, the babysitting.

"So you're the mommy-hero now?" my mother asked.

"I'm not a hero. I did my job. And no, I'm not trying to be his mother, either. I'm just a person helping a friend in need." It was hard to keep irritation out of my voice.

Mom sat at the opposite end of the table, so it was impossible to avoid her glare.

"Then why does he seem to look at you like...," Kelli paused in thought. "I don't know, like you've got history?"

Ricky tapped a finger on his lower lip. "Now that you mention it, he does look at her like he's infatuated. Hell, now that I really think about it, you look at him the same way."

Sharice stared at me in surprise. Apparently, the thought of me and Trevon as a potential couple never crossed her mind. "Hold up, you and my husband's best friend are an item? How come I haven't heard about this? Andre tells me everything!"

"Oh, this is good," Miri mumbled. She held her nearly empty cup in Ricky's direction for a refill as he got up from the table.

"History?" Mom leaned forward, her elbow resting on the edge of the table. She sipped her drink and stared at me with the look she used when I was a child. It demanded truth without it being a verbal threat. But it was still a threat.

I slid back to my chair, trying my best not to squeeze the life out of my refilled cup. How much could I say without giving away too much? A quick glance at the nosy people at the table answered that question. "We don't exactly have a history." I stared down at the wine then drank nearly half of the contents. "We just...met once. I had no idea he knew Andre...or Malik."

Sharice leaned forward in her seat. "Define 'met'." She used air quotation marks for emphasis.

I took a deep breath. "Our paths crossed one night in a bar about a year ago. We talked...connected."

"Connected as in...," Ricky leaned forward and demonstrated by sliding his index finger in and out of his closed fist.

The room was so silent it seemed no one was breathing.

I pursed my lips, shut my eyes, and nodded once.

Everyone howled.

"You go girl! That is one fine man!" Ricky reached over the side of the table to give me a high five.

Efforts to hide my grin were lost. I gave in and accepted the gesture.

"Ooo..." Kelli said, her eyes as big as saucers at the bit of gossip.

Miri laughed. "Damn, this is better than my daytime soaps!"

Across the table, my mother had a weird grin on her face.

"Hold up," Sharice said. "You got your ho on with Trevon Campbell and let him hit it?"

I held my cup to my mouth and mumbled, "Yes." I swallowed the remaining liquid quickly as more shouts, howls, and hands slapped the table.

Now that I'd admitted it, I might as well own it.

"And a year ago? Weren't you engaged to my brother-in-law at the time?" Sharice asked.

That bit of news quieted the merry band of women. Well, everyone except for Miri who now mumbled something in a language I knew nothing about.

"It was the night I called off the engagement, okay? And...," I drawled for emphasis. "It was only one night. We didn't realize our circle of friends was so small until the night you invited us over after Junior was born." I looked pointedly at Sharice, whose eyes grew so wide I thought they might pop out.

"Hold up, you're all friends, right?" Miri pointed around the circle. "How did you not know who he was?"

"Because of my crazy work schedule. I'm a firefighter and sometimes I'm not available to go to the parties. That day was a random incident."

"But you were with Malik that day," Sharice confirmed.

I could tell her new line of questioning was leading up to accusing me of something.

Across the way, mom's eyebrows lifted. "On again, off again. Girl don't know when to let the man go. Him, I never liked." She shook a finger in my direction.

"Yeah, well, after seeing Trevon that day, I realized something about my relationship with Malik, and myself. I deserved better. That one night with Trevon was better than the years I put into my relationship with Malik. Yet for some stupid reason, I went back to him after realizing better existed." I shrugged and stared into the empty cup in my hand. "Either way, he and I are done."

Alcohol had a way of making you say things you normally would keep to yourself.

"Who? The Malik guy?" Miri asked. She was so engaged in the conversation, I almost thought she would be making notes the moment she reached her car.

"Both. Never again will I allow myself to lower my standards in search of the perfect man. As far as Trevon is concerned, we've decided to keep our friendship strictly platonic."

"No sex?" Ricky asked, disappointment on his face.

I nodded.

The room was silent.

"Was it good sex?"

Everyone's eyes went to my mother who was the one asking the question.

"What? I was young woman once. Your father and I didn't wake up married. Women have needs like men." Snickers were hidden behind hands by all sitting at the table.

"Stop acting like you are virgins." She pointed at everyone before her attention came back to me. "So, Kai, good sex or no?"

"On a scale of one to ten, to be fair," Kelli amended.

I put my hands up in the air. "Twelve and a half!"

Shrieks of laughter forced me to cover my ears even as I laughed along with them.

"Okay, so now that you are an official member of the *Black Lilies* club, you need a flower." Kelli looked over at our mother. "As matriarch of this family and leader of this group, do you want to do the honors?"

She nodded and took a moment to study me. "You, my daughter, are a special woman. You have been hurt on your path to love, but it has made you stronger. You could be bitter, but you are not. You look for the good in people, in family, and friends." She stood, examined the buckets of unused flowers sitting nearby, and selected one before walking to my side of the table. I accepted the flower as she kissed my forehead. "The yellow Calla Lily. It means friendship and happiness. Both are coming to you, my daughter. Keep on your path and you will find the happiness you deserve."

Chapter 17

"Tre, man, I can do this job in my sleep."

"I'm sure you can, Derrick. That's why I wanted you on it." I watched as he studied the floor plans for the renovation.

The minute corporate sent them to me, I forwarded the email. Now it was one o'clock in the morning, Justin was bathed and in bed, and we were talking via Skype.

"Got a start date for me?"

Derrick scratched his chin and turned his back to the camera. I could see a huge calendar hanging on the wall. "Let me call my guys. I know a few who don't mind traveling and will want in on this gig. All I have to do is set it up. I'm thinking with a large enough crew, we can drive down and get this done in about four to six weeks, tops."

"Can you step away that long?"

Derrick faced the camera again. "When you're part owner of the company, you can do what you want, when you want. Not to mention, the construction industry is a bitch, so you take what you can when it comes in and store up that shit. A flux in the stock market can rip a great paying job out of your grip like that," he snapped his fingers for emphasis. "Shit, 9-11 changed a lot. Remember how my dad went from working in the union to unemployed in less than a month?"

"Yeah, that was a crazy time." I sat back in my chair and scratched my head.

"Then a few years later, the housing industry crashed. No more subdivisions. Half-built houses were everywhere. The one thing I learned from my dad was the importance of being a multi-skilled carpenter and to never turn down a job unless the customer is going to be a pain in the ass."

I laughed, remembering the long talks Coach used to have with Derrick and me when we were teens. Everything he taught us didn't have to do with basketball. One thing he never did was hold back the truth about life, women, and working.

"How is the old man? I know he quit coaching a while back, but is he still running the business?

"Nah. He retired and passed the reins over to me. How do you think he's doing?"

"Sounds like he's on vacation."

"Pretty much. I ain't mad, though. He's the kind of man my mother needed. After all those years working her ass off to care for me and my brother after the sperm donor left her high and dry…" He chuckled, shook his head as if in memory. "My brother and I used to give her hell until he stepped in, married her, and put our disobedient asses in check. Best damn dad ever."

"It takes a lot to be a good father. I realize it every day I look at Justin." It was my turn to laugh. "There are moments when I see the devilish twinkle in his eye and realize he's a miniature version of me. I gave my dad a run for his money. I got the feeling he's going to be laughing at the payback. You know, Justin turns three on Tuesday."

"Wow. Got plans?" Derrick punched a few buttons on his keyboard, apparently closing the file on his computer screen.

"Nothing major. I'm letting him spend the night with his grandparents. They want to throw him a party."

Derrick stopped typing and glared at the camera. "You're in the middle of a custody dispute. Why the hell would you do that?"

"My lawyer says it would be in my best interest in the eyes of the court to be cordial. Putting distance between him and the family that helped raise him since birth would make it look like I'm not willing to work things out."

"Mighty big of you." He shook his head. "I couldn't do it."

"You'd be surprised what you'd be willing to sacrifice in order to keep your son happy."

"Better you than me. Kids…family? Nowhere on my to-do list." He went back to pecking at the keyboard.

"That's what I said. Now that I've got him, I wouldn't have it any other way."

Except for the part where I lost Trina.

Derrick smirked on the screen, one eyebrow cocked. "The day I feel that way will be the day I find *the* woman who's willing to put up with my shit. And believe me; that shit is deep and I ain't looking."

I shook my head and checked the time. "Anyway, I'll be checking in with you later. Let me know what your start time will be and the estimated end date. I have to let my interior decorator know when to be ready. Time is of the essence because she's pregnant."

"That sucks. I'll get back to you in a day or two. Tell little man I said what's up."

"Will do."

We disconnected. I headed to bed, wondering how Justin would take to my father/son plan for his birthday. After being spoiled by grandparents, aunts, and uncles, there was no need for me to try to top that. Simple would do.

I told Trina once that we needed to have a family day and go to Centennial Olympic Park. I'd been a few times and watched the kids play in the jumping water sprays that were set to music. She said okay, but our schedules always seemed to collide and we never had the time.

Then we ran out of time.

I massaged my temples then opened the door to Justin's room. He appeared so peaceful. I'm sure he would love the chance to play in the water again. He had fun at the birthday party for Andre's son when we played with water guns.

Out of nowhere, an image of Kai came to mind. I was holding Justin's hand and she stood on the other side, doing the same. We walked through the park, Justin between us, laughing and jumping as we held our arms up high to let him swing between us.

Kai instead of Trina.

God, what was wrong with me? Why did I imagine her in Trina's place?

Finding a woman to play the role of mother to Justin was not in my future plans. If I stumbled into a romantic relationship, then my son's needs would come before her. What were the chances a woman would be strong enough mentally and emotionally to deal with me, or a child who required specialized care?

Justin was by no means on his deathbed. He was a child whose recovery from his illness was a day-to-day concern. As long as his body continued to accept the donor tissue then he was considered cured of the sickle cell disease. That didn't mean he no longer needed medical care. Just not as often.

As much as I wanted to remain positive about his situation, a part of me still worried about the side effects from the medications he took and the possibility of a setback that could turn his medical situation into another downhill spiral.

Between my son and my job, I couldn't imagine falling in love again. Ever.

I walked into Justin's room and scooted him from the edge of the bed and placed him next to the wall. A pillow went between him and the edge. He was a wild sleeper and had the tendency to hang off the bed at night. Once or twice he'd fallen to the floor and woke up yelling. I made a mental note to install a bed rail on the open side of his bed. An injury was the last thing he needed.

In my room, I set the alarm and climbed into bed. No matter how hard I tried, the image of Kai sitting on the sofa with Justin and watching TV or playing games when I came to pick him up from her house came to mind. He was happy with her. She seemed to have a good time with him. It was as if they had formed a bond over the weeks she'd babysat for me.

Kai was a friend, a fact I needed to remember. We both agreed any attempt to go forward in any kind of way, even if it was just physical, was out of the question.

Yet, I still dreamed about her at night.

****

"Hey, it's about time you got here. Justin and I were going to start without you." Kai stepped aside and let me enter her apartment.

"Daddy!" Justin ran up to me, arms raised, fingers grasping the air.

"Hey, little man." I picked him up and kissed his cheek. "Start what?" I peered around Justin's head as he hugged my neck.

"Peeza!" Justin yelled in my ear.

"Whoa there," I pulled back and tickled his belly. "Peeza? What's that?"

Kai laughed as she walked by and rubbed Justin's head. "He means pizza. We were about to make one."

"Oh." I followed her to the kitchen. "So I take it I have to stay for dinner?"

She shot me a look over her shoulder. "Unless you've got other plans?"

"No, not at all." I studied the spread on the table. Onions, bell peppers, shredded cheese, a can of spaghetti sauce, pepperoni slices, and pizza crust. I glanced around the kitchen. "Where's the box?"

"Of what?"

"Pizza."

Kai looked at me as if I was an idiot. "I'm making homemade pizza."

"Homemade pizza? Wow."

Kai laughed, then sat down at the table and pulled the cutting board and the nearest ingredient to be chopped before her.

I sat down across from her with Justin in my lap.

She placed a bell pepper on the cutting board and began to chop it into circular pieces. "I take it your mother didn't make it this way?"

"My mom cooked big, extravagant meals, you know, down home Southern cooking. I was at the dinner table, not in the kitchen. I left my sisters to have that fun."

Kai stopped chopping and pointed the knife in my direction. "Hold on, you mean you manage a major eating establishment, but don't cook?"

"Manage; operative word in the sentence." I grinned.

Kai cracked up. Justin, who had no idea what the big fuss was about, laughed too.

I joined in. "Hey, somebody's got to make sure the line cooks, chef, and wait staff stay on the ball. Plus, I cut the checks."

"But still, what do you eat?" She wiped the corners of her eyes.

It was a pleasure to see her laugh that hard.

"Food."

"From where?"

"Applebee's and other places."

Her expression went from laughter to serious. "What do you feed Justin? You said he has certain dietary needs. He can't just eat Applebee's every night."

"He doesn't. I didn't say I can't cook…I'm just not that good at it."

Kai shook her head. "You need more help than I thought. Okay, here's what we're going to do. Justin," she sat the knife down and stood. "Do you want to watch another movie?"

"Yes!" He jumped from my lap and went straight for Kai's outstretched hand.

"Traitor," I mumbled, then laughed.

I watched as they walked out of the kitchen, hand-in-hand, and tried my best not to feel like the world's worst dad.

I knew what Justin's dietary needs were. My workplace wasn't the only place I purchased fast food from. There were several soul food restaurants on my speed dial. I made sure he had the best mixture of fruits and vegetables, along with protein.

But, Kai had a point. I couldn't keep doing this.

Times like this made me contemplate packing up everything and moving back to Charlotte. I needed my mother. She would make sure Justin had everything he needed.

The problem was, his doctors were here. My job was here.

Trina's family, he'd known since birth, was here.

I was on my own.

Kai returned. "Come on. Cooking Lesson 101; how to make homemade pizza." She grabbed the cutting board, knife, and the bell pepper she'd been cutting. "Grab the rest of it, will you?"

I did as instructed and found myself standing beside her at the counter.

"I feel stupid for asking this, but do you know how to chop?" She looked up at me.

It had been a long time since we stood this close together. I forgot how tall she was. Her head stopped just short of my shoulder.

"You take a knife and you slice stuff up. Simple. Who doesn't know that?"

A smile spread on her face as she shook her head. "Show me." She handed me the knife, handle first.

I felt like an idiot, but did it anyway. When I was done, Kai had laughter in her eyes, but not so much in her voice.

"Trevon, you just massacred an innocent vegetable. That was horrible."

I looked down at my handiwork. "Okay, I don't know how to chop like the chefs on TV, but it's cut up, right?"

Kai shook her head and let the laugh she'd been holding out. "Thank God you don't make love the way you use a knife."

My attention went directly to her face, which grew crimson after her comment.

"Sorry. My point is, you need to approach food preparation the same way you'd approach sex, with passion. Understand?"

I scratched my head and tried to ignore the visual that came to mind. Kai on top of me, my hands on her hips as I pushed up inside of her. Long silky strands of jet-black hair brushing my chest as she leaned down and our mouths met…

That same silky hair now rested in a neat bun on top of her head.

I gripped the edge of the counter top to keep from reaching out to touch it.

"Trevon?" Kai looked at me with a puzzled expression.

I blinked. "Huh? Oh, yeah, right. Cook with passion. Got it."

She removed the outer layers of an onion and placed it on the cutting board. "Try again."

I grasped the onion. The thing was large and filled my fingers completely. I held it in place. Kai took my hand that held the knife and lined it up over the onion. The contact sent an image of her hand on mine when her breast had been in my hand. The soft, yet firm weight of it. The texture. The taste.

Focus.

I sliced through it, cutting it in half, then I looked at Kai. A smile was on her face, so I assumed I did well. I repeated the process over and over until there was nothing but small chunks left.

"Better?"

"Much better." She was genuinely pleased.

Satisfied, I ran a hand over my brow. "Oh, shit!"

"What's wrong?" Kai's hand was on my arm.

"I got onion juice in my eye!" I blinked rapidly, trying to aid the natural tears raining down to clear out my tear ducts.

"Here, sit down." She guided me to the nearest chair. "I've got saline drops in my purse. Hold on." She disappeared, and was back in a flash.

Could I make myself look more inadequate?

"Hold still." Kai leaned over; spreading my eyelid open, she dripped the solution in the affected eye.

I shut my eyes and hung my head down, trying my best to resist the urge to rub it again with my onion infected hands. "Damn, that hurts."

"Why on earth would you wipe your face when you haven't washed your hands yet?" She laughed her disbelief.

I blinked, then blinked again. The burning sensation in my eye took a second seat to the awareness of Kai's body between my legs.

She wore shorts, while I had on a pair of dress slacks, yet I could feel the heat from her body as it radiated against my leg. For a moment I was transported back to my bed and the way our bodies had rocked and bucked against one another. The mindless need to feel her again begged for me to pull her into my lap.

Kai cleared her throat and stepped back, breaking the connection. "Better?"

"Yeah." I leaned forward and started to rub my eye again, but she grabbed my arm and led me to the sink.

She squirted dish liquid in my hand; I scrubbed furiously. When done, I turned to see she'd returned to chopping the remaining toppings for the pizza.

"Justin's birthday is on Tuesday." I blurted the news to fill the uncomfortable silence that had formed.

Deep brown eyes looked my way. I imagined getting lost in them again, as I had that night.

"Really? Got plans?"

"His grandparents are throwing a traditional party. Then he's spending the night. I'm trying to find something to do to fill the morning hours with before taking him over there."

Her finely arched brow rose. "That's going to be awkward."

"Tell me about it. My lawyer advised me to go with it because it makes me look good."

"I could see how that would make sense. Do you need someone to go with you?"

I read her expression; she was serious. "Thanks, but showing up with another woman would misconstrue things."

Not to mention they'd already seen me with Kai at their daughter's funeral. Nobody asked questions, but it had come up in their request to get custody of Justin. A fact I hadn't mentioned to her.

"I understand." Done cutting, she removed the pizza crust from the package and began spreading on spaghetti sauce.

"How come you're not using tomato paste?"

Her attention left the crust as she smirked. "I thought you couldn't cook."

I shrugged. "I didn't say I didn't know what the ingredients are."

She chuckled. "Tomato paste is plain and boring. Seasoned spaghetti sauce heightens the flavors. Besides, it's all crushed tomatoes in a can."

"You're the chef."

She grinned.

When the toppings were added, she bent over to put the pie in the oven. When she stood, our eyes met.

"You said his birthday is on a Tuesday, right?"

I nodded.

"If you're looking for something to do with him before taking him to his grandparents', you should try the library. They have a children's reading program in the morning. I've never been, but I was there one morning and heard them. They seem to have a lot of fun. From what the librarian told me, they read books, dance, and sing, and at the end, they do an art project based on the theme of the book. I think he'd have fun and make a few friends."

"Sounds like a book club for kids; I like that. I read to him as much as I can because I want him to fall in love with books the way I have. Do you know what time it starts?"

"I'll look it up and send you the information."

"Thanks."

"No problem." She gathered the cut scraps and threw them in the trash as she cleaned up.

I grabbed the empty containers and assisted. "I'm taking Justin to Centennial Park on Sunday. Do you want to join us?"

Kai's brow rose in surprise. "Me? Are you sure?"

"Positive. Justin likes you. Besides, it's going to be our private celebration."

"Private? I'd be in the way."

The image of both of us holding Justin's hands came to mind again.

"No, you'd be a perfect fit."

She angled her head as if studying me. "If that's the way you feel, then my answer is yes."

Chapter 18

"Okay, who's ready to have fun this morning?"

"Me!!!" The chorus of yells coming from the kids around us was louder than I would have expected to be allowed in the library.

"Come on, Justin, why don't you go join the reading circle?" I tried to pull my son off my leg, but his grip was fierce.

He shook his head no and resumed sucking his thumb. It was hard to tell what made him more uncomfortable, the enthusiasm of the fifteen kids jumping around to the music that now played in the middle of the reading circle, or the fact there were a lot of unfamiliar faces around us.

It was Tuesday, the morning of Justin's third birthday and upon Kai's suggestion, we were at the library for preschool story time. The librarian who led the group had an infectious personality that encouraged the kids to open up and have fun. Unfortunately it wasn't something Justin was ready to do.

I noticed some of the parents, or rather moms, were dancing around and being silly with their kids. I was the only dad in the group, which had already gained me more than enough attention. I ignored their stares and focused on Justin.

"You sure you don't want to dance?"

He shook his head no.

"Alright, you leave me no choice but to go into goofy dad mode." I swept him off his feet and into my arms. We stepped into the middle of the dancing and jumping kids and joined in. Justin bounced along with me in my arms. His thumb was out of his mouth as he held on and laughed. Just the reaction I wanted. My attention stayed on him, but I couldn't ignore the pats on my leg. I looked down and was surprised to see most of the kids had formed a circle around us and were laughing and jumping with us.

"Okay, that was fun!" the librarian said as the song came to an end. Parents and kids clapped. Justin even managed to clap a little. "Everyone take a seat in the circle."

I tried to put Justin down, but he refused to let go. Not wanting to carry him back to the chairs where the adults were sitting, I found a spot on the edge of the circle and sat down, putting Justin beside me. I wanted him to be a part of the group, not an outsider.

"Good morning, everyone! I'm glad to see so many bright and happy faces. We have a lot of stories to read today and a fun activity to do, but first we have some new friends in our group."

I looked around, hoping she was referring to someone else. Unfortunately, the entire group focused on us. I smiled while Justin laid his head on me.

"Hello, my name is Ms. Becky. What's your name?" Her smile was warm as she waited for Justin to reply.

He didn't, of course, despite the fact I nudged him with the arm he was holding on to. "His name is Justin and today is his birthday."

"Welcome and congratulations, Justin! Can everyone say happy birthday to Justin?"

"Happy birthday!" The voices of the kids melded into a chorus.

Justin's eyes widened, but this time he smiled.

"Thank you." I said since he was too shy to reply.

"Dad, what is your name?"

"Trevon."

"Welcome Trevon and Justin. Let me tell you how our group is run. As you see, we start off with a song and dance to get our little bodies ready to listen and learn. Next, I read stories and get the kids to participate. Another song and dance happens, and we finish by making an art project that is about the books we read. Sound like fun?"

"Yes, it does." I nudged Justin again, but it was to no avail.

Ms. Becky selected a book that was on display on the table nearby and sat down. "Okay, let's begin!"

Ms. Becky gathered the kids in the circle and captivated them with her voice and animated storytelling abilities. The kids clapped and giggled as she made up robot voices for the characters in the book. I glanced over at Justin and saw he was just as entranced as the other kids. I took a chance and quietly got up from the spot on the floor and made my way back to the seats where the other parents sat. I pulled out my phone and sent Kai a text message.

At the library. This was a great idea. Justin is having fun…finally. Thanks for the suggestion!

I was about to add, *Wish you were here, too*, but decided against it.

A few minutes later, she replied: *Glad you went. Have fun!* ☺

I smiled and was about to slip my phone back in my pocket when I looked up and realized that over half the mothers in the group were staring at me. I smiled at the woman closest to me, and she sat up a bit straighter and smiled back. She ran a hand over her hair and let it linger. There was no wedding ring.

I kept my face straight and tried not to show that I felt like…eye candy.

Across the room two other women watched me with a skeptical expression. They were probably wondering why a man was at the library at ten o'clock in the morning attending a children's program instead of working. I'm sure the assumption was that I was either lazy, out of work, or a stay-at-home dad. The reality was I worked in the evenings, so my mornings were spent with Justin.

Before long, Ms. Becky directed children and parents to tables in the area in order to start the arts and crafts portion of the class. Everything needed to make paper robots -since that was today's book theme- lay before them. Somehow I managed to settle my large frame on the kid sized chairs and help Justin handle the glue without making too big of a mess. He laughed the entire time.

"Trevon?"

I looked up to see Ms. Becky standing next to me with a clipboard and pen in hand.

"Would you be interested in signing up for the weekly classes?"

"Definitely. What do you need?"

After giving her my contact information, I pulled out my phone to get a picture of Justin and his completed robot, then texted it to Kai. I knew she'd love it.

Next stop was the Waters' home so he could spend the day with his grandparents, aunts, uncles, and cousins to celebrate the start of his third year of life. I was sure when he came home he would have a ton of gifts of the extravagant kind meant to buy his affection. Maybe I was making that up in my head, but it could still be true. Why wouldn't they pull something like that in a custody battle?

To be sure I avoided that type of game; I kept the gift I'd given him when he woke up simple. His favorite toys were trucks. As a kid, I loved cars, too. I decided we would do something together as father and son, something I wish my father had done with me. I gave him a Hot Wheels Racetrack, complete with cars. We didn't have time to put it together and take it for a test spin before it was time to eat breakfast and make it to the library. But I promised him the moment he came back from his grandparents' home, it would be the first thing we did.

The expectation of more gifts sated him. Hopefully he'd still feel the excitement when he returned home.

"Are you sure you don't want to stay for the party?" Felisha asked when I handed her Justin's overnight bag.

I could see through her attempt to be sincere. Like her mother, she wasn't a fan of mine.

"Thanks for the invitation, but we both know that wouldn't go well. I don't want to ruin Justin's day with any negativity. Take care of him, and I'll be back to get him in the morning."

She smirked a little. "You know we will."

I squatted down to Justin's level and straightened his shirt. "Be a good boy for grandma, okay?"

"'Kay." He squirmed in anticipation of the events he knew would be coming. As it was, there were balloons decorating the railing and a big 'Happy Birthday Justin' sign on the front door…not that he could read it.

I gave him a hug and savored the feel of his returned love as he kissed my cheek. Then he was gone, running as fast as his short legs would take him into the house to be with the family he'd known since the day he was born.

Felisha didn't wait for me to leave the porch before closing the door in my face.

Anticipating the way I'd feel when I dropped him off, I'd taken the day off work. I reached into the pocket of my jeans and pulled out my phone as I walked to my car. By the time I opened the driver's side door; I'd typed a group text message and sent it to my boys.

Both Andre and Derrick responded in record time.

Perfect, because I didn't want to drink alone.

****

"Okay, gentlemen, here are your beers. Are you ready to place your order?"

"Yes, we are," Derrick drawled, not hiding the fact he was exploring our waitress's curves with his eyes.

Andre and I placed our orders, sat back, and watched him go to work. The waitress wasted no time flirting back. In the end, I was surprised he hadn't asked for her number. No doubt he'd do that as he left her a tip after we paid the bill.

"You haven't lost your touch." I popped the top off my beer and took a long sip. With the way I felt, I needed the amber liquid to rush to my empty stomach and give me something to feel really good about.

Knowing my son was spending the night with relatives who wanted to take him away did not sit well with me. Yet, it had to be done.

"Shit, I'm just playing with her. Do you see how young she looks? I'm thirty-years-old, man. I don't have time to waste dealing with a girl who's wet behind the ears." He popped the top of his beer, his eyes following her as she walked across the room. "But damn, she looks good in those micro shorts. That should be against the law in this place."

"It's *Hooter's*, Derrick, she's supposed to be dressed like that." Andre's eyes followed her, too.

"I still say we should have gone to a strip club. At least there I had a better chance of having some fun and I know for sure the ladies are beyond legal."

"Derrick, the girls here are legal, they have to have a license in order to sell alcohol. Look at it this way, we did you a favor. You'll leave here at the end of the night with money in your wallet, less what you spend in food and beverage. At the club, you'd be broke from lap dances." I pointed my bottle in his direction before taking another sip.

Andre chuckled. "Ain't no way I'm going near a strip joint. I'm a married man and Sharice don't play. One thing I can say about my wife is she makes sure all my needs are taken care of, and I mean all of them." He grinned, wagged his eyebrows, and drank.

Derrick smirked. "Yeah, alright, that's your story, but that has nothing to do with my man over here." He slapped my shoulder and shook me, nearly causing me to drop my bottle. "You're single and have no woman. What's your excuse for refusing to surround yourself with a bunch of hot, naked, and willing women?"

I shook my head and laughed. "Do I need one?"

He looked at me as if I'd grown another head. "Uh, hell yeah."

I grabbed a napkin to clean up spilled liquid. "I got one. Child custody case." He huffed. "I'm serious. My attorney already said they think I had a woman on the side while trying to get back together with Trina. The last thing I need is to get to court and have the opposing attorney pull out pictures of me hanging out at a strip club with half naked women gyrating on my lap."

"He's got a point." Andre nodded in agreement.

Derrick's head swiveled between us. "Hold up, what woman?" When it was obvious I wasn't about to answer, his attention fell on Andre.

"Not my story to tell, dog." He shot me a side glance.

"Hold up, there's actually a *woman* involved somewhere? Tre, you mean you've been holding back on me? What's up with that?" He appeared to be genuinely hurt.

I shrugged. "There's not really a story to tell."

Andre nearly spit out his drink and laughed his butt off. "I beg to differ. There's a story alright, you just don't want to tell it."

Derrick punched my shoulder. "So it's like that, huh? It's okay to ask me to drive down from North Carolina to save your ass, but a story that involves a woman and it's not something you think you should share? That's some bull."

"It's not that I don't want to share, it's just…" I looked up to see both men staring at me with raised eyebrows. "Shit." I mumbled. "If I'm going to talk about it, we need another round of beers." I waved my hand to signal the waitress over. Our order placed, it was obvious neither would accept waiting for our beverages to arrive for me to decide to start talking. "It's like this—"

"He's taking too long. I'll give you the short version." Andre took over the conversation. "Trevon's got this thing for a woman he slept with a year ago. I can't blame him though, because the woman is fine. She saved Justin and Trina's life…she's a firefighter," he explained when Derrick opened his mouth to ask a question. "The only problem is he didn't know she was engaged to my brother at the time they slept together."

Derrick's attention came back to me as his fist went to his mouth. "You slept with his brother's woman? Damn! I didn't know you were hittin' 'em like that, bruh."

"They weren't engaged at the time and I had no idea, okay? Andre knows that." I glared at him as he laughed.

"So hold up, I don't understand. That was then, this is now. What does that have to do with anything?"

Andre chose now to keep his mouth shut and pointed at me.

"Kai got injured when she rescued them. Our paths crossed again, after the funeral. Now she's babysitting Justin a few days during the week. It's strictly platonic."

Andre laughed.

Derrick looked at him, then faced me. "Hold up, let me get this straight. Some fine honey you smashed saved the life of your son and is now babysitting him and you have no plans on hittin' that again, much less having a relationship of any kind other than being her friend?" He watched me nod. "Is she gay, bi-sexual, got some kind of infectious disease that would keep you from gittin' it in?"

I bit back my annoyance. "No. It's like I said before…"

Derrick waved me off. "Yeah, yeah, you got no time for relationships, sex, or anything that equates you to being a healthy male. I'll believe that shit when pigs start to fly."

Andre let loose a big laugh.

"Look, I don't know where your balls are or if you even have a pair anymore," he continued. "The fact of the matter is, if you tasted her goodies once and got hooked, it doesn't matter what is going on in your life. You're gonna want to hit that again. True?"

"Amen, my brother." Andre pounded fists with Derrick in agreement.

I fidgeted in my seat. His comment was beyond true. The fact that the erotic dreams of being with Kai had never truly gone away was a testament to the fact that I was still attracted to her on a physical level. The problem was, now that we spent time getting to know each other and having real conversations without the expectation or opportunity to have sex on the regular, I wanted her even more.

"It's not an option." I drank.

Derrick watched me for a moment, something he did a lot when we were kids and he was trying to read between the lines of what I said. Nine times out of ten, he was correct.

"Keep telling yourself that. But I can guarantee you, the first chance you get; you're going to hit that again. And when you do…" He let his words hang in the air.

It didn't take much to fill in the blanks because I knew the answer.

I was going to be screwed.

Chapter 19

"Daddy, daddy, look at me!" Justin spun around on slippery bricks as jet after jet of water leapt over his head.

"Justin, be careful!" Trevon sat forward as if preparing to grab his son the moment it appeared he might fall.

While I understood his fear, my research about living with children who had sickle cell anemia suggested parents keep an eye out for the kids wellbeing, but not overdo it when it came to everyday activities, such as playing in the Fountain of Rings water fountain at Centennial Olympic Park. In Justin's case, he was practically cured, so there was nothing to worry about.

"Trevon," I put my hand on his bicep. "It's okay. If he falls it will be a little bump. He's bound to get a few. After all, he is a boy."

"And a lot like me, that's what scares me. Justin…"

I shook my head, but at least he settled back on the ledge we sat on.

My sunglasses in place, I tilted my head up and scanned the buildings around us. The park was in the middle of downtown Atlanta, site of the 2006 Olympics. I remembered coming out to the site with my parents and sister. Watching the fountain made up of humungous rings that represented the symbols of the worldwide event was a featured attraction. The periodic synchronized water shows put to music entertained locals and tourists alike.

It looked nearly the same today as it did then, well, with a few new additions. Either way, it was the perfect place to spend the afternoon on a hot summer day with a little boy who was full of energy.

"Daddy, come on!" Justin trotted over, dripping wet from head to toe, and grabbed his father's hand.

"No," he laughed. "I can't leave Ms. Kai alone."

Justin glanced over at me then pulled Trevon's hand as much as he could. "Pweese?"

"Why don't I come? Unlike your daddy, I'm not afraid of a little water." I stood, stripped off my shirt, and revealed the bikini top beneath.

"Oh, that's harsh." Trevon laughed.

I dropped my shirt in his lap, winked, then picked up Justin and went straight to the middle ring of the leaping water jets.

Justin giggled and squirmed in my arms, ready to be let down so he could run along with other kids who did the same. The minute his feet touched the ground, he ran circles around me as the nearby jets came on out of nowhere, soaking me in an instant. I laughed, and shielded my face. When the water subsided and sprouted another jet a few feet away, I pulled plastered hair out of my face and secured it in a makeshift hair knot. I should have brought a ponytail holder with me.

When I looked up again, Trevon was smiling and his phone was aimed in my direction. Assuming he was either filming or taking pictures, I played along and posed for a few. When Justin ran by, I grabbed him and encouraged him to pose as well.

"Okay, that's enough. Is your camera water proof?"

"Yeah…" The moment Trevon realized what I meant, he started shaking his head. "No way, Kai."

I ran over as he stood up from where he sat, with Justin on my heels. Catching up to him, I grabbed both of his hands and pulled, using my firefighter training to move this man who was easily one hundred pounds heavier than I was.

In the spirit of the moment, I forgot about my back injury. "Oh sh–!" I let him go then leaned forward, resting my hands on my knees. The pain shooting up my back froze me in one spot.

"Kai! Are you okay?" Trevon reached for me, his hands going to my shoulders tentatively.

My eyes squeezed shut, my breath ragged from the sudden flare up, I forced myself to breathe deeply and slowly and let the pain wash over me. "My back…give me a second …"

Trevon walked behind me, put his large palms on my lower back, and began to knead the muscle with his knuckles in a gentle circular motion. "Does this help?"

"Oh yeah, that's good. Please don't stop." I forced the pain off my face when I opened my eyes and found Justin staring at me.

"Ki-Ki, you 'kay?" Since I was bent over, it was easy for him to place his wet hands on my cheeks. His little brown eyes were filled with worry.

"I'm fine, baby. Just had a bad pain in my back. I'll be okay in a few minutes."

He nodded and then walked around to see what his father was doing. I felt his little hands try to join in to help, but Trevon gently moved his hand and explained that he was taking care of me.

As the back spasm passed, I forced myself to stand and ignore the pain shooting down my hip. Trevon's hand stayed in place as he guided me over to the seating area and helped me into a sitting position.

"Are you sure you're okay?" His concern was evident on his face.

"If you hand me my purse I will be." He retrieved my small bag from the inside of Justin's backpack, which held a towel and some dry clothes. I dug in for my pill bottle and took the pain meds prescribed to me by my doctor. Trevon handed me a bottle of water.

"I thought you stopped taking these." He read the label on the bottle.

I gulped the pills and liquid. "I did, except for when I feel like this." I managed and then grimaced.

His eyes narrowed. "How often does this happen?"

"Once a week? Two tops?"

He looked me over. "When is your doctor going to release you?"

"Not soon enough," I mumbled.

Silence had me looking over to see Trevon studying me. He wasn't satisfied with my response.

"Not soon enough? Kai, you just strained your back from trying to drag me, and I was standing up. You want to go back to work. How are you going to—?"

"There are other things I can do at the fire department," I snapped, a bit too forceful.

He put his hands up. "Look, I'm not saying you can't do your job, just…don't rush back. I don't want you to get injured again and be sidelined because you haven't healed. You love your job too much; it would crush you. I know how that feels."

I stared at him. "Yeah, right. What do you know about being sidelined?"

He was about to reply, but looked away; Justin was standing in front of us. He turned to his son. "Ms. Kai is feeling better. You can go play. I'll be there in a minute, okay?"

His eyes lit up. "Kay, Daddy!" We watched as he ran back to the fountain.

After a moment, he faced me. "I went to college at Georgia Tech with a dream to be the next Michael Jordan. I was good at basketball, still am. I had a few teams scouting me over the years. But during one of the last games of my senior year, I got knocked down by an opposing player; blew my knee out. I had to have surgery, twice. I was benched for the rest of the season, and all the scouts turned their sights onto the next hot player."

I grimaced, but this time it was because of his story. "That had to hurt."

"More than you know. I spent the last part of my college education trying to figure out what to do with my life."

"What did you do?"

Trevon stretched out one of his legs, bending and flexing what had to be the damaged muscle. "Came to terms with the fact I wouldn't be playing pro basketball and used my education to get a job."

"Is that how you ended up at Applebee's? The food service industry is a long way from professional basketball."

"Nothing beats being part of a fraternity. My brothers looked out for me. My major was business management. I got the hook up on a management training program and well, here we are. Six years later, I'm an assistant manager with the opportunity to become GM of my own location…if I can get this rehab done and get customers back in the building."

"Is that what my sister is helping you with?"

He nodded. "So like I said, I know what it feels like to be sidelined." He dipped his head. "Do you have a backup plan if things don't work out for you?"

Annoyed, I looked away. "Don't need one."

He studied me, skepticism on his face. "Everyone needs a backup plan, Kai."

"I know, and I have one. Working temporarily for my mother is one thing. Having it become my bread and butter? Not about to happen."

****

A few hours later, I followed Trevon into his home. It wasn't the first time I'd been there. Every now and then I'd drop Justin off instead of him coming to my apartment to pick him up. The living room was the farthest I'd gone.

"Where do you want me to put this?" I pointed to Justin's backpack, hooked over my shoulder.

"You can bring it to his room. I still don't understand why you insisted on carrying it." He glanced over his shoulder. Justin lay spent in his father's arms. The fresh air and exercise had worn him down.

"I told you, I'm better now. The meds worked." I smiled, but his expression read that he wasn't buying it.

I followed him down the hall, glancing around to take in the house. It was in a nice neighborhood with houses that had to be less than ten years old. It wasn't fancy, just a three-bedroom, single-story home that lacked the touches of a woman. It said 'man cave', but it had potential.

Justin's room was as I imagined it to be, filled with sports posters and toy cars. He had a racecar themed spread on his bed and a toy box overflowing with an abundance of toys. One thing was for sure, Trevon made sure his son wasn't lacking anything he wanted or needed. I sat the book bag down beside the dresser then examined the pictures of various basketball teams beside the closet door. Beside the Georgia Tech logo, an old picture hung next to what I imagined was Trevon's college jersey. I looked at the photograph and smiled. A much younger and slightly slimmer Trevon stared back at me. Happiness and a future with potential showed in his eyes. Too bad life had taken him in another direction.

"Subliminal messages?" I pointed to the wall.

Trevon laid Justin on the bed before he looked up to see what I was referring to. His smile was thoughtful. "I guess so." He removed Justin's clothes. "I've got to give him a bath. If you don't have plans, you're more than welcome to hang out with us. I usually order from the Chinese restaurant from around the corner and pick something from Netflix or Hulu to watch. It's not much but…," he smiled.

The sincerity of his invitation was heartwarming. "That sounds like fun. Let me make a phone call." I walked out of the bedroom, down the hall to the living room, and stuck my head in the other rooms along the way. Talk about being nosy. I couldn't help being interested in the way this man lived. Having visited his condo the night we met and loving the extravagance of it all, the amazing views from the terrace, and the clean and modern lines of the place, this house seemed to show a different side of him.

One thing was for sure, regardless of where he lived, Trevon had good taste. Though it was obvious he lived alone, it held a sense of home. Welcoming and inviting.

I pulled my phone out of my back pocket and called my neighbor to see if she minded dog sitting for a few more hours.

"The menu is on the fridge." Trevon yelled down the hall as he carried Justin, who whined, to the bathroom. It was obvious he wasn't in the mood to be awake.

"What do you want?" I yelled back.

"Pick one of whatever is circled on the menu."

Before I could ask what he wanted me to order for Justin, the sound of water being run in the bathtub, mixed with even louder cries, floated down the hall before the door was shut.

Okay then.

Menu in hand, I studied the choices, reviewed what was circled, then dialed. Order placed and set to be delivered; I explored the kitchen of the man who said he wasn't a good cook.

The fridge and cabinets were full of food, fresh fruits, and juices. A few microwave meals, and especially frozen pizza. The memory of teaching him how to cut up vegetables in my kitchen made me smile. Off the kitchen sat a small dining room with sliding glass doors leading out to the back yard.

The blinds were closed, so I pushed them aside and took in the breathtaking size of the back yard. It was fenced in and some of Justin's toys littered the open space. On the patio sat a grill and two chairs. I could imagine Trevon cooking hot dogs and watching Justin run around the yard. I could also see Sugar running the length as well, chasing after squirrels that ran for their lives up the few shade trees within the gated area.

Maybe Trevon would allow me to bring her over sometime to get some off the leash exercise.

My curiosity sated, I settled on the couch and turned on the TV.

Trevon had what I liked to call a 'man's' TV. The thing was huge. Had I seen a flat screen this big before? An image came on and speakers hidden around the room blared a newscaster's voice from the sports channel. I fumbled with the complicated remote to find the volume button and turn it down.

"Sorry!" The bathroom door was closed so I doubt he heard me.

Not sure what type of movies he liked, I logged into Netflix and flipped through the options and I reviewed his recently watched TV shows and movies.

Sports, of course, mixed with Sci-Fi and mystery themed programs. My kind of man. The night we met at the bar, we agreed that Science fiction was one of our favorite genres to read, or more specifically, anything related to Star Wars. He told me he had a huge collection of Star Wars books along with collectible figurines.

I sat up on the sofa and looked around the living room. I didn't see any of those things. Could he have been lying about it in order to connect with me that night?

I glanced down the hall. That didn't sound like the man I'd come to know. Trevon was, if anything, honest. He didn't like being lied to, and avoided telling lies himself at all cost. I appreciated that about him. After years of being stuck in a relationship with a man who lied as if he would make millions because of it, Trevon's honesty was really refreshing.

If he said he had a collection of books and figurines, then he did. It was probably in one of the rooms I peered into, but since the lights were off, I left them alone, not wanting it to be obvious that I was looking around. If I asked, I'm sure he would be happy to show me.

The doorbell rang as Trevon emerged from the bathroom. Justin was wrapped in a towel and appeared just as sleepy, but at least he was quiet.

"My wallet is in my pocket." He started to walk my way.

I grabbed my purse. "Don't worry about it; I've got it."

"Thanks." He walked into Justin's room.

A short time later, he reappeared without Justin. "He's down for the count. I tried to get him to come eat, but he refused to open his eyes. Guess it's just you and me. Hope you don't mind."

Trevon went to the kitchen and came back with a set of cups and a bottle of unopened soda. I guess it had been hidden in one of the cabinets I hadn't checked.

My heart kicked up a notch. Why did this feel like a date?

I smiled, liking the sound of that more than I should. "No, that's fine. Let's eat."

Chapter 20

"Thursday's the big day, huh?" Kai dug into the bucket of the house fried rice with a fork. "Are you ready?"

"Not sure I'll ever be ready, but," I shrugged and accepted the pint of rice, spooning some on my plate. "My lawyer thinks we'll win. I've got to, Kai." My attention left my plate and went to the closed door to Justin's room. "It's crazy how my life has changed in a year. I've gone from a man who lived in a condo on the expensive side of Atlanta with no responsibilities, to being a homeowner and single dad. I couldn't imagine going back to that again. I love my son." I chuckled and shook my head. "I can't believe I'm about to say this…"

Kai looked up from her plate. "Say what?"

A slow smile spread across my face. "I really do want a family. I'm talking about straight American Dream stuff. Wife, two kids, white picket fence. The works."

She looked around, appraising our surroundings. "It seems you're halfway there. A bit out of order, but," she laughed a little. "That's modern life." Her attention went back to her plate as she scooped broccoli and jumbo shrimp onto her plate.

I accepted the container when she handed it to me and took my fill. It appeared we liked the same dishes.

"What about you, Kai. What do you want out of life? Besides your job, I mean. You can't be a firefighter forever."

I felt as if I were about to disturb the hornets' nest. I made the same statement earlier in the day, and shared with her my past. Yet as we sat here, I realized, she never really answered the questions I asked.

"Says who?" She glared as if I'd insulted her.

"Says life. After you reach a certain age, the wear and tear on your body can make it impossible for you to keep up with the younger generation. What then, a desk job?"

"Maybe." Her voice was flat. "There are other careers in the firefighter field besides riding the truck."

I paused before taking a bite of my food. "Look, I have no idea where your career path could take you, and I'm sorry if what I said offended you. What I'm really trying to ask is what do you have planned for your personal life? Most women want the American Dream, too. You are not most women. What else do you want out of life?"

Kai used her fork to keep her mouth busy, but she appeared to be uncomfortable and refused to give me eye contact.

"Did I cross a line? It's just…I felt like today our relationship evolved into something else. We've spent the past two months dealing with each other, yet, I feel there's so much we still don't know about each other." Her gaze stayed on her plate. "If you want to change the subject then, that's fine."

She didn't respond. I took that as a sign that this part of the conversation was over. My attention went back to my food.

"I can't have kids."

My head snapped up from my plate; she continued to stare at hers.

That wasn't the kind of response I expected. Not knowing what to say, I kept silent.

Kai set her fork down and leaned back in her seat. "No matter what I want out of life, or what I can achieve with my career, being a mother is the one thing I will never be able to do. No matter how much I love other people's children, I will never have one of my own." Sorrow filled eyes met mine. "So no, Trevon, I can't say I have the same dream as you."

Her attention went back to her food, but instead of eating, she stabbed at it.

Pain hit my chest. She couldn't be a mother? After months of watching how well she took care of Justin and how much he had grown to love her, it was hard to imagine Kai not having that same type of affection for a child of her own.

"I'm sorry." A part of me felt the need to reach out and pull her in my arms. Instead, I stayed in my seat and watched as her facial expression changed ever so slightly. She seemed to be holding back tears with a facade of strength.

Kai shrugged. "Nothing for you to be sorry about."

She was right, but I couldn't help but feel the way I felt.

"I'm not sure how to ask you this, or if I should. Feel free to tell me to go to hell and mind my own business and I will."

She pushed her food around some more then looked up. "What?"

I swallowed, ignoring the dull ache in my chest. I'd never seen her look this sad before. "How do you know…that you can't have kids?"

She sighed. "I've had two miscarriages. The problem isn't my ability to get pregnant. The problem is that the embryo doesn't make it to my womb. Once it was an ectopic pregnancy."

My brow furrowed. "Ectopic? What is that?"

"The fertilized egg was stuck in my fallopian tube and didn't implant in my womb. It caused a medical emergency and I nearly bled to death internally from a ruptured tube. My doctor had to go in and remove it."

"Oh, man." I leaned back in my chair.

"The second time the egg did get to my uterus, but it didn't implant like it should. My body eventually dispelled it, so that was a natural miscarriage."

That was a lot for her to experience. I had a newfound respect for this woman.

"You know, that was one of the reasons why things didn't work out with Malik. As much of an ass as he can be, he wants a family. Losing both babies hurt him. He didn't start cheating on me until we realized I wouldn't be able to give him what he wanted. He's pretty envious of his brother." She paused, eyebrows furrowed. "If I'm not mistaken, I think he's finally got some woman pregnant."

I stared at Kai in disbelief. "Your relationship issues were because of not being able to have a baby?"

She nodded, but stared at her plate again.

"Kai, look at me."

After a moment, she did. Her eyes glistened with unshed tears, having lost the battle to appear strong.

"Your ability or inability to have a baby has nothing to do with your worth, Kai. You are an amazing woman. You're passionate, strong, have an open heart, and are willing to sacrifice your life and health to save people you don't know. If he couldn't appreciate that about you then it's his loss, not yours."

She smiled a little. "Thanks for the kind words. Too bad it doesn't change the truth about my future." Kai took a deep breath. "Well, that's enough about me. Let's talk about something pleasant."

"Are you sure there's something pleasant to talk about right now? I think we just managed to discuss the two most depressing issues in our lives."

Kai looked at me and several emotions went over her face. In the end, she laughed, hard.

I chuckled, not sure what the joke was. "What?"

She pointed at the both of us with her fork. "If someone had told me the night we met that you and I would be having this type of conversation instead of sex, I would have thought they were crazy."

I grinned and shook my head. "Yeah, I would have lost that bet, too."

After a few minutes, the laughter subsided. "So what now?"

Kai sat back for a moment; her eyes met mine and held. "I'm curious. You told me about this huge book collection you're supposed to have, yet I don't see it in your living room. Were you lying?"

I smiled. "That was not a lie. I have it, but to tell you the truth, once I bought this house and moved in, dealing with Justin's hospital visits and stays took a priority to unpacking. If it wasn't something needed for everyday use, it's still in a box."

Her attention went to the living room. "Um, it looks like you're unpacked to me."

"That's because the boxes are in the third bedroom, you know, the one room down the hall that has a closed door?"

One of her eyebrows arched. "Oh, well then…"

"But, if you really want to see something, I can show you my DVD collection. That's sitting over by the TV."

That seemed to get her attention. "Do you have anything Star Wars related?"

I scoffed. "Did you forget who you're talking to? Original or re-mastered?"

"You have both?"

I nodded as my grin went wide.

"Do you have all six?"

"Which one do you want to watch?"

Kai rubbed her fingers together, a true fan.

"Episode three is my favorite. I love watching Anakin spiral downhill and turn into Darth Vader."

I stood, grabbed my plate and drink. "To the living room then."

She settled on the sofa with her food as I selected the DVD, slid it into the player and joined her on the couch. The moment the theme song blasted out of the speakers Kai turned to me in wonder. The surround sound made it feel as if we were in a movie theater instead of my living room.

"This is so much better than watching it on my regular old TV. I've got a flat screen, but it's like half the size of this!"

Her attention was on the screen as the opening movie sequence played. The pain that had been on her face only moments ago seemed to have dissipated. So had the tightness in my chest.

For the first time since the birthday party, I let go of the stress and worry about the court date and did the one thing I hadn't done in months. Enjoy life. I had to admit, today had been more than I expected it to be. And Kai was a part of it.

What happened in the future could not be predicted. What happened now was important.

Right now my son was safe and asleep in his bed in my home. On my plate sat a good meal, and beside me…the company of a good woman.

Of a friend.

****

The crack of my knuckles sounded like gunfire in the quiet courtroom. My nerves were on edge and my heart raced. It took Herculean effort to keep from tapping my foot on the floor. I glanced at my lawyer sitting beside me as he reviewed the notes for my case. He, of course, didn't seem fazed. Then again, he wasn't about to find out if he was losing his son.

Across the room, Trina's parents sat, along with their lawyer. I tried not to stare at them and get a reading on what the judge would decide.

A pat on the shoulder reminded me I was not alone. My parents had driven down from North Carolina as witnesses on my behalf and to provide moral support.

My sisters, LaShana and Ebony, had messaged me in the morning with their well-wishes.

Kai had called.

I glanced at the clock on the wall and noted the time. We'd been waiting for the judge to enter the courtroom for nearly ten minutes. To keep from losing it, I imagined what Justin was doing at this very moment. It was a court-mandated order that he be present in the courthouse during the session. Though he wouldn't be brought before the judge, I had to have him present in case the ruling didn't go in my favor. If Trina's parents won custody, he would leave the courthouse with them.

Giving him over to the court appointed caregiver to wait in a playroom down the hall during the hearing was the hardest thing I had to do in my life.

My attention went to the dark paneled walls around the courtroom. Though the lighting was adequate, I still felt stifled between the walls and the raised podium where the judge sat. I loosened the tie around my neck and wished I had a bottle of water for my parched throat.

A side door of the courtroom opened and a deputy entered, followed by the court stenographer. She took her seat near the front of where the judge sat and began opening up the equipment she would use to record every word spoken.

"Trevon, make sure your phone is turned off." My lawyer whispered, then removed his phone from his suit jacket. "No need to piss off the judge."

I reached for my phone to comply, but paused to review the photo I'd taken of Justin before we left home. He was handsome in the khaki pants, vest, and bowtie combination. He looked just like me.

My heart swelled with pride at the same time pain stabbed me in my chest.

What if…

"Stop focusing on the negative." Kai's words during our morning call forced me to stay positive.

I took her words to heart as I pocketed my phone and stood along with everyone else when the judge entered, then settled in to wait and see how the rest of my life would begin.

Or end.

Chapter 21

"Kai, you hit like a girl."

I shot a look of pure hatred at my physical therapist. The only thing keeping me from hitting him was the punching bag he held steady between us.

"That's because I am a girl!" I growled and went into the next round of punches and ended with a high kick. "Shit!"

Pain shot up my back and had me leaning down, hands resting on my knees. Tears mixed with sweat, burning my eyes. I wiped at them, but it was impossible to do with the oversized gloves.

"Hey, you alright?" My therapist let go of the bag and leaned down to meet me in the eye.

Not willing to give in, I forced myself to stand up straight and walk it off. Limp it off was more like it.

I waved him away as he started to speak again. "Give me a minute, Josh."

He nodded and went to his water bottle.

Less than a week had gone by since the injury to my lower back had been aggravated when I tried to pull Trevon into the water fountain. Until that time, I'd felt fine. And because I did, I'd avoided the suggested physical therapy appointments from my doctor. He wanted me to do kickboxing to strengthen my core and increase my cardio. As a firefighter, I exercised every week to keep fit in order to do my job. But the two month down time was evident.

Maybe age had something to do with it as well. I was at the midpoint of thirty, an age where my level of physical fitness should have me snapping back from the injury.

Should be, but wasn't.

Trevon's question of what I had planned for the rest of my life if I couldn't return to work had been floating around in my head for the past couple of days. The obvious answer would be to continue to work for my family. Following in my family's footsteps would mean doing what they wanted and giving up my dream, one that I was already living.

Starting from scratch at the age of thirty-five was not what I wanted to do with my career.

I stopped circling the gym and took a second to lean forward to touch my ankles, a stretch I did on a daily basis to loosen up before work.

Unbearable pain shot through my body before I could reach my toes.

"Okay, that's enough for the day. You need rest, Kai." Josh screwed the top on his water bottle. He'd apparently been watching me. "You're going to hate me for this, but I've got to let your doctor know you're not fit for active duty yet. To be honest, you need to have your back X-rayed again. I've got a feeling you have damaged your back more than you know."

I bit my lip to keep tears from flooding my eyes. He was right. I was in no way ready to go back to work. I cursed as he pulled the gloves off my hand, and plopped down on the nearest bench.

After a few moments, I gathered my things and made my way to the locker room. The minute I reached home, I did the one thing I tried my best to avoid…resort back to pain medication.

****

The ringtone of my cell phone woke me from a drug-induced sleep. I grabbed at it, wiped sleep from my eyes, and squinted to see the screen. It was Trevon.

My eyes were heavy, my mouth dry, and my voice thick from sleep. "Hello?"

There was a pause. "Kai, are you okay? You don't sound too good."

"Huh?" I rolled onto my back, testing for soreness. It was a lot better than it had been when I came home. "I was taking a nap." I stole a peek at the time on the phone. "Crap, I didn't mean to sleep that long. It's nearly five!"

"I know. What time did you go to sleep?"

"Twelvish?" I yawned and realized I had to pee.

"That was a long nap. Is everything okay?"

I could hear the concern in his voice.

"Yes…and no." I was in no mood to discuss my physical set back. Knowing Trevon, he would go into concern mode and have a list of 'do's' and 'don'ts' for me to adhere to. I scooted to the side of the bed and sat up. As my mind cleared, I realized my physical problems took a major backseat to what was going on in his life. "That's enough about me. What about you? What happened in court?"

"That's what I wanted to talk to you about. Is it okay if I come up?"

I blinked. "Hold up, you're here?"

"In the parking lot. I've called you three times on my way here, but you didn't answer. I got worried when I arrived and saw your car. If you didn't pick up this time, I was going to call the police or something. You scared me."

I ran a hand over my face. "Sorry. Blame it on the Tramadol."

"What?"

My attention went to my room and my attire. "Never mind. Come on up, but be warned, I'm looking a hot mess."

Trevon chuckled. "Thanks for the warning. I'll see you in a sec."

He disconnected and I drug myself into the bathroom. Sugar rose from her doggie bed in the corner of my room, stretched, then came over to lick my hand. She whined a bit, her way of telling me that she needed to take a trip outside to relieve her bladder, too. "In a minute, girl. Let me get myself together first. We've got company."

After using the toilet and washing my hands, I splashed water on my face to counteract the effects of the medicine. It wasn't enough. I needed coffee.

I did the best I could to cover the bags under my eyes, but gave up, pulled my hair out of its rubber band, and let it fall over my face. Maybe it would hide some of the sleepiness. Short on time and not in the mood to find something else to wear other than my sleeping shorts and tank top without a bra, I grabbed a robe and slipped it on. What you see is what you get. If it scared him, he could leave.

The doorbell rang and I made my way over. One look through the peephole and I really felt like crap.

I opened the door to find Trevon dressed in a suit and tie. His low cut hair had been freshly cut; his face was as smooth as a baby's bottom, except for the small tuft he left under his bottom lip. I don't know why that was sexy, but on him, it was.

His rich brown eyes studied me the moment I opened the door. "Damn, you weren't kidding about the hot mess look." He laughed when I rolled my eyes.

"Ha, ha, and ha." I gathered the lapel of my robe and walked towards the sofa, leaving Sugar to greet him with licks and expressed interest in the bag he held in his hands. He shut the door.

"I wasn't sure if you were hungry, so I stopped and got some wings." He held up the bag and went to the kitchen with dog in tow.

I lay back on the sofa, pulled my legs up, and after an attempt to get comfortable failed, added a throw pillow at the small of my back. The pain medication and rest had worked wonders. The pain, while still there, was less pronounced. The dizziness from getting up after lying down for hours was lingering, though.

"Thanks, I could use something on my stomach. But wait a minute, are you going to leave me hanging or tell me what happened?" I looked over the edge of the sofa and watched him move around my kitchen as if he owned the place.

Trevon closed a cabinet after retrieving two plates, and then searched for cups. His smile went wide. "I am officially and legally the sole provider and custodian of my son. The judge awarded me full custody and the right to determine visitation with Trina's family."

"Yes!" I sat up as he walked around the edge of the sofa. I meant to give him a hug, but instead, moved a bit too fast, which started a very nasty round of nausea.

"That's it, Kai. I'm taking you to see a doctor. You should be better by now. Hell, I thought you were better."

I waved him off and lay back down. "There's no need. I made an appointment to see him next week. Believe me, I'm going." I looked around. "Wait a minute. Where is the little munchkin?"

"Justin? With my parents. Tonight's their last night in town. After court, we went to Chucky Cheese to celebrate. I called to see if you could join us, but, no answer." Trevon joined me on the couch and set the plates, cups, and food on the coffee table. "That's why I came over here. I was worried about you." He reached out and put a hand on my leg, rubbed a bit.

My heart warmed at his thoughtfulness, but it was hard to decide what did it the most, his wanting to invite me to spend time with his family or the genuine care shown by his actions.

"I appreciate your concern."

"Hey, you've gone out of your way to help me. I'm not sure I could ever repay you." That charming smile I'd grown to love appeared.

I rubbed Sugar as she came to sit beside me. She sniffed the air, her focus on Trevon and the bag of chicken that was now in reach.

"Hey, girl." Trevon reached over, let her sniff his hand.

She responded with a quick lick and then sat in rapt attention. Which reminded me…

"Can you do me a favor?"

"Sure, what do you need?"

"Do you mind taking her out so she can use the bathroom? She hasn't been since I came home and knocked myself out with the drugs."

"Sure." He stood and went to the coat closet where I kept her leash. "How much of that stuff did you take?"

"Half a tablet. Anything more than that and I would be asleep until tomorrow."

His brow went down as he called Sugar over and attached the leash to her collar. "That's some strong stuff, Kai."

"And addictive, which is why I refuse to take it if I don't really need to."

The expression on his face read as if the fact I needed to take the medication at all meant more than I was letting on. "I'll be back in a minute."

To show my appreciation for his taking Sugar out and for dinner, I went to the kitchen, washed my hands, and grabbed a bottle of blue cheese dressing from the refrigerator. He'd forgotten to get something to drink, so I popped a can of frozen apple juice out of the refrigerator and proceeded to make some fresh juice to drink.

I was nearly done when he returned. "That was fast."

"She really needed to go."

I smiled. "I hate to think what would have happened if you hadn't called and woke me up. Thank you."

"What are friends for?" He disconnected the leash and put it back in the closet before joining me in the kitchen.

Friends. The fact that that word continued to float in the air between us felt awkward. Yet, despite the way I felt, we had both drawn a line when it came to our relationship.

"My offer to help with Justin still stands, by the way." I opened the freezer to retrieve a tray of ice cubes.

When I turned, Trevon was standing right behind me. I bumped into him and he caught me before I lost my balance.

I was immediately aware of his strong hands on my shoulders. The connection was electric. Though there was nothing sexual in the moment, it was impossible to ignore the attraction I felt for this man.

Hurt back and all.

The expression on Trevon's face reflected a ton of emotions, as if he were truly touched by my offer.

"Kai, have I told you how much I appreciate you? You've gone above and beyond for Justin…for me. And I'm not just talking about your job. With our…history…you've stepped in to be a friend when you could have just walked away. Why?"

I bit my lip as his hands slid slowly down my shoulders and to my wrist. Tiny shivers ran across my skin at the memory of what it had felt like to have those very hands explore every inch of my body.

"Because…I like you, Trevon. The night we met, I slept with you because I really did like you. I knew that if I ever saw you again, I would want to get to know you."

Trevon's brow rose ever so slightly. "Really? Why?" His hand stayed on my wrist, squeezing as if testing the pace of my beating heart.

I swallowed hard. "Honestly?"

He nodded, focused on my eyes.

"Because you made me feel things Malik didn't. We'd been together for nearly three years, yet a few hours with you left me feeling like a woman." I shook my head. "That didn't come out right. What I mean is, I not only felt beautiful, I felt…it felt like you really did give a damn about me. You asked questions and listened as if you cared about what I had to say. And when we went back to your place, you treated me like a lady. You even tried to convince me not to have sex, but talk instead. I mean, what man who's about to get some does that?" I shook my head. "But you did. You made it known you'd rather get to know me instead of just having sex." My attention went to the place where I could feel his bare skin against my own. "God, Trevon, you're making me feel that way right now."

I fought to keep sultry and sexy out of my voice. The expression of Trevon's face told me I'd failed. Big time.

"I looked for you that morning, you know. I got out of bed, realized you weren't in the bathroom, and jumped online to see if I could find you on Facebook. I kicked myself for falling asleep without getting your full name, phone number, email, or something so that I could find you. I even went back to that bar every night for a week hoping you'd show up looking for me, too."

"You're kidding." Guilt took over as I imagined him sitting at the bar watching the door.

"Then out of the blue you show up at Andre's house. Kai, you have no idea how many emotions I went through. I don't know what was worse; seeing you again or realizing you were Malik's woman."

I cringed and looked away. I remembered that day, too. After being with Trevon, I went back to Malik's cheating ass. I had felt like an idiot seeing him again.

"Crossing paths with you that day is what made me realize I needed to break things off with Malik for good. You reminded me that I deserved better."

His hands went to the side of my face. "You do, Kai, you do. Even though life took me on a different path since then, somehow, it's brought me back to you. I still want you. I want you more than before because now I know the kind of woman you are." He ran a hand through my hair, pulling it away from my face. "I know what I said before, about not wanting to be in a relationship, but, when I was with my parents and Justin today, I realized something was missing. It was you. Celebrating didn't feel the same without you. You've become a part of our lives, Kai. I like that. Justin likes that." Trevon's warm eyes stayed on mine, as if he was at war with himself about something. "I'm falling in love with you."

My breath caught. "Are you serious?"

Trevon's reply wasn't verbal. Instead, he lowered his mouth to mine. The kiss wasn't rushed or passionate. It was simple. An answer to my question. He pulled away, repositioned the hold he had on my chin, and came back for more.

A moan escaped as I melted into him, my hands coming up to hold the back of his head, allowing myself to be claimed by this man.

When we separated, Trevon rested his forehead against mine. His breathing was a bit heavier, as was mine. It was obvious we were both turned on.

Trevon released my face and slid his hands down the front of my robe, to the tie. He undid the knot, taking his time, as if waiting to see if I'd protest.

The minute his fingers found the edge of my tank top, he slid a finger under and teased me by running fingertips along the skin of my belly and the underside of my breast.

I sighed and let my head fall back. It was amazing how the barest of contact could mean and say so much.

"I want to take you to bed, Kai," he murmured in my ear, then kissed the side of my throat. "I've wanted you since that night. You've been in my dreams for months…" He kissed my shoulder. "Now that we have this chance to be together again…" He pulled back, his breath soft against my skin. "I'm not going to take you. Not now, because no matter how much your body is calling to me at this moment, you're not ready."

My head snapped up, breaking the trance his kisses and words had put me in. "Excuse me? You have no idea how ready I am."

His seductive touch slid across my rib cage; I shuttered. His lips curled in a slow smile.

"Oh, I know you're ready, but you're also in pain. I won't ask you to make love if you're hurting. We've held ourselves in check this long; I can be patient."

I fought the urge to pout like a kid. "What if I can't?"

He chuckled, kissed me again. I melted as he explored my mouth before pulling away.

"Then by the time we do make love, I'm going to be a sex god because you're that horny." He wagged his eyebrows.

I couldn't help but laugh. "You proved that the night we met." My arms went up around his neck before sliding down the front of his dress shirt. I tugged on his tie and sighed.

As much as I hated to admit it, he was right about the pain and discomfort.

"When do you see your doctor?"

I sighed and rested my head on his chest. "Next Tuesday."

"Good." He kissed the top of my head, then reached between us and pulled the edges of my robe together and tied it back. He met my gaze when I looked up. "Let's see what he has to say, and then we'll go from there." Another kiss left me speechless. "How about we eat dinner before it gets cold?" He took my hand and led me back to the sofa in the living room where our food sat on the coffee table.

Sugar lay nearby, eyes staring at the plates full of treats as her tail wagged hard.

"I forgot she was sitting there. She didn't touch a thing." Trevon's shock came out as a laugh. "I don't know who trained her, but damn, they were good."

"Good girl, Sugar!" I called her over and rubbed her head as we sat down again. Trevon reached over and rubbed her too, then offered her a chicken wing full of meat.

I held up a hand. "She can't eat it like that. If she does, those small bones will get lodged in her throat and we'll end up spending the evening at the vet's office. I think one disabled person around here is enough."

Trevon pulled back the chicken wing before Sugar could get it. "Oh, man, sorry. My sister was always the one good with animals; that's why she's a veterinarian. I played sports."

I looked at him in surprise. "I didn't know you had a sister?"

"Two of them actually. Ebony is my twin, well, fraternal twin."

Between us, Sugar whined, unhappy about her loss of a snack. "If you want to give her a treat, I've got carrots in the refrigerator. Those are better for her."

Trevon dug into the bag of wings until he pulled out a Styrofoam container. He opened it to reveal a mixture of carrots and celery sticks. "Will this work?"

"Perfect."

He retrieved one and held it in Sugar's direction. She sat without waiting for the command. When he lowered it towards her mouth, she slowly moved to sniff, gently took it from his grasp, and then trotted off with her spoils.

"I had no idea dogs ate vegetables." He popped one into his own mouth after dipping it in blue cheese dressing.

"Dogs will eat nearly anything you put in front of them. I learned a long time ago to put up my underwear and my shoes in the closet. Sugar will get chewing urges from time to time and decide the toys I bought her are not enough." I pointed to the large dog kennel in the corner. "That's where she goes when she has one of those chew on anything moments. It used to be worse when she was a puppy, but since the training, there have been fewer incidents."

"Guess I have a lot to learn if I want to get a dog." He pulled out a few wings and set them on his plate.

I laughed. "But wait a minute; let's get back to the family thing. You said you have a twin?" He nodded while stuffing his mouth. "Then why am I just hearing about her?"

He shrugged. "I guess we've both had too much going on in life to focus on those details. I'll make you a deal. Once you talk to your doctor, spend the day with me. We'll go out and do something fun and talk about all the stuff we've never addressed."

I tilted my head in surprise. "You mean, go on a date?"

"Exactly, as long as you're up to it."

"Um, yeah…I'd like that. What do you have in mind?"

He tilted his head and studied me as he chewed on a wing. "If you're feeling better and up to it, I think we should go to Stone Mountain. I haven't been in a while and I'd love to see the laser show. Besides, I've always wanted to walk the mountain trail. The exercise would be good for you, too."

I grinned. "Look at you trying to be all thoughtful. Okay, I'm game. I'm sure Justin will, too."

Trevon shook his head. "No, I'm getting a babysitter for him. I want this to be about you and me. We'll pack a lunch, go for a challenging walk, and get to really know one another. Sound good to you?"

I nodded in agreement, and watched as he went back to work on the chicken bone in his hand.

Trevon was happy and in love.

With me.

And then it hit me.

I loved this man and I hadn't told him that.

What was holding me back?

Our relationship status had just gone from friends to being a couple in a matter of minutes. Though I loved Justin and had deep feelings for Trevon, it didn't change the fact that I couldn't give him everything he wanted. I told him that.

Had he forgotten or did he not care?

At this moment, I was too afraid to ask.

Chapter 22

"Sorry, Trevon, but we didn't pass inspection."

I studied the papers Derrick handed to me from the county inspector. "You've got to be shitting me. How did that happen?"

Derrick threw his hands up, frustrated. "It's these damn city ordinances. Georgia has different regulations than North Carolina. Apparently they made changes to the code over the past few months. I researched this the moment I got the plans. We were good. But now, shit. It ain't like they send out a memo when they make the changes. That's how they make their money, in fines."

My head started to hurt as I reviewed the paperwork again. "Two thousand dollars?" Corporate would not be pleased. "Once the pipes have been upgraded…"

"Then we can start moving in the kitchen equipment." Derrick walked over to one of the drainage pipes in question and kicked it with his steel-toed boot. It sprung free and dark sludge bled out. The smell was horrible.

"All right then. I'll make the needed calls and delay a few things. Keep me advised, D." I held out the paperwork.

"Of course." He accepted the list.

I took a seat at the bar and made my first call to the company scheduled to deliver and install the kitchen equipment in the next forty-eight hours. Then it was time to inform my boss. After a few choice words and a not so veiled threat to lose the management opportunity if we went over budget again, I got off the phone and looked behind the bar. The alcohol that had lined the glass shelves was boxed up and put away due to the renovation. Damn, I could really use a drink right about now.

The last person on my list was Kelli, who was in charge of the final touches of interior decorating. Of all the calls to make, this one would be the easiest.

"Oh hell, no. Trevon, that's not going to work for my schedule, that's two weeks! I need that time! My due date is a week after that. I need to be done with this job before I go into labor. What if something goes wrong and I need an extension of time? I won't have it. What do you expect me to do? Tell my baby to hold on for another week, mommy's still working?"

I scratched my brow. Okay, it wasn't so easy. Mental note: never piss off a pregnant woman. "Kelli, that's just crazy. You know that's not my intention…"

"I'm sure it's not, but let me tell you something…"

I held the phone away from my ear as she vented her frustration. That was the problem with working with friends and family in business. All sense of professionalism went out the window.

The moment she paused long enough for me to get in a word, I pulled the phone back to my ear. "If you don't believe me, Kelli, talk to the contractor. I'll give you his number and the two of you can work out the scheduling." Across the room, Derrick shot me a look of disbelief. I ignored it.

She ranted for ten more minutes before hanging up. If we weren't on cell phones, I'm pretty sure the phone would have been slammed down in my ear.

"So you sic her on me, like the shit is my fault." Derrick shook his head, grabbed a broom, and swept up debris from the day's work.

"Gotta keep the in-laws happy."

"In-laws?" The broom stopped moving. "Did I miss something?" Derrick studied me as if I'd grown a horn on my forehead.

I laughed. "No, and saying 'in-law' is a bit premature. Her sister and I just decided to be a couple yesterday. But yeah, I'm pretty sure she's the one." The thought of the new path my relationship with Kai was taking was enough to dissipate the anger and frustration I felt about my current work situation. I held on to the image of kissing her in the kitchen, and then before leaving, for as long as I could.

Derrick cleared his throat to get my attention. He stood the broom in front of himself and rested both hands on the top of the handle. "Is this the same woman you kept a secret from me?"

"Her name is Kai, and yes, it's the same woman." I checked my phone for any missed messages or emails just in case she'd sent one while I was on the phone. Nothing. Fighting the disappointment, I stuffed the phone in my pocket. When I looked up again, Derrick stared at me with a continued look of disbelief.

"Kai? Firefighter Kai? One-night stand Kai? The-woman-I-slept-with-once-but-decided-we-would-only-be-friends, Kai?"

"Yep." A smile spread on my face.

"Okay, it's official, hell is freezing over." He threw a hand up and then resumed sweeping.

I laughed. "That's overkill and you know it."

"No, it's not. You're the one who said, and I quote, 'hell will freeze over before I get married or have a kid'." He counted off a finger. "You got a kid, now you're talking marriage. I'd say hell was fifty percent frozen."

I grinned. Leave it to Derrick to remember the comments of a nineteen-year-old kid who was horny and in full player mode. "If you need a coat, Burlington Coat Factory is having a sale."

Derrick laughed. "Uh, hell no, I'm good. Besides, I know how to dodge that bullet. Give 'em what they want in bed, but make no promises. If you're straight with them in the beginning, then chances are they won't get attached." He shrugged. "Single, detached, and free to do whoever, whenever. I'll be sure to share stories so you know what you're missing."

I chuckled and pulled up the text app on my phone to send Kai a message. It was Tuesday and she was scheduled to meet with her doctor. I wanted to know what the prognosis was. Since she hadn't sent me a message, I decided to avoid the delay and send her one first.

"When's the big day?"

"What day?" I focused on my typing. When I hit send and looked up, the smirk on Derrick's face said it all. "There's no wedding date because I haven't asked, but I'm sure she'll say yes when I do."

"Because..."

"Because we've been in each other's space for four months and haven't slept together. We've been getting to know each other. She's gone out of her way to help me with Justin and it wasn't her responsibility. I've thought about what you told me that night at the bar, and as much as it pains me to say it, you're right. The next natural step in our relationship is about more than sex though."

"Natural?" Derrick resumed sweeping. "Call me the Devil's Advocate, but we've been boys since the fifth grade. I know you. Taking on the role of father, I can see that, admire it even. But you were in love with his mother. How can you go from trying to get back together for the sake of your son, to mourning her death, to falling in love with another woman?" His hand went up as I opened my mouth to reply. "I get it, man. She saved your son. You've tasted the goodies and liked it. How does that make her the one? Are you scared to raise Justin alone?"

I blinked.

Afraid?

I wasn't sure how to answer that question.

And Trina…

A pain in my chest made it hard to breathe. So much had happened since her death.

Was I sad? Yes. Did I miss her? Yes. Would we have gotten back together if she hadn't died?

My intention and focus had been on making that happen. Her agreement to move in with me before she died had been the first indication that she might have been ready to give us another try. The question I hadn't asked myself was how long would it have worked? Was her decision based on wanting the same thing or convenience?

Knowing her, it could have been a way to keep her private life out of her mother's controlling grasp. While she loved her family, she loved her independence more.

And then there was Kai.

The one-night stand that stayed with me even when I was in Trina's presence.

Our connection was about more than the fact she had saved my son. Saved Trina. Our connection had started the night we met, well before I learned of Justin's existence. What would have happened if we had crossed paths before Trina and Justin came back into the picture?

I would never know. What I did know was that the situation with Trina made me want to try to get our family back together. Seeing Kai again made me want to explore and find out what our connection could lead to.

If Trina had lived, would I have been able to leave Kai alone?

I massaged my temples as the stress of the day came back with the added realization that some of what Derrick said could be true.

Was the love I felt for Kai about the woman or just convenience?

Chapter 23

"Derrick, I'll holler at you later. I've got to go handle some interviews for new employees when we do open up."

"Go do your thing." I watched Trevon walk to his car. His hands were in his pockets and his head hung low. My questions must have hit closer to home than I thought.

I hated to point out the defects in his plan to find Happily Ever After. What kind of friend would I be if I didn't keep it real?

If there was one thing I knew about Trevon that he didn't know about himself, it was that he is a flat out romantic. He tried to hide it, but he wore it on his sleeve like a neon sign. In high school, girls tried to take advantage of his soft spot. At 6' 3" and the star player on the basketball team, he had a future as an NBA player, which made him a magnet for every girl who wanted to be there when the checks started rolling in.

P.B. Pretty Boy.

That's what the other players called him behind his back. I was his friend so I got away with saying it to his face.

While I had my own share of good looks, putting us both side by side was like night and day. While we were the same height and shared the same dream, I was a different shade of chocolate. I pulled my share of women, too, but unlike Trevon, I knew exactly what to do with them. It didn't take long for him to pick up on my tutelage and run with it, though.

And now it appeared he'd dropped the ball.

My back pocket vibrated. I dug for the phone and read the screen. Not recognizing the number, I ignored the call. If it was important, they'd leave a voicemail.

Done with the cleanup, I grabbed my notebook and took a final trip around the kitchen, reading the inspector's notes, taking measurements, and making plans for ordering the needed materials to get the job completed as soon as possible. My boy didn't need any more issues.

"Hello?"

Startled, I looked up from my clipboard and saw a woman entering the premises from the back doors of the restaurant. My workers and Trevon had left for the day, while I stayed behind. There was a huge sign out front that said 'Under Renovation.' For some reason, this woman felt she needed to see what was going on for herself. Either that or she was at the wrong place for a job interview.

"Excuse me, Miss, we're closed. Did you see the sign?"

The woman held onto the doorjamb while peering down at the floor as she took her time stepping over the cords near the threshold. Long dark hair hung in front of her face, but she looked up at the sound of my voice.

Her skin was a beautiful shade of cream. Her eyes were dark orbs set in a sexy catlike slant. And her body was…

I whistled. "Damn, I'm sorry I missed the opportunity."

Her thin eyebrows drew tight. "Opportunity for what?"

"To get you pregnant."

Her lips grew tight at the same time her hand went to her very round belly. Most women would have laughed and took my words as a compliment. She didn't.

"If you're trying to be funny, you failed. I'm going to assume you're Trevon's friend."

Feisty. "So that must make you Kai's sister, the very pregnant interior decorator."

"My name is Kelli." She frowned. "You know my sister? She's never mentioned you."

"No, we've never met. I've just heard a lot about her." I crossed my arms, amused at the irritation on her face.

"Heard a lot about her how?" A thin eyebrow arched.

Without realizing it, I found myself studying her body. Despite the pregnancy, it was obvious she had somewhat of a petite frame. She wore a dress that fit her every curve, too. Not the kind of maternity wear I'd seen on a woman before. She was confident for sure. My attention went back to her face, and got stuck on those dark chocolate eyes that glared at me. Her face was oval shaped, yet her cheeks were a bit rounder, no doubt from the baby weight. Her lips were…perfect.

If her sister looked anything like her, minus the pregnant belly, I could see why Trevon was hooked.

"Uh, hello? I asked you a question." A hand went to her belly.

I chuckled to buy myself some time to get my thoughts together. Since when did I study the body of a woman carrying another man's seed? Yeah, I seriously needed to find a woman in Atlanta and get laid. Forget going out with Trevon and his married friend. Tonight I was going solo and if things went my way, I wouldn't be going back to my hotel alone.

"Apparently you don't know." I folded an arm against my chest and held the clipboard in place while scratching my chin.

"Know what?" Those already slanted eyes got narrower.

Watching this woman's irritation morph to curiosity was rather entertaining. A part of me wanted to continue to rile her up to see what other types of expressions she would make, but that would be flirting, and I didn't flirt with —yep, that was a ring on the hand resting on her belly— pregnant or married women.

"They've hooked up, Kai and Trevon, you know, doing the couple thing? She didn't tell you?"

"They did what?" Surprise was all over her face, as was disbelief and even more irritation. Was that possible? Maybe it was due to pregnancy hormones.

"Guess not. Anyway, you didn't come here to discuss their love life. I assume you're here about the construction delay."

It took a moment for her thoughts to get back on track.

"Yes. Trevon said I would have to wait two weeks before I can start. I don't have that kind of time." She pointed to her obvious belly. "As you see, I have other plans. I'm working with a small team and we need that time. My schedule is to have this project completed before I go into labor. I don't like leaving things unfinished or putting it into someone else's hands to complete. So this is what you need to do…"

I looked around the empty kitchen to see if she was talking to someone else who had snuck into the building without my knowledge. When it was obvious I was the one she was addressed, I burst out laughing. "What *I* need to do?"

She dug into the oversized purse on her shoulder and pulled out a humongous planner. Her attention went to the pages as she flipped through to the one she was looking for. "What you need to do is," she continued as if I hadn't spoken, "have your guys done or at least out of my way by—"

This woman was serious. A smirk crossed my face as I took a wide legged stance and listened with interest as she rattled on and on about her personal deadlines and how my time to reach completion should be handled.

I had to give it to her, she was damn good at scheduling, but she had no idea of the reality of the situation.

Out of respect for her femininity, I let her go through her plan without interruption. Maybe saying it out loud would release some of the pent up frustration she was dealing with.

Finished, she slammed the book shut and put it back into the depths of the thing she called a purse. When she looked at me again, her expression read of satisfaction as if she'd found a way to make the situation bearable for all parties involved.

I clapped my hands.

Her lips thinned. "I don't do sarcasm."

"And I don't do unskilled labor, or in your case, what's your job title again? *Interior decorator*, telling me how to do my job."

"Excuse me?" Her hands went to her hips as her voice went up an octave.

I sighed and massaged my eyebrows. What the hell was wrong with me? Was I really about to get into it with a pregnant woman? I was about to apologize and reword my statement, but the snarky expression on her face made me think twice.

We stared at each other, at an obvious impasse.

My phone vibrated in my pocket again. I looked at the name on the screen and sighed; more urgent matters needed to be addressed.

"Look, I was trying to make it easier on you and your…," I waved a hand in her direction. "Delicate condition, as you southerners like to say."

"My delicate condition?" Her lips thinned as she got madder by the minute.

I ignored the attitude. "Look, when those grease traps and pipes are removed in the kitchen, the smell is going to be unlike anything you've smelled before. It won't matter where you're working at in the building by the way. But if you're hell bent on having things done your way then do your thing. I am not claiming responsibility for you being uncomfortable with the work conditions." The phone chimed, indicating a missed call and new voicemail. "Now if you'll excuse me, I've got to return this call."

I felt daggers on my back as I walked away, pressing the button to redial the missed call. "Hey, Pop. How is she?" I held my breath and waited for my stepfather to reply.

"Today wasn't a good day. Making it to her doctor's appointment was a struggle. She's resting now so she'll be fine in a few hours."

I closed my eyes and massaged my brow. My guilt was a problem I'd never be able to get rid of. "I should be there. It's my duty to make sure mom is taken care of."

"Actually, son, it's my job to make sure she's taken care of. Believe me, what you're doing right now means a lot. She understands why you can't be here. Lupus is a manageable disease. You know as I do this is a day-to-day situation. What you're doing is helping, believe me. Less stress about how her medical bills are going to get paid makes it easier on her and on me."

I shook my head. "Dad, it doesn't matter what I do; we both know it's impossible to make her stop worrying."

"True," He chuckled. "You know how much she loves being in control. Not being able to do something as simple as walking in the mornings because her body aches is really starting to affect her mood. I'm doing everything I can to make it better for her, but it's hard."

Knowing Charles had my mother's best interest at heart didn't ease the tension in my shoulders.

"Is she still having a problem remembering things?"

"Unfortunately. Her doctor's referred us to a psychologist. The only problem is the insurance will only cover part of it."

I sighed and massaged my brow. Helping pay for her medical insurance was one of the reasons why I worked my ass off. The last thing I wanted was for him to come out of retirement and go back to work. My mother needed him to be home to support her emotionally and see that she made it to every appointment more than she needed money. That was my job.

Not that I didn't need the help. If my brother's lazy ass wasn't unemployed and living at home making matters worse, the family business would be more lucrative. As it was, I could only be in one place at a time.

"Did Shawn make it to the interview?"

Pop sighed.

"So that's a no." I shook my head in disgust.

If it weren't for his drug habit, he would be running a division of the construction company. A work injury had him addicted to painkillers, which led to stronger street drugs. He had gone into rehab once and made a change. That alone had drained the company financially, but was worth it. He got better and was released.

His wife, Lydia, had kicked him out of the house and wanted him to stay away from the kids because he couldn't be trusted. None of us wanted to run the risk of him having a setback. Shawn moved back home with mom and dad because staying with me wasn't an option. We bumped heads too much. Mom knew if we were left alone for too long, one of us would end up in jail.

Then she was diagnosed with her illness.

The drugs she took proved to be too much of a temptation for Shawn and before we knew it, her expensive medications went missing and his job performance at work turned from one gigantic failure to another and nearly bankrupted the company. Dad had no choice but to fire him and retire early so he could take care of mom.

The success of the company now rested on my shoulders alone.

"Shaun made it all right. The problem is he failed the drug test."

"How? He knows how to get around that. Shawn isn't dumb; he's just lazy as hell. I swear, Pop, he's doing that shit on purpose because he knows that no matter what he does, Mom wants him to stay around."

"That may be true, but I'm at my wit's end with him. I'd put him out if it wouldn't upset her and cause her to have a flare up. She needs to be as stress free as possible."

So did I. Unfortunately, I didn't see a way for that to happen at all. Not now, not ever.

"I know, Pop. Damn." I looked around and saw Kelli had let herself out the back door. "Pop, don't forget to put the medicine up. That stuff is too expensive to have Shaun's slippery fingers all over it again. I had a failed inspection at work today, stupid code issues, so it'll be a few more weeks before I get that final check."

"That's the nature of the business. Do what you have to do, son, but don't worry. We're good here. Don't worry about the meds, I've put them in a lock box, and only your mom and I know the combination. Hold up," He paused and I could hear my mom's voice in the background. "Your mother wants to know when you think you'll be home again."

"Tell her I'll try and slip away this weekend and spend the day with her if I can."

"Will do. I won't hold you up. I'm about to make your mom something to eat and then we're going to watch a movie. I refuse to let her focus on the fact she doesn't feel well."

"Pop, I'm so glad she has you. I don't know what she would do without you…or any of us for that matter."

He sighed. "I know."

The call ended and I looked around my current workspace.

Two weeks. It was the deadline I gave myself to get this job completed and have a check cut. Then it was back home to North Carolina and the next job. Momma's medical bills wouldn't pay for themselves.

Chapter 24

"Damn, Kai, why is Kelli givin' you the evil eye?"

"Ricky, I was about to ask the same question." I sat the flower stem I was about to insert into the arrangement on the counter.

My sister put her purse down next to it then glanced around the shop. "Where's mom?"

"Out to lunch. Why?" Wary, I kept my eye on her as she walked around the table that separated us while staring me down.

Her hands went to her hips as she waddled. "You're really not going to say it?"

"Say what?" I looked at Ricky in confusion. All he could do was shrug.

Having reached where I stood, Kelli grunted and pinched the crap out of my arm.

"Ow! What the hell?" I pulled away and fought the reflex to punch her back.

Ricky shook his head and rubbed his arm. "I felt that all the way over here."

My arm ached as I massaged the spot in disbelief. "I'd pinch you back if it weren't for the fact you're carrying my nephew. What's wrong with you?"

"When were you going to tell me you're sleeping with the customers?"

"Say what?" Ricky stopped rubbing his arm and abandoned the floral arrangement in front of him. "Spill it." He snapped his fingers.

Boxed in between the two of them and a table at my back, I slipped between them to get out of pinching range. "Sleeping with customers? How did you—"

"Trevon didn't tell me. His obnoxious contractor friend did."

"Trevon? You're with him again? Ooo…" Ricky laughed, his attention set in my direction.

I rolled my eyes and walked away to put more space between me and my nosy family. "First of all, 'sleeping with' sounds cheap. We've decided to have an official relationship." In my peripheral, I saw Ricky's mouth open. I held up a hand to stop him. "No, we're not cut buddies, so don't ask."

Ricky's mouth stayed in the shape of an O.

"And don't even think about asking me about our sex life ever again." I turned and walked towards the back office.

"Well…damn. You are no fun at all." He sucked his teeth and went back to work.

"You're not getting off that easy, sister. Why are you with him?"

I glanced over my shoulder and saw Kelli hot on my heels. "You act as if it's a bad thing, Kelli. Trevon's a good guy and you know it."

"Yes, he is. He's also a friend of mine who's gone through a lot. He's vulnerable right now. You've got your own issues, too. I don't want to see two people I care about end up hurt. Then I'll be in the middle."

I glanced over my shoulder, irritated. How did my decision of whom I dated end up being about her?

"First of all, you act as if I have a track record of breaking men's hearts. I don't. I'm the one who's been screwed over time and time again by a man who was supposed to marry me. Don't you think I've thought this through? I have no intention of taking advantage of Trevon in any way. I've got feelings for him. He has feelings for me. We know what's going on in each other's lives. This isn't something that just happened."

"Like hell. 'It happened'", she did air quotation marks, "when you guys met at a bar and slept together. Everything since then has been coincidence and some weird kind of obsession on your part."

I stopped dead in my tracks. Kelli had lost her mind. "Excuse me? How dare you—" I stopped myself before I said something that I would regret. Instead, I cocked my head to the side and processed what my sweet, angelic, baby sister had said to me.

Then I faced her. Sweet and angelic had been replaced with bossy and bitchy, and it wasn't because she was nearly nine months pregnant.

"For a moment, I thought your comments were because you cared about my wellbeing and wanted to be sure I didn't get hurt again. Now I know what the problem is." I pointed a finger in her direction. "*You* are jealous."

Kelli scoffed and took a step back. "Like hell I am."

Her words said one thing, but the expression on her face told another story completely.

I put my hands on my hips and stared her in the eyes. "You're jealous because for the past five years, I was bold enough to step out from our parents' shadow and do exactly what I wanted with my life. I got the job I wanted, live where I want, do whatever I want. So what my track record with men hasn't been the best. Who cares? So what I can't have a baby of my own?" Tears gathered in the corners of my eyes as my voice went up an octave. "Have you ever stopped to think that I could be jealous of you? Perfect, bossy, All-American Kelli. You married the perfect man with a kick ass job. You've got a beautiful home with just the right amount of space to raise those two point five kids of yours. The only thing missing is a dog and that's just because Alonso is allergic to them." Damn, a tear fell, but that didn't stop my rant. "Kelli, Kelli, Kelli, what could *possibly* go wrong in your perfectly planned world?" I plopped down in the office chair.

Kelli made her way to the only other available chair, lowered herself down, and sniffed.

I rolled my eyes. Leave it to her to become dramatic about my rant.

"Oh please, you need to stop." I reached across the desk for a tissue and dabbed my eyes.

When I looked in her direction, I paused. Her face was flushed red and tears ran down as if a water faucet had been turned on.

Kelli's hands went up as she mumbled, "Alonso is cheating on me."

For a moment I thought my hearing was messed up, but the expression on her face said what I heard was true. "Say what?"

Kelli wiped her face with the back of her hand. "I found lipstick on his pants the other day when doing laundry. He's been staying out late, saying he's working, but I don't buy it. He gets phone calls and leaves the room so I can't hear him. He's put a lock on his phone." She blew her nose in the tissue I handed her. "I'm big, fat, and carrying his second child. He looks at me as if I'm a barge and he no longer wants me. We haven't had sex in months, and he spends more time with our daughter than with me. I don't know what to do, Kai."

Regardless of how much she pissed me off, my big sister defensive instincts kicked in. I got out of my seat and squatted down next to her. "I had no idea."

"Nobody knows. I made sure of that." She blew her nose. "Not so perfect after all, huh? It's okay, you can laugh. I deserve it."

I shook my head in disgust. "It's not funny, Kelli. Just because you piss me off doesn't mean I don't love you. I've been where you are before. Remember Malik?" I sighed. "Have you sat down and talked to him about it?"

She huffed. "In my condition? He'll probably claim I'm imagining things because I'm pregnant. Then I'd get emotional and end up in labor and he'd have to rush me to the hospital. That's not how I want my baby to be born… in the midst of an argument."

I couldn't help but laugh. "Uh, no, I don't think so. You'd squeeze your legs together and demand the baby wait until you're ready to go to the hospital."

That made her smile. "Am I really that bossy?"

I looked at her sideways. "As if you didn't know."

"Okay, okay, I'll admit it. But, I'm not bossy…I'm organized. If it weren't for me, Alonso wouldn't have the job he's got now. When we met, he was fresh out of design school and unsure of how he'd work his way up in a design firm. Now, thanks to me, he's the first Hispanic to be a lead designer at the number one architectural firm in Atlanta."

She was right; she had pushed her husband to get to where he was. He had talent, no doubt. What he'd lacked was confidence. Kelli made him see past the racial glass ceiling and helped him break through it. There was truth to having a good woman behind you. Supporting those she loves was her strong suit.

"By the way, you were right; I am jealous of you."

I huffed in disbelief. "For what?"

"Like you said, you did your own thing and got the job you wanted. You're living your life to the fullest and didn't plan a damn thing. Me? I plan the hell out of mine in the pursuit of perfection. It's a curse." She shook her head in disappointment. "There are times when I wish I could be you and just…be. No worries, no cares, no—"

"Husband to love or children to cuddle?"

Kelli closed her eyes and a tear dropped. "That was insensitive of me, Kai. I'm sorry."

"No need to apologize. We deal with what life gives us." I pushed up off the floor.

"That's what scares me about Trevon." Kelli watched me as I moved around to the chair opposite of her. "He's dealing with a lot. You don't know him like I do."

"He's Andre's friend, Kel. I don't get the feeling Alonso and Trevon run in the same circles."

"Not really, but women talk. Trevon has always been a ladies' man. Not a bad one like Malik, but still."

"I know, he told me."

Her lips tightened. "Did you know he was trying to get back with Trina before she died?"

"Yes."

She scowled.

"Like I said, we've been friends since the funeral. We've aired our dirty laundry and are ready to move forward in our lives. It's not complicated."

"So you're in love with him and his son. You can see yourself taking Trina's place."

I took a deep breath. "I'm not trying to take her place. I'm trying to find one of my own. And yes," I looked down at her belly. "My not being able to have a baby of my own has planted Justin in my heart." I placed my hand on my chest for emphasis. "I want this, Kel, more than I realized. For once, I feel like I can have my cake and eat it, too. A job I love and a family."

"Without gaining a single pound," she murmured, balled up a sheet of paper that had been sitting on the desk, and threw it my way.

I caught it and cracked up. "Well, when you put it that way, that's not a bad trade off."

We sat in silence for a moment as Kelli wiped at her eyes again. "When are you going to tell mom and dad?"

I shrugged. "I figured I'd spring it on them at our grandparents' anniversary party."

"Crap, that's coming up soon, isn't it? I've been so stressed with Alonso that I forgot all about it." She frowned. "Wait, are you sure you want to introduce Trevon to the entire family in one night? You may want to wait until you get a ring on that finger and he's invested first."

"I'm sure he'll be fine." I pulled out my phone; saw I'd missed a text message from Trevon. I was about to call him back when my phone rang.

"Hi, stranger, I was just talking about you." I pointed to the phone and mouthed an apology to Kelli.

"It was all good, I hope." Trevon's laugh seemed forced.

"It was if your ears were burning. But hey, what's wrong? Is Justin okay?" Worry hit the pit of my stomach. I looked up to see Kelli working her way out of the chair and heading to the door.

"I'll give you two some privacy," she whispered.

I nodded my thanks and shut the door behind her.

"Yeah, I'm good. It's just been a long morning. I'm interviewing possible employees for the re-opening. I've done this before as Assistant Manager, but as GM, I'm looking at things differently. I need a staff that will be on point with customer service and experience. I've seen too many people from the community that need a job but don't meet the qualifications. It's frustrating, that's all. With corporate watching me, I feel like I've got performance anxiety."

I stifled my laugh, realizing my head was in the wrong place. Performance anxiety when it came to sex was not a problem for him.

"You'll do fine, I'm sure."

"Thanks. I was calling to see how your doctor's appointment went."

So much had happened that I nearly forgot. "I should be released in a few weeks!"

"What? How? You were just in some serious pain last week."

"He thought I may have had a muscle tear, but it turns out I just aggravated the sprain," I laughed. "That makes no sense; basically, I irritated the muscle that was healing that day at the fountain. He gave me a strong shot of steroids and wants me to come back again for another shot next week. If all goes well, then he'll release me to go back to work on light duty. As of right now, I feel great!"

There was a slight pause. "I'm happy for you, Kai."

It was not hard to miss the sadness in his voice.

"Trevon, what's wrong? Seriously, talk to me. I thought you'd be excited about this."

He sighed. "I am, seriously. It's just I get this feeling that once you start working again, I won't be able to see you as much."

My heart warmed. "It won't be too bad. My schedule can be reasonable. It's usually one day on, two days off, unless I decide to pull a double. But don't worry, I'll still be able to watch Justin when I'm off and still have time to see you. We'll work it out."

"I'm sure we will. So you think you'll start when?"

"He didn't say, but I'm thinking maybe two or three weeks, why?"

"We definitely need to keep our date for this weekend, then. We had a few issues with the restaurant that put completion behind schedule, but if everything goes well, it will be opening in three weeks."

"Oh, wow, anything major?"

"No, just time consuming and bit more expensive. It'll work out." He paused. "I'm really looking forward to seeing you Saturday."

I felt my skin warm from his remark. "Me, too. By the way, if you're up to it, week after next, my grandparents are celebrating their forty-ninth anniversary. You could meet my family and then we could spend the rest of the night getting reacquainted."

Trevon's voice went low. "Reacquainted…is that what we're calling it?"

"I could have said something like getting our freak on, but I didn't want to put more performance pressure on you."

To that, he laughed. "When it comes to you, Kai, there is no pressure. I've imagined the scenarios countless times. The only question is which one will we do first."

I fanned myself, wondering if what he imagined our time together would be like was anything like my own.

"What do I wear to the party?"

"Suit and tie. I'll have on a dress. It's going to be held at the community rec center, which isn't far from the restaurant."

"Really? Hmm…We'll have to go by afterwards so you can see what's going on."

"Sounds like a plan."

There was a muffled sound on the line. "Crap, I gotta go. My next interviewee is here. I'll talk to you soon. I miss you, Kai."

A slow smile spread as my heart warmed even more. "I miss you, too."

Chapter 25

"Are you ready to have some fun?"

The enthusiasm on Trevon's face when I answered the door was infectious. I grinned back. "Yes. Let me get my backpack."

I held the door open, let him in the apartment, and walked over to where it sat on the sofa. When I turned, he still had the same goofy grin.

I inclined my head, curious. "What is up with you?"

Trevon walked over, slipped the bag off my shoulder, and kissed me. The minute our lips connected, I felt my eyes roll back in my head and my breath caught. Without thinking, my hands went over his shoulders and gripped the back of his neck, holding him to my mouth.

He pulled away. "Glad to see we're on the same page."

I stood on my tiptoes and kissed him again. "You can say that again. That kiss has been on my mind since last week."

His eyes glinted with mischief. "You don't want to know what's been on mine." He stepped back, grabbed my pack, and slipped my hand into his. "Come on, I want to get there before it gets too hot outside. The forecast called for an overcast day, but that doesn't mean the humidity is going to keep it any cooler."

Since Sugar had already been taken across the hall to my neighbor's home, there was nothing else for me to do except lock the door behind me and follow him down the steps to his car.

"I've never said this to you before, but this is one sexy ride!" I released his hand and walked over to the jet black Dodge Charger, running my hand over the shiny hood. It was obvious that he'd just washed it. Though I'd seen it plenty of times when he picked up Justin, I'd never been in it.

Pride was on his face. "Thanks. It was my gift to myself last year."

I peered over the hood as he unlocked the doors with a remote. "Seriously? It must have been a good year."

He nodded and slid in behind the wheel. "Actually, it was. That and the fact I was tired of doing repairs on my old car. I was able to patch it up and trade it in. Even managed to get enough to go towards the down payment."

I sat on the black leather seats with yellow accents, and, unable to resist, ran a hand over the black dashboard. The interior was clean, too. "What did you drive before?"

"An old Mustang. It was a gift from my parents when I got accepted at Georgia Tech. It wasn't new and had some miles on it, but it was paid for and mine. I got a lot of good use out of it for sure."

"I bet. How many women have you seduced in this thing?" I shot him a side glance and watched his lips curl up.

"You sound like my sister. She said the same thing when she visited last year."

I slapped his arm. "That's right, your twin! Tell me about her." I sat back in the bucket seats, my head on the high headrest, and listened.

He glanced my way as he backed out of the parking space. "I'm not sure what you want to know, but I guess the best place to start is that yes, we're twins, fraternal of course, so we don't look anything alike. We're close. We played together a lot when we were kids."

"Seriously? What could you two play that was fun for a boy and girl?"

He looked my way as we left the apartment complex and headed for the highway. "One guess; I'm sure if you think about it hard enough, you'll get it."

My brow creased. "Star Wars?"

"Yep."

I cracked up. "So she's a fan girl like me?"

He nodded.

"I think I'd like to meet her. Where does she live?"

"Ebony and her husband live in Los Angeles and are expecting their first child in a few months." He smiled. "I'm going to be an uncle again. My oldest sister, LaShana, lives with her husband and two daughters in my hometown of Charlotte, North Carolina, along with my parents. Justin is spoiled because I'm the only one who had a son."

"Lucky him. I remember seeing your parents, a lovely couple. I mean, I didn't get a chance to talk to them, but I did see them at the funeral."

"You'll meet my family soon enough." He seemed pleased to make that statement.

"Just like you'll be meeting mine."

He glanced my way. "I'm looking forward to it."

The rest of the ride was in silence as we hit the highway, music blasting and windows rolled down. I couldn't remember the last time I felt this good about anything in my life. I was with a man who appreciated me for who I was. A man who seemed to genuinely love me.

I had deep feelings for him, too.

And today, I was going to make sure he knew it.

****

"Our lunch is in here." Trevon pulled one of those temperature controlled lunch bags out of a cooler in the trunk.

I opened it and laughed. "Um, this doesn't look like anything that was homemade."

"You and I both know my cooking skills are limited." He grabbed his backpack and handed me mine.

"It's a sandwich. You don't have to be Emeril Lagasse to make that." I teased.

"Look, woman, it's a Publix deli sandwich, which means it's special. I didn't want some lame meat and bread combination on our first date."

My smile spread. Score one for making a moment special.

He stuffed the lunch bag in his pack then closed the trunk. We headed for the entrance to the Stone Mountain walk up trail along with several other groups of people. We stopped to read the sign at the entrance that covered the rules and regulations about using the trail.

I looked over at him. "It's a mile. Can you handle it?"

He huffed. "Please, a mile will be a piece of cake." He adjusted the straps of his backpack on his shoulders and led the way.

I kept my giggle internal. While Trevon was a nice physical specimen of a male, and it was nice watching his backside as he walked ahead, I wasn't too sure about his athletic ability. As it was, he said he *used* to play basketball. That had been years ago. I, on the other hand, had years of daily physical training as a firefighter that made running steps while wearing full gear, tools, and an air tank manageable. Walking this inclined trail would be nothing.

To my surprise, he set a nice pace. For the most part we were silent, taking in the beautiful sounds of nature as we hiked. Since I had never walked this trail before, I had done research on it by checking out the details and pictures posted by park visitors online.

This wasn't going to be an easy walk. From what I could see, the trail was painted directly on the mountain. There were no trees to take cover under so I was thankful for the cloud cover to keep the sun from beating down on us. Families with young kids and people who were apparently walking in fitness groups walked at different paces. Some we passed, others passed us.

We didn't do a lot of talking, each of us conserving energy and focusing on breathing as we traveled the ever increasing incline.

Halfway up the trail, Trevon peered over his shoulder; he was drenched in sweat. So was I. "How are you doing? Your back okay?"

"I'm good." It wasn't an exact lie. The pack stretched my back in ways that were uncomfortable, but it was in a good way. I had to get used to carrying weight on my back again. I needed to wear heavy equipment to do my job. If I couldn't handle the weight of this pack, then there would be a problem. I was in my top physical condition, or else, my doctor wouldn't have set a tentative release date to return to work. The problem was it would take more exercise to get back to my pre-injury stamina.

Trevon studied me. "Why don't we take a break for a moment?"

I was about to protest, but he walked off the path to a large pile of rocks and leaned against them, slid his bag off, and pulled out a bottle of water.

Hydrating sounded like a good idea. Without trees to shade us and with the sun peeking out from the clouds periodically, the heat coming from the granite was a bit intense. Add the fact of the Georgia humidity and well, you got thirsty pretty quick.

I followed his lead. The water he'd given me was still chilled from its time spent in the cooler. It was beyond satisfying.

My attention went to the trail and the way we'd come. "Oh my God, Trevon, look at that!"

He followed my line of sight. "Wow, now that's a beautiful view."

The path up the mountain wasn't a winding one, but one that literally led up the face of the mountain. From where we sat, the parking lot was barely visible due to the trees that lined the walkway, but we could see over the tree level of the park and into the surrounding areas.

"I can only imagine what it will look like when we get to the top."

"Me too." I looked his way in time to see him watching me.

"Better?" he asked, screwing the top back on his now empty bottle.

"Yeah, thanks." I continued to drink.

He stretched out one of his legs and adjusted the knee brace. "I'll be honest; this trail isn't bad, in a sense of wearing me out. I may not go to the gym as often, but I do still play basketball every now and then."

"Really? I didn't know that." I drank some more.

He nodded and stuffed his empty bottle into the depths of his pack. "I mentored some kids at a community gymnasium. We met every Saturday, but then Justin came into my life and well…my son became the focus."

Nearly done, I finished my water then put the empty bottle away. "Have you thought about doing it again? I mean, now that things have calmed down a bit, you may still be able to work with them. Take Justin along. I'm sure he'd like to be a part of something you love doing. It's one thing to see your picture on the wall and watch a game on TV with you, but it's another to actually see you play."

He angled his head in my direction. "We play on the goal I have in the driveway sometimes."

I shook my head. "Not the same thing as seeing dad in real life on the court."

He pursed his lips. "Good point. I'll look into that. I have to admit, I miss those kids. A lot of them looked up to me as a big brother." He laughed a bit. "Some of those mothers liked me a bit too much, though."

I let my eyes travel over the brown skin of the man next to me. Trevon wore a sleeveless gym shirt and a pair of baggy basketball shorts. The muscles of his arms and the sexy calves made me bite my lip. As good looking as he was now, he was even sexier naked.

"I can see why. I'd be more than happy to show up and set them straight if you want." I shrugged when he looked at me and laughed. "What?"

"I'm just imagining my firefighter girlfriend giving them the evil eye. I like it." He leaned over and kissed me.

A whistle from a group of hikers as they walked past broke the moment. I felt my cheeks warm and ducked my head, embarrassed. When I risked a peek up, I saw the group was full of college-aged guys who were giving Trevon thumbs up.

"You ready to finish this thing?" He stood, his attention coming back to me.

"Yes. I'm feeling pretty good, to be honest. I got a little winded at first, but it's nothing. If I'm going back to work soon, I need to be at my best. Thanks for suggesting we do this."

He held a hand out to me as I stood. "You're welcome. We can do this as often as our schedule allows. There are plenty of trails to try, some not as intense as this, while others will push us."

"We should bring Justin when we do the shorter ones."

His smile widened. "Yeah, I think he'd have fun. I'm pretty sure he'd love the nature trails." Trevon turned to retrieve his pack from where it sat. "Oh wow, Kai, look at that."

My attention went to where he pointed. I gasped. A butterfly sat on his backpack, its black and yellow wings opening and closing slowly. It looked just like the one I'd seen months ago…the same day my path crossed Trevon's again.

The symbolic meaning of seeing the same butterfly again meant only one thing: Trevon was my shot of happiness. I walked over to him and planted another kiss on his mouth.

"Not that I'm complaining, but what was that for?"

"Because you make me happy." I turned to get my pack, and when I looked at his again, the butterfly had disappeared.

We resumed walking. By the time we neared the summit, the sky had disappeared behind darkened clouds, which was perfect. There were no trees atop the mountain and standing in direct sunlight would have been too much.

"Trevon, this is amazing!"

No matter which way you turned, there was a stunning view. We could see downtown Atlanta in one direction and the North Georgia mountain range in another. According to a nearby sign, when the horizon wasn't hazy, you could see sixty miles in either direction. We stood in line and waited for a telescope to come available and took turns seeing the far off sights up close.

What amazed me the most was being able to see the city of Atlanta drenched in a rainstorm and see the difference in visibility between where the rain started and ended.

Thunder rumbled in a distance. I jumped a bit, and Trevon put his arms around my waist. I leaned into him and absorbed the feeling of his body against mine.

"You guys look so lovely together."

Our heads turned as an older couple walked by, holding hands. I smiled.

"Thank you," Trevon said.

"Don't they remind you of us when we were young, Fred?"

The elderly lady's husband looked at us and smiled as if he was a bit embarrassed by his wife interrupting our moment. "Yes, they do. Come on, Bernice; let's leave the young people alone." He tried to tug his wife away, but I held up a hand.

"Wait, can you do me a favor and take a picture for me?" I angled my head to see Trevon. "Do you mind?"

"Not at all."

I stepped out of his embrace and pulled my phone out of my pocket. I set the camera up and showed her how to take a photo. Satisfied that she could do it, I slipped back into Trevon's open arms and smiled.

"Beautiful," Beatrice said when she handed the phone back. "I wish you a life of happiness like we have." She blew a kiss in our direction while Fred winked. Then, they were on their way towards the gift shop.

Thunder boomed again, and rain began to fall.

"Oh man, this is crazy!" I held my arms up in the air and embraced the falling drops. It felt good to cool off.

Trevon laughed. Around us, people made their way to the gift shop to find cover. It looked crowded, so we decided to make our way to the cable car that would take us safely down the side of the mountain. Any attempts to walk down the slippery slope, especially in the middle of a rainstorm, would be suicidal. By the time we reached the ride, we had to wait for the next one that came up the mountain.

Trevon watched me with an expression that was hard to read.

"What's on your mind?" I reached for his hand, and with my free one, wiped water out of my eyes.

He angled his head in my direction. "Did they think we were married?"

The thought made me nervous. “Oh man, I hope not.” I laughed a bit.

The cable car arrived and we entered alone. Apparently we were the only ones who made the trek over in the rain.

We leaned against the large window and stared out at the scenery for a moment, enjoying the up close and personal view of the enormous carving of General Lee and others on the mountain’s side.

After a moment, Trevon pulled me into his arms. “You don’t like that idea?”

Unable to answer, I tucked my head into his chest and shrugged. “It’s just a lot to process on a first date, you know?” I listened to the beat of his heart and tightened my grip around his waist. “What about you?”

“Haven’t decided yet. But there is one thing I do know…”

“What’s that?” When he didn’t answer immediately, I pulled back and looked into his eyes.

His expression was intense. “I want to spend the night with you. There’s nothing for us to wait for…besides, I think we’ve held ourselves back long enough, don’t you?”

My body heated at his suggestion and my breath quickened. The thought of spending another night with him even if it wasn’t as intense as it was the night we met, had me gripping the edge of his shirt.

“What about Justin?” The urge to jump him in the private space of the tram was as powerful as the way he looked at me.

“All I have to do is make a phone call.” Then his lips were on mine. “Tell me, Kai,” he whispered in my ear when he pulled away. “Should I make that call?”

My body was on fire and it was hard for me to find my voice. “Yes…”

Chapter 26

Asking Kai if she wanted to go to her place or mine was a no brainer. She lived on the north side of town, while I stayed thirty minutes past her.

Plus she would need to get her dog from her neighbor.

At least it made sense to me.

The drive back took twice as long because of the torrential rainstorm. I gripped the steering wheel so tightly that the pattern felt as if it would be imprinted on my palm. Knowing our destination would end in getting the woman beside me out of those wet clothes that clung to every sensual inch of her body left me impatient. The urge to pull over and take her in the back seat of my car had every nerve in my body pulsating.

After months of dreaming about our one night together, it was about to happen again.

I glanced over and saw her shiver a little. "Are you warm enough?"

Despite the fact that it was summer, getting caught in a downpour could leave you a bit cold when inside an air-conditioned car.

"A little." Her teeth chattered, though she smiled.

I shut off the air and turned on some heat before reaching over to rub her rain soaked thigh. That brought on another round of shivers I was sure had nothing to do with the cold. Deciding it would be best to keep our skin-to-skin contact at a minimum to keep from being distracted, I reached for her hand instead and kissed the back of her wrist.

"Did you make that call?"

Crap. We'd been so preoccupied with getting back to the car and on the road that I had forgotten to do the number one thing I needed to do.

I connected my phone to the car's Bluetooth system and went to speed dial.

Andre answered on the third ring. "Hey, man, everything alright?"

"Yeah, everything's fine. Got caught up in the rain, though. Guess we should have paid a bit more attention to the weather. How are things going?"

"Good, hold on…Junior, let the cat's tail go!" A round of giggles and the mewing of a very unhappy cat filled the car. Kai muffled her laugh. "I told Sharice we shouldn't have gotten that damn cat. Boys need dogs. A dog wouldn't care if the kid tugs on its ear or pulls its tail. This cat jumps around like…" He sighed. "Never mind. Justin is fine, if that's what you wanted to know."

"That's good, but that's not why I'm calling." I glanced over at Kai who was staring straight ahead, but a hint of a smile splayed on her lips.

"Okay…"

"Do you think you guys could…um…watch him until tomorrow?"

There was a moment of silence on the phone as he processed what I had asked.

"Trevon, are you—"

"You're on speaker and Kai is in the car with me." I prayed he heard me before saying something that could embarrass everyone on the call.

He coughed a laugh. "Hi, Kai."

"Hi, Andre," she sang.

"Sure, he can spend the night and you can pick him up whenever you're ready. We don't have any plans for tomorrow and I'm sure Junior will have a ball knowing he's having a sleepover. Does he have enough medicine in his bag?"

"Yeah, I always pack extra for emergencies."

Kai glanced in my direction with laughter in her eyes.

"Sounds like this is one of them," he laughed. "Have fun, guys. Don't do something Sharice and I wouldn't do."

Kai laughed and I grimaced.

"Thanks, Andre. Later." I disconnected before he could say anything else. But his advice made me remember something very important.

"I've got to make a stop before we get to your place."

The minute we were off the highway, I pulled into the first gas station I could find. "Want anything?" I parked as close to the door as I could. I was nearly dry from riding in the car with the heat on. I had no intention of starting the drying process again.

"An orange juice?"

"Sure thing."

I jogged to the door and went inside. Not wanting it to be obvious that my main reason for stopping lay behind the register, I forced myself to walk down the rows, grabbing random stuff until I reached the refrigerated juice section. Selections in hand, I stood in line and waited my turn.

"Did you find everything you were looking for, sir?" The man behind the register appeared old enough to be my dad.

Why did I suddenly feel like a teenager buying condoms for the first time? "Yeah, thanks."

After ringing up my purchases, the attendant looked up in time to see me staring at the products over his shoulder. "Anything else?"

I nodded and pointed to the box I wanted. He grabbed one; I shook my head. "Two, please."

A hint of laughter lit up his face. He gave me my total and I paid. "Have a good evening, sir."

I smiled and left. Now it was time to take Kai home.

****

The trip from the car to her apartment door left us both wet again. One thing was for sure, the leather seats of my car would need to be detailed as soon as possible; they were soaked.

Kai's apartment was on the second floor. When we reached the top of the steps, she dug into her purse. "Here's my key, go in and make yourself comfortable. I have to get Sugar from my neighbor's house."

I accepted the key ring, slipped an arm around her waist, and backed her up against the door. "Does it have to be now? It's still early." To reiterate my point, I leaned down and explored her mouth. My self-control had reached its limit.

Kai's body trembled a bit, either from the cold or from the unspoken promise of satisfaction from the kiss when we parted, and her eyes drifted from my lips to my eyes. "If I don't get her now, I'll have to climb out of bed and go back in a few hours."

"Good, let's do it that way. We've waited long enough." I looked past her, fumbled with the key.

Sensing the urgency, she twisted in my arms and slipped the keys from my hand. "I'll do it."

The brush of her body against mine made me groan in anticipation. "Hurry, Kai." I gripped the bag from the gas station before slipping my arms around her again and pulling her butt against me. I ground my hips, imagining what it would feel like to be inside of her again.

The door opened and we tumbled inside. All sense of tact and finesse went out the window. I knew what I wanted, what she needed, and it was beyond time to take it.

I kicked the door shut behind us and dropped the bag to the floor. Kai spun around, grabbed me by my shirt, and pulled me to her body as she fell against the wall in the entrance of her apartment. Our mouths fused together, our tongues at war to see who would dominate in this private battle. I won, taking her arms from around my neck and pinning them above her head, a move she apparently liked since she gasped and wiggled her hips.

With my free hand, I explored the top of her breasts before reaching down and yanking the damp fabric up the side of her body. Progress was hampered by the fact the wet material was skintight and stuck to her.

"Damn…" I let go of her wrists and went at it again with both hands.

Kai laughed, but aided me in the struggle to get her breasts free. The minute they hit the air, my hands were on them, so was my mouth. Beneath me, I felt her squirm and pulled back in time to witness her attempt to remove the equally stuck shorts. Ever willing and able, I helped. Satisfied she was naked, I stepped back to enjoy the view.

"You're everything I remembered from that night. Perfect."

Kai smiled, and reached for my shirt. Fortunately, my clothes were baggy and despite the fact they were wet, it was nothing to get them off. Stripped naked, I gripped her hips and lifted her off the ground; her legs wrapped around me and I could feel the heat of the one place I needed to be resting just above my erection.

We needed a flat surface, right now.

I forced my attention to what was available in the small living room. Sofa, table….floor. Looking down the hallway, I saw the place that would be most desired, her bed, and decided that would be where we made love.

I put one foot in front of the other, balancing the weight of the woman who moved in my arms. She wasn't shy about anything. She kissed my face, my mouth, ran her fingers over my head. The grip of her thighs around me was tight, evidence of just how strong she had to be in order to do her job.

We'd nearly made it past the edge of the sofa when Kai nipped my ear with her teeth. "What are you waiting for?" she gasped, kissed the side of my throat and grinded her naked body against me.

The direct contact of her heated core on my manhood sent desire through my system so fast I nearly lost my grip on her slippery bottom.

"Shit…" I sunk to my knees, and lay her on the floor beneath me.

My mouth went to hers while my hands continued down the length of her body. Skin that was equally hot and damp from the rain and current physical activity slipped beneath my fingertips, and got more intense the closer I got to finding the glorious spot between her thighs.

I felt the damp and pulled away from her mouth to look down the length of her body. Kai was open to me, ready to give everything that was her. And God, she was beautiful.

"Trevon, hurry, baby, please…" Kai's hips rose off the floor, demonstrating the urgency she felt.

Never one to keep my woman waiting, I slipped my hand where she wanted and was rewarded as I watched her orgasm within seconds. The sensual movements of her hips as she worked herself against my fingers mixed with the beautiful face she made as her eyes squeezed shut and her mouth opened in a muted shout of appreciation made me desperate to follow her into that feeling of complete and utter satisfaction.

I sat up and searched for the bag that held the condoms. When I found it, I couldn't get the foiled package open fast enough. All the while, Kai lay on the floor, biting her lip and watching me as she ran her hands over her body. She loved putting on a show, and I loved to watch.

Distracted, I fumbled with the package; it slipped out of my fingers and landed on her belly. Kai grabbed it, finished the job, then sat up and slid the condom in place. My head fell back at the softness of her fingers as she gripped me, then on my thighs as she lay back down and guided me to her body.

Wasting no time, I entered. Slow at first, testing, not wanting to hurt her in any way. Beneath me, Kai's hips wound up in a breathtaking motion that not only worked me in deeper, it teased the hell out of me. I leaned down, rested my elbows on either side of her body, and watched her eyes as I pushed and retreated until every inch of me was inside and our bellies touched.

My rhythm was precise, no erratic movements, not yet anyway, as I wanted to experience everything as if it were our first time being together.

"You feel so good…so damn good…" I dropped my head down to her shoulder, sucked the soft skin and was rewarded with a moan.

Kai ran her hands over my head and down my shoulders. "So do you, baby, so do you. Don't stop what you're doing, please…don't stop."

I followed her instructions, pausing only to reposition her thighs for even better penetration. I must have hit the spot because she threw her other leg around me and grabbed on tightly, her hips pumping so hard against me that they came off the floor.

Spurred on by her reaction, her cry of passion got louder as I pumped harder. Then out of nowhere, Kai slapped my ass. It was so unexpected that it threw me off. I looked down at her in surprise.

Her smile was sexy; her eyes a bit wicked from what she'd done. "What? You didn't like that?"

I took a second to process what had happened. I never had a woman do that to me before.

Beneath me, Kai moved her hips again, drawing me back to what was more important. My head dropped to her breasts; being inside of her while suckling her nipples was a high I never wanted to end.

And then she did it again. This time it wasn't as much of a shock, but more of a turn on.

"Keep that up, and I'm going to come sooner than—" Another whack made me groan. "Kai…"

She bit my shoulder. "I want you to come…"

A fourth slap had me lose all sense of control and give in to my primal need of taking her. I spread my knees apart for better balance and went all in, not giving a damn about control and dug in to take her the way she obviously wanted me to. Hard.

Both of us cried out as she came again, but somehow, I managed to hold on for a minute longer, enjoying the tug and pull of her body until I pushed deep and let go.

I felt as if I would black out from the sheer force of the orgasm. My head spun, and my breath caught for I don't know how long. But down below, my body continued to pump out everything it had to give, which after months of short-lived self-gratification in a shower, was a lot.

When the spasms rocking my body ceased, so did all sense of muscle control. I collapsed on top of Kai. I breathed deeply, taking in the fragrance of our mountain walk and sweat from the sex we just had.

I was about to move when her legs tangled with mine and she gripped me tight in her arms, both hands locked behind my back. Her body also began to tremble, but this time, it wasn't from an orgasm.

She was crying.

Chapter 27

"Oh damn, Kai, did I hurt you?" Trevon pulled away from me and sat up, worry on his face.

I wiped at my eyes. "No, no, I'm fine, I swear." Tears continued to leak, though, confirming the lie. I cursed silently.

No better way to ruin a moment than to have a woman start to cry. I sat up too, took one look at him, and felt another wave of crazy hit me.

I drew my knees up to my chest, laid my head in my hands, and gave up. The tears rained down.

"Kai…," Trevon's voice was soft as he pulled me into his arms, which only made matters worse.

"Talk to me, love. What's going on? If I didn't hurt you, then what?" His gentle fingers slid hair from my face, tucking it behind my ear, before pulling my hands from my eyes and lifting my chin.

The warmth and sincerity of his eyes was unbelievable. My heart filled with so much joy that it was hard to explain. I forced myself to swallow the next round of sobs, reached over, and pulled his mouth to mine.

Though I knew my outburst confused him, he didn't deny me what I wanted.

When we parted, I sniffed. "You are just too good to me…you know that?" I ran my hand over the side of his chin and put my forehead to his.

Trevon didn't speak, but it was obvious he was confused.

"I'm not crying because you hurt me." I hesitated, letting the happiness felt in my chest become evident on my face, in my voice. "You really don't understand what it's like being with you."

"Um…no. I thought it was pretty good, but now that you're crying, I'm not so sure." He reached over to wipe my damp cheeks. "Care to explain?"

I grabbed his hand and brought it to my lips, kissed it. "You make me feel like a woman." I closed my eyes and smiled. "You have no idea how many times I've questioned my self-worth when I was with Malik. I told you this before, you listened, but I know you'll never be able to understand." I pulled his hand to my heart. "Today has been amazing. Simple and amazing. We had our first official date and did something we both enjoyed. You made sure I was comfortable and able to handle the climb. You brought us lunch," I chuckled at the memory of his explanation of not wanting to ruin our date with food that was subpar, even though the rain cut off any chance of eating it. "You kept me warm on the ride home. And the passion you showed in the cable car and at my door let me know everything you felt was about you wanting me, not something done for the sake of convenience, like it was sex because I was there and you were there. I haven't been made love to in a long, long time." I shrugged, unable to explain my actions any better. "The beauty of it all got to me. I promise I won't cry when we do it again."

After a moment, Trevon shook his head and chuckled. "Well, at least if it happens it's because I managed to hit all the right buttons for you."

A tingle went up my spine at the memory of what it felt like when he'd found that spot. "That you did, for sure. Care to do it again?" I threw on my sultry voice and flipped my ponytail around to cover the side of my face.

Trevon's head went back as he laughed. "Give me a few minutes and let me catch my breath. But yeah, believe me, I'm more than willing to do it again, and again, and again. You, Kai," he leaned over and caressed my lips with his thumb, "have nothing to worry about. You will always be the woman for me; the only one I want. You and I will never have sex for the sake of convenience." He paused as if in thought. "Unless the power is out and there's absolutely nothing else for us to do except entertain each other."

I grinned. "Deal."

After a quick kiss, he stood and leaned down to help me up. He grimaced for a second and reached for the brace on his knee.

"Are you okay?"

He limped over to the sofa and sat down to remove it. "Yeah, I'm okay. I guess the hike followed by an intense session with you on the floor wasn't good for my injury." He massaged the area then stretched his leg, bending it back and forth and glanced in my direction. "Not that I'm complaining in any way."

I smiled and headed for the kitchen. "Do you want some ice for that? I've got Ziploc bags to put it in."

"At the risk of sounding old, I'll say yes, thank you."

I laughed. "Trevon, how old are you?"

"Thirty." He accepted the homemade ice pack and set it on his knee, then sprawled back on the sofa and stretched his leg out. "Why?"

For a moment, I was speechless. Why hadn't I thought of this before? It should have been obvious since he was such good friends with Malik's younger brother, Andre.

"What?" He repeated, curiosity on his face. "Does it matter?"

"You know I'm older than you, right?" I sat down beside him and pulled a pillow across my chest. Why did I feel the need to hide my body from him? We were both naked.

His brow creased slightly as his eyes followed my actions. "I've never given it any thought. How much older?"

I wrinkled up my face. "Five years."

Trevon grimaced before removing the ice from his knee and massaging the spot. "That doesn't exactly throw you into Cougar territory, if that's what you're worried about."

I couldn't help but laugh. "You do realize that I was in kindergarten when you were born, right?"

He shrugged. "You've also got five more years of sexual experience on me, too. I liked that butt slap move you did, by the way. I've slapped a few in my time, but never had a woman do it to me. What else you got hiding in those invisible gray hairs of yours?" He leaned over and ran his fingers through my hair.

Unable to stop myself, I laughed so hard, my stomach hurt, but stopped when I realized he'd sat the ice on the floor and was trying to remove the pillow from me.

I allowed him to take it and watched as he tossed it on the floor before pulling me over to straddle his lap. He slid his hands over my hips and down my rear, while his eyes stayed on mine.

"Kai, I want to be with you. When I told you I was falling in love with you, I meant it. I am in love with you. A part of you has stayed with me ever since we met, ever since the first time our lips touched. You are in here," he pulled one of my hands to his heart. "I like having you there. Now that we have decided this is the kind of relationship we want, don't back out on me now. I've never cared, nor thought about our ages. When it comes to you, Kai, everything I feel is real. This relationship is about you and me. Obstacles have been put in our way, and yet we still want to be together. Don't try and find an excuse to back out."

I ran a hand over the light hair of his chest, drawing a circle around his heart. "I've had five years of bad luck and bad men when it's come to relationships. I'm willing to bet it's because I was in serious need of learning the difference between a good man and a bad one. You, Trevon Campbell, are a good man…a good father. I like being with you and would have it no other way." I tilted my head to the side in contemplation. "It's funny, I never thought about our ages either until you made the comment about the old knee."

He smiled; his hands moved from my rear and slid high on my back. Desire ran through my body and ended in the most sensitive area between my legs. Unable to help myself, I rocked my naked body against his and felt his immediate arousal beneath me.

"An old knee injury is just that, because nothing about me is old…" His eyes lowered as he traced a finger around one of my nipples that, because of my position in his lap, made it line up perfectly with his mouth. "Nothing about you is old either." He leaned forward and teased me with his tongue before sucking the engorged nipple into his mouth.

I pulled my hair free of the damp band and let it fall, enveloping his head in my private curtain. Trevon slid a hand up to it; twisting the long strands in his fist before lifting his head up and pulling me down to meet his. Man did he know how to work that tongue of his.

He moved from my lips to my chin. "So, got any good moves for sofa sex? I know a few, but I'm an eager learner."

I laughed and reached for his head, looking him straight in the eye. "Have I told you I love you?"

His brow knitted momentarily. "No, I don't think so, but there's no need to rush if you—"

I placed a finger over his mouth. "I'm in love with you, Trevon Campbell."

A slow smile spread across his face as he ran his hands over my back again. "Good, now, make love to me."

I smiled, reached into my bag of tricks, and proceeded to give him exactly what he wanted.

Chapter 28

"Are you ready to meet my family?"

I opened the car door for Kai. The moment she was out of the car, she gave me a once over, then adjusted my tie.

"Sure. This won't be bad. I know Kelli, so it's a start."

"Yeah, my sister, but not my mom and definitely not my dad." The expression on Kai's face was hard to read. She seemed to be excited, yet a bit wary at the same time.

I peered down at my girlfriend. "Is there something I should know?"

She made a weird face. "My family isn't typical?"

I laughed. "Whose is?"

Kai took my hand as we walked to the rec center. The minute we entered, I knew exactly what she was talking about. Everywhere I looked, there were Asian people. Nobody appeared to be related to Kai in the least.

I leaned down to whisper. "Um…are we in the right spot?"

She laughed. "Yes, this is the right place. This is my mother's side of the family."

I turned to her for clarification.

"My mom's Cambodian and my father is African-American." She turned to study the room, no doubt searching for them. "There they are. Come on and I'll introduce you."

Cambodian and African-American. That explained why I couldn't place her nationality.

"I never would have guessed that."

"What?" She turned back to look at me as we made our way through the crowded room.

"When we first met, I tried my best to figure out your nationality. Eventually I gave up. Getting to know you was more important. Now I know something else." I pulled our linked fingers to my mouth and kissed the back of her hand.

She blushed.

"Well, well, well, what do we have here?" The deep voice brought my attention from the love of my life to a heavyset man.

Mr. Malone was not a small guy. While I was an inch or two taller, his thick frame showed the fact that he was a force to be reckoned with, no matter what his age. He cleared his throat and stared at me over his daughter's head.

"Hey, Dad…Mom." She released my hand and went straight into her father's arms. His glare didn't waver, though. Next she hugged her mom and kissed both cheeks. "I'd like to introduce you to Trevon Campbell, the man in my life."

Without thinking, I stood a bit straighter under her parents' appraisal.

"Trevon, this is my mother, Nary and my father, James."

I shook her father's hand and held her mother's for a moment. While Kai looked a lot like her mother, it was obvious she got her height from her father's side of the family. The combined genetics of her parents had produced a beautiful woman.

"I can see where Kai gets her good looks from."

Her mom cocked her head to the side and stared up at me. "Sucking up gets you nowhere, young man," she shook a finger. "You want me to like you, be good to Kai, then you are okay with me."

"Yes, ma'am." I managed, trying my best to keep the sudden jolt of nervousness from showing on my face.

Her father laughed. "Good luck, son. My wife doesn't play."

I forced out a laugh. And I thought he'd be the tough one.

Kai rested her head in her hands and shook her head. "Mom, please don't give him a hard time."

Her mom slanted her eyes in Kai's direction before walking around, examining me from head-to-toe. I felt like a piece of meat at auction.

She was nodding her head when she stopped in front of me. "Not a bad choice, Kai." The next words she said were in a language I couldn't understand. Her father apparently did because he nearly choked on the beer he was drinking.

Kai, on the other hand, blushed and looked embarrassed.

"Okay," she grabbed my hand then pulled me away. "Dad, keep mom away from the liquor," she shot over her shoulder as she drug me into the crowd. "That was embarrassing," she mumbled.

"For who? You or me? I felt like I was on the bachelor auction stand. What did she say?"

Kai shook her head. "You don't want to know. Now, where are my grandparents?"

Meeting them was just as interesting as meeting her parents, less threatening and more entertaining. It was easy to see where Kai got her spunk and tenacity for life. It appeared to run in the family.

After being introduced to a variety of cousins, uncles, aunts, and friends, all who seemed to think I was a catch, we settled at a table with Kelli and her husband, Alonso. Though I didn't know him well, it was nice to be in the company of someone who wasn't watching me like a hawk.

The minute the ladies took a trip to the bathroom, I took advantage of the situation and asked some questions that had been rolling around in my head since we arrived.

"Is this family as crazy as they seem? And I mean crazy in a good way. They appear to be pretty accepting."

Besides Kai's father, I was the only black man in the room, yet her grandfather was Caucasian and Alonso was Hispanic. I watched the room, taking in the way the family interacted with one another. Smiles were on everyone's faces. Maybe it had to do with the abundance of free alcohol that sat on a table in the corner of the room near the food. Everyone seemed to have a drink in hand.

Alonso gave me a side eye look as he drank his beer. "You thinking about marrying in?"

I couldn't stop the grin that spread across my face in response to the question. "If things work out with Kai, then yeah."

He smirked. "My advice? Don't rush. This family is filled with controlling women. You would think because they come from an Asian background that they'd be docile." He shook his head. "Nope. Then you mix in black," he looked my way. "No offense. My point is, if Kai is anything like her sister, walk away now. I used to think that controlling thing with Kelli was enduring. Don't get me wrong, it's been helpful in my career and she's a great mother. It's even better in the bedroom. But now?" He stopped talking when we heard the voices of both women as they made their way back to the table.

I sat back in my seat, unsure of what about Alonso's comment offended me most. The 'black' statement, the negative attitude he had toward the family, or the fact he had the balls to tell me in so many words that he was no longer in love with his wife.

Kai slid her hand over my shoulder and rubbed my back for a moment before sitting down. I glanced at her and smiled. She smiled back, but her eyebrows dropped as she leaned over to whisper in my ear. "Are you okay?"

I forced myself to forget Alonso's comments and enjoy the evening with Kai and her family. While Alonso may not be happy, his issues had nothing to do with me.

I leaned over and planted a quick kiss on her mouth. "I'm good."

In my peripheral, I saw Kelli look away while Alonso rolled his eyes. There was indeed trouble in paradise.

An announcement came over the P.A. system saying that it was time for everyone to find their seats.

The table we sat at was round. In order to see the main table in front of us we had to turn our chairs to face forward. Kai moved her chair beside mine and leaned towards me. Instinctively, I placed my arm on the back of her chair, which allowed her to scoot a bit closer and rest against my shoulder. Her hand went to my thigh.

She smiled up at me and we kissed again. Across the room, I noticed her mother watching us. The moment our eyes met, she smiled her approval.

The way we interacted with one another felt as though we had been together for months instead of just a week. Our day trip to Stone Mountain was about us spending time together as a couple, something we'd unofficially done for months.

The sex was icing on the cake.

The room burst into laughter and clapping ensued. Having been deep in thought, I didn't pay attention to the fact that everything being said was in Cambodian.

"What did I miss?" I whispered.

Kai squeezed my thigh and laughed. "My grandmother's been talking for the past five minutes about the day she met my grandfather. You just realized you missed something?"

"I was thinking about us and stopped paying attention." I smiled as she looked at me, a question on her face.

"Thinking about us? What about us?"

I stared deep into her eyes then ran a finger under her chin. "How much I enjoy being with you, right here, right now."

"Hmm…nice answer. You sure you're not thinking about later?" She wiggled her eyebrows and slid her hand up and down my thigh.

I had to stop her before she slipped and went too high on my leg. The way our chairs were turned, anyone looking in our direction would see what she was up to.

"Yeah, it's crossed my mind for sure. But right now, I'm liking this." I gestured between us and her family.

Before long, dinner was served. The opportunity to have authentic Cambodian food was a new experience. Between the sliced pork that lay in a tray with the cooked pigs head in the middle, and the rice that featured baby squid, chicken, and beef, I was wary of what to select. Kai pointed out dishes that were her favorites and encouraged me to try them. In the end, I was full and very satisfied.

Then it was time to dance. I'm not sure what type of music I expected to hear, but the moment the DJ started playing songs from the top forty lists you'd hear on the radio mixed with some old school hip-hop, I turned to Kai in surprise.

"Told you we weren't typical." She grabbed my hand and pulled me out on the dance floor.

Dancing wasn't exactly my thing. With my height, I felt like a fish out of water. I mean, I had moves, but they were best done in a nightclub, when the lights were low and it was hard to see. Here, all the lights were on and I stood at least a foot above nearly everyone in the building.

Yet I had to admit, I was having fun and was glad she invited me to take part in her family's traditions.

The next song to play was the Cha-Cha Slide. I howled with laughter as I watched a room full of Asians try and do their best to follow the instructions. It didn't matter that most were unable to keep up, everyone was enjoying themselves.

My phone rang and I stepped away from the dance floor to pull it out of my pocket. Andre's number was on the screen. He and Sharice were babysitting Justin for the evening.

"Hey, everything okay?"

"Yeah, we're good here. Justin was about to go to sleep and wanted to tell you good night. Let me put you on speaker."

My son's voice came through the line. "I lub you, Daddy. Night, night!" His enthusiastic declaration was followed by a weird sound I assumed was him kissing the phone.

"I love you, too. Be good and I'll see you in the morning."

There was a giggle and the sound of running feet before Andre was back on the line. "I don't think he heard the last part. He and Junior have been having too much fun. Sharice treated them to milk and cookies a little while ago. She's setting up a movie in the bedroom so they can watch it while going to sleep."

"Thanks for babysitting again. I hate it that his grandparents weren't feeling well enough to take him today. Two weekends in a row…you guys have gone above and beyond."

"Told you we had your back. How's it going with the family thing?"

I chuckled. "Very interesting."

There was a pause. "Is that the Cha-Cha Slide I hear in the background?"

"Yep. Apparently they love listening to a lot of different types of music. It's not what I expected."

"Yeah, Malik said the same thing." He paused. "Can I be honest?"

Not sure what to expect after he mentioned his brother, I steeled myself. "Sure."

"I haven't had the chance to see you guys together, but I've noticed a change in you over the past few months. If this has anything to do with Kai being in your life, then I'm happy for you. You guys seem to be a good fit. I'm not just saying this because you're my boy, either. I know my brother took her for granted. She's a good woman and didn't deserve what he put her through. Go be happy, Tre, and if you know what's best for you, you will not show up at my house in the morning. You feel me?"

I laughed. "Message received, and thanks."

A tap on my shoulder had me turning to find Kai behind me. "I saw you walk outside. Is everything okay?"

I shut the phone down and slipped it in my pocket. "Yeah, Justin wanted to tell me good night. He's having fun."

Kai slipped her arms around my waist. "That's good to know. I think it's time we have some fun, too." Her voice was seductive, the fragrance she wore inviting.

I returned the gesture, pulling her body against mine, and ran my hands over her back. "Miss me?"

"Every day. Have you missed me?"

"Always."

That made her smile. "How about we say goodnight to my family and go spend some time alone?"

"Sounds good to me. We just have one stop to make first."

Chapter 29

"What do you think?" Trevon flipped on the lights as we entered the back door of the restaurant and walked into the kitchen.

I toured the room, taking in the sights of the spotless stainless steel equipment. "Wow. I've never been behind the scenes of a restaurant before. Well, one that hadn't been burnt down, that is."

"Hey, don't jinx the place with fireman talk." He walked over and tested the gas controls on the stove making sure they were really in the off position.

"What can I say? I'm excited about going back to work. Two more weeks and I will be back on duty, Trevon, two more weeks. Can you believe it?" I threw my head back and laughed as loud as I could. My voice vibrated off the equipment.

Trevon shook his head and walked through the swinging doors that led into the dining area.

I followed, but stopped when I stepped through the doorway. It was a completely different world. The last time I'd come to this location was the night I ran into Trevon after the birthday party. The lighting had been low and the seating and decorations were dated. But now...

"Is this what my sister did?" I looked to him for confirmation.

"Yes."

"It's amazing!" I walked over to the bar and tested one of the comfortable seats, swinging it back and forth. "Oh yeah, this is good. And the bar?" Trevon flipped a light switch. I pointed to the newly lit up glass background where the liquor would be held. Instead of plain white lighting, there were now colors. Even the TVs had been upgraded.

He placed his hands on the counter behind the bar and stood, pride on his face. "Kelli is good. Worth every penny."

"Yes, she is. I can do arrangements, but she's got the eye for design and the creativity to pull it all together. She is a great interior decorator." I slid off the chair and walked to the nearest wall and studied the aged photograph of one of the city's oldest buildings.

"She fought tooth and nail to get it done on time. Gave Derrick a hell of a time, too." He was silent for a moment. "She's due to have her baby next week, right?"

"Yes. She can't wait, either. This pregnancy hasn't been the best. Not like her first one."

"Hmm…"

"Why do you ask?" I faced him.

"Something Alonso said tonight, that's all."

I rolled my eyes at the mention of my brother-in-law's name. "Let me guess, he said—"

"Nothing you're thinking, I'm sure." He scratched his chin. "I get the feeling there are problems in that marriage."

"You hit the nail on the head. Kelli thinks he's cheating on her. You're a guy; did you pick up on that?"

Trevon threw his hands up. "Whoa, nope, not going there." He turned to flip off the light switch behind the bar before walking towards the kitchen again.

I followed. "Why not?"

Trevon's route took us through the kitchen and off to a small room. He turned on the light as we entered.

"Kai, the night we met, our first conversation was about cheating and men lying. Once was enough."

I looked around the space. A desk sat against a wall with a chair nearby. On the floor were a few unopened boxes. A quick examination showed a computer, printer, and other office equipment waiting to be set up.

"If memory serves me right, that conversation led to sex." I walked over to the desk and ran a hand over it while watching him out the corner of my eye.

"What it led to was me having to defend the fact that I was a man who had the ability to be honest."

I shrugged. "Either way we ended up in bed." I walked around Trevon, grabbed his shoulders, and backed him in the direction I wanted.

He looked down at me in surprise. "What are you up to?"

I pushed him once, he lost his balance, and his butt landed on the desk. "Christening your office."

Before he could ask another question, I cut all chances of communication off by stepping in-between his legs and putting my lips to his. My tongue was in his mouth as I pushed his suit jacket off his shoulders. Trevon didn't resist. He shook the coat off and slung it to the floor before gripping my hips and pulling me against him.

I unbuttoned his shirt, but kept my lips locked with his, savoring the connection of our mouths as we explored one another. It had been one agonizing week since we had spent the night together and every moment spent alone in my bed was torture.

My mouth left his and went for his Adam's apple before journeying down to the revealed flesh of his pecs and sucking his nipples.

"Kai…" His voice was thick and heavy as if formulating words were a struggle. He may have been unable to speak, but his hands had gone from my hips to the back of my hair, digging in and holding on. It was obvious he liked what I was doing.

His pants were next. I slid my hands along his thighs and between his legs and found him getting hard. Annoyed by the buckle of his pants, I wasn't gentle as I undid it and pulled the zipper down. Trevon moaned when I started massaging him with both hands.

"Oh God…Kai…this isn't how I planned to—"

My mouth went to his again, while my fingers continued to tease. The way he kissed me back made me gasp for air when I pulled away to speak. "Do you really want to climb back in the car and drive back to my place? That's at least twenty minutes from here."

Trevon's eyes were heavy with passion, and his body was showing all the signs of impatience.

"Hell, no." Trevon slipped from my grasp, grabbed my hips, and switched places with me so fast that I was sitting on the edge of the desk before I could blink.

I grabbed his face and pulled it down to meet mine. The kiss was hot; I felt as if my body would catch fire. He pushed my legs apart before sliding his hands up the inside of my thighs while shoving my skirt out of the way. The muscles in my legs trembled as he repeated the motion, this time caressing the bare skin before stopping at the juncture between my thighs that silently called his name. I moaned and rocked my hips in invitation. Trevon responded by sliding a hand over my panties.

"Oh yeah…" he murmured, leaving my mouth and exploring the side of my throat as he stroked me.

"Please…please…" I panted.

Trevon gave me what I wanted by pushing my panties to the side and teased me.

Unable to hold still and not wanting to slip off the edge of the desk, I let go of my hold around his neck and lay back. My change of position caused him to lean forward, which put my breasts in line with his mouth.

He teased my nipple through the fabric of my dress with his tongue. "Pull it down for me, baby. Let me have it."

I complied, sliding the straps of my shoulders and pushing the cups of my bra out of the way. Trevon latched on as if my breasts were the air needed to live.

Between his mouth and his fingers, I was beyond gone. I grabbed on to him and gave in to everything he did to me. When I came, I called his name. But he didn't stop there. Instead, he repositioned himself between my legs.

"Kai…watch…"

My mouth open as I gasped for air, I looked down his half-naked body and watched as he gripped himself and teased. I nearly exploded again.

Trevon didn't waste time. He slipped in and out, pushing harder until every inch of him was inside and our skin was slippery with sweat. He leaned down, his elbows resting on the desk beside me, my head in his hands. His mouth was busy as his hips pumped and twisted, fast, then slow, then fast again. I lifted my legs as high as I could, wrapped them around his waist, and held him in place.

And for once, I was thankful we were not in my apartment. The amount of yelling and moaning coming from the two of us would have had the neighbors knocking on the walls.

My hands were in his hair as his lips left mine and he nipped my ear, his breath heavy as he whispered, "I love the way you sound when you call my name. Say it again..."

I did.

The gentle creaking of the desk from our passion and the sound of slick sweat as we moved to please each other were the only sounds to rival our moans.

"Kai…I can't hold out much longer…" He slowed, sat up, and looked at me. His arms trembled.

But I didn't want him to slow. I wanted him to feel the same gratification he'd given me from multiple orgasms. I wanted the same need and sex starved passion that had built inside of me to be the same for him. I wanted this to culminate into one mindless act.

No thinking, no planning. Just doing and letting go.

I placed an elbow on the desk and pushed up so that my mouth was inches from his and gripped the back of his neck, establishing control of his body. "Look at me…," I panted.

He did, with deep brown eyes that made my heart sing.

"Let go, baby, let go…" I pushed against him, rocking and grinding my hips as he thrust, harder and harder until his head fell down and rested between my breasts as his body gave way to orgasm.

Unable to support our combined weight on one arm, I lay back and pulled him with me. Trevon panted as his body continued to spasm. I smiled; satisfied that I had gotten my man off to the point that he had lost complete control. I took advantage of the situation and ran my hands over his head, his shoulders, and down his back. The connection was amazing, even in this awkward space. I couldn't wait to repeat this again in my bed when we were completely naked and every inch of our bodies were touching.

Trevon mumbled, then sat up a bit and kissed that space between my breasts.

"What did you say, lover?"

He pushed up a bit more so we could see each other, eye-to-eye. "I said that has got to be the best sex ever."

I laughed and wiped the bridge of his nose where sweat had collected. "I agree."

He leaned down and kissed me. "Then again, when it comes to this, to us, I'm willing to bet every time will be the best."

"Too bad we don't have a bed nearby, huh?"

He nodded. "Getting completely naked would have been nice. I like seeing you naked."

I grinned. "It still beats waiting, though. Plus the memory of this every time you come to work should make your day."

He groaned. "Or torture me to death." He kissed me once again then retreated from my body, slow and deliberate. His pants were around his ankles, so he reached down to pull them up. "I hate we have to put our clothes back on."

"But," I wiggled my eyebrows, "we get to play strip tease and take them off again."

"My kind of woman." He grinned and walked over to where his shirt and my panties lay.

I stood when he handed them to me.

And that's when I realized our mistake.

I looked down and closed my eyes. "Oh, no."

"What's wrong?" Trevon shrugged his shoulders back into his shirt, a look of concern on his face.

It was obvious he'd missed it as much as I had.

"We didn't use a condom."

His brow creased as he started buttoning his shirt. "You're on something, right?"

At that point I wasn't sure who to be mad at. Myself for being lax about birth control since my breakup with Malik, or Trevon's presumptive question.

Instead of responding, I slipped my panties on and walked out of the room and to the back door.

I heard Trevon curse, then come after me.

"Kai, wait a minute. Talk to me."

My back still turned, I only had three words to say. "Take me home."

Chapter 30

"Eating a pint of Mayfield ice cream is perfectly good comfort food, Sugar, so stop looking at me like that."

My words meant nothing because my dog continued to stare at me as if thinking, "Yeah, right."

"Whatever," I mumbled, and crammed another large helping of Banana Split into my mouth.

The combination of fudge, nuts, and cherries mixed with creamy vanilla ice cream did nothing to appease the uneasiness I felt in the pit of my stomach. A week had gone by since I demanded Trevon take me home. A week since we had sex. A week since I allowed the one mistake I swore to avoid happen again.

Unprotected sex.

Not that I was worried about sexually transmitted diseases. I had annual checkups as part of my mandated yearly physical for work. Trevon did, too. The problem was mistakes like this with Malik are what led to my prior pregnancies. Two opportunities to bring a life into the world that failed miserably. Though neither pregnancy made it past the first trimester, it was a loss that hurt deep. I wanted to be a mother as much as I wanted to be someone's wife, even though I put on the front of not wanting to give up my career.

I needed something that defined me as a woman. If I couldn't have a baby then I would excel at my career.

At least that's what I thought until I started babysitting Justin. An innocent act of friendship turned into a desire to have a chance at happy…a chance to be someone's mother. Even if the word 'step' was in the front of it.

I closed my eyes and imagined Justin sitting in my lap, the warmth of his arms around my neck, and the feel of his sloppy kiss on my cheek before leaving when his father picked him up.

My phone vibrated yet again. I checked; it was a text from Trevon.

I sighed and placed the phone face down, unable to read his message. We had talked a few times since that night, but I wasn't ready to have the conversation he wanted to have. He wanted to know why I flipped out after discovering we hadn't used a condom. How could I tell him that I was scared that I could end up pregnant? The minute I came home, I checked my calendar and counted the days until I had my cycle.

The blood drained out of my face when I realized I was on the fertile end of things.

My period was due to start any day now…but if Trevon's sperm managed to fertilize an egg…I was going to be a ticking time bomb of pain, sorrow, and disappointment.

How could I tell him that?

Unsure of how to handle it, I threw myself into work. My time working for my family was nearly over. I was now mentally preparing myself for what I would face once I went back to the firehouse. Being placed on light duty meant my responsibilities would include cooking and cleaning, paperwork, and helping with truck maintenance. I would still work the twenty-four on/ forty-eight off shift schedule, something Trevon was well aware of.

My phone rang again, and I ignored it, not even looking at the screen. The voicemail chime went off. I tried to stave off my curiosity with a few more scoops of ice cream. Then the phone rang again. One thing Trevon didn't do was call back to back. When I didn't respond, he'd wait a few hours before calling again. Unless it was something that had to deal with Justin.

I checked the phone, saw Kelli's number on the screen, and hit redial.

"Hey, what's going on?"

Panting came through the line before she spoke. "Kai, I've gone into labor. I can't drive to the hospital and Christina is here. I need you to come and get me."

I sat up with a start and pulled my phone away from my ear to check the time. It was past ten o'clock at night. "Where is Alonso?" I rushed into the kitchen and threw my leftover ice cream into the freezer.

"I have no idea where that son of a—," she gasped and growled in the phone. "I don't care. This baby is coming and I don't have time to give a damn about where he is or who he's screwing!"

Glad I was still dressed; I laced up my tennis shoes and put Sugar in the kennel kept in the living room for emergency purposes. She wasn't happy, but I didn't have time to knock on my neighbor's door and ask her to dog sit. I dashed down the steps and jumped behind the wheel.

"I'm on the way. If Christina isn't dressed, tell her to put on some clothes and grab your hospital bag. Put some shoes on yourself, unlock the door, and sit on the sofa. And for the love of God, keep your legs shut! I don't want to end up delivering this baby for you!"

****

"Kelli, you can do this! Push!" I grimaced and held back my yell as my sister squeezed the crap out of my hand.

The moment we reached the emergency room, she was rushed to the Maternity ward, given a room, and started pushing.

"Okay, momma, we're almost there, I can see the head!" The obstetrician said.

"You hear that, they can see the head!" I squealed and leaned forward to see if I could see it too.

Kelli fell back against the pillow and panted. "Where the hell is he?"

Wasn't that the question of the hour? It was nearly midnight and her husband, Alonso, had yet to respond to my text messages or calls.

"Don't worry about him right now. You need to focus on getting this baby into the world. Christina is excited about seeing her baby brother!"

My comment got me the side eye from hell. "Alonso needs to pull himself out of whatever ho he's lying with and get his ass down here right now!"

I looked up at the doctor in time to see his eyebrows shoot up in the air, while one nurse whispered a comment to another that made them both giggle.

I rolled my eyes. "We're not worried about his cheating ass right now; we just want this baby to be born so stop thinking and push!"

Kelli did as I instructed as soon as the doctor told her to.

"Here's the head, momma. Hold on a minute before you push again. I've got to get the cord from around his neck and clean out his mouth."

I leaned forward again to take another look, and what do you know? A head full of black hair and a squished up face that was red as could be was in the doctor's hands. He used his thumb to pull the cord gently from around his throat and then a syringe to clear his mouth.

Tears came to my eyes. "Oh my God, he's beautiful!"

"Okay, one more push and your baby will be born."

Kelli dug in and gave it her all. Two seconds later, the rest of my nephew's body slid out and into the doctor's hands.

"Aunt, would you like to cut the umbilical cord?" The doctor asked as he clamped the cord off in two places.

I looked at Kelli. This was something Alonso was supposed to be doing, not me. I remember how much it had meant to her that he'd done it when Christina was born. Alonso not being here now hurt her to the core. She bit her lip and nodded.

I accepted the scissors and steadied my trembling hand as I did the job, making the birth official. My nephew was then whisked away into the hands of several nurses as they did their jobs weighing, cleaning, and writing down measurements.

"Why isn't he crying?" Kelli asked as she tried to sit up, something nearly impossible to do while her legs were in stirrups.

I put a hand on her shoulder and held her down. "He's okay; they're just cleaning him up." But my attention stayed on the nurses.

It wasn't long before the wail of a newborn was heard. Kelli lay back in relief.

After what felt like forever, one of the nurses stepped forward with a bundle of baby. "Here you go, Mom. You have a healthy baby boy. He's seven and a half pounds."

Arms spread wide, Kelli accepted her son, kissed his cheeks, then pulled the blanket from his face to examine the fruit of nine months of hard work.

I leaned in and kissed them both. "I'm so proud of you!" More tears came from my eyes.

I was at work when Christina was born and unable to witness the miracle; now I knew what I was missing. A moment like this would never happen for me. Being able to witness a new life enter the world was a miracle I would never forget.

It was then my phone rang. I excused myself and left the room, sliding the phone out of my back pocket without looking at the caller ID.

"Where the hell are you, Alonso? My sister just had your baby!"

"That explains a few things."

I pulled the phone away from my ear and stared at the screen. Crap. "Trevon, hold on for a moment." I put the phone to my chest and walked down the hall to an empty waiting area. It took a moment to gather my thoughts because I was too emotional to have a conversation with him right now.

"Okay, I'm back."

For a moment, neither of us spoke.

"So you're at the hospital because Kelli had the baby. How is she?"

Safe territory. I found a seat in the corner, propped my feet up, and leaned my head against the wall. "She's okay, so is the baby. It happened so fast. One minute I was at home watching TV, next I got a call that had me rushing to her house and driving her to the hospital."

"I take it Alonso isn't there because you nearly cut my head off when you answered the phone."

I sighed. "Sorry about that. He's MIA and hasn't returned any of my calls, or hers. She's stressing about it right now, but I'm trying to keep her focused on her baby." I rubbed the bridge of my nose. "Trevon, I don't know what is going on in that marriage, but it's not good. I have a feeling after tonight; the countdown clock of that relationship is going to start. I can't imagine what she's going through right now." Feeling my sister's pain mixed with my own, I wiped the corners of my eyes from silent tears.

Trevon was quiet, but I could hear the background noise of a television through the phone. "I feel the same way about us, Kai. Is there a clock on our relationship, too?"

I could hear the pain in his voice and it cut me to my heart. Everything that I'd been stressing about before getting Kelli's call came to mind. How would he handle the possibility of me getting pregnant? How would he handle the loss? Could I? The rational part of my brain said to speak up now and address the issue. The part that was scared that my words would indeed start that countdown clock kept the words in the back of my throat.

"No…we don't have a clock ticking…"

"Then why does it feel like since the night we were together, you've been avoiding me. You won't tell me what's wrong. Did I do something wrong? Did I ask the wrong question? You have to talk to me, Kai. I'm hanging on by a thread here. We've gone through too much over the past few months to suddenly hit a brick wall and for you to just cut me out of your life. I need you, you know that." He sighed heavily. "Justin misses you. You know how much you mean to him. Even if it takes some time for us to work through whatever this is, you can't keep avoiding him."

Images of the sweet little boy that I loved came to mind and it was a struggle not to give in to the urge to break down and cry.

"Oh no, Christina!" I jumped out of my seat and walked towards the nurses' station.

"What's wrong?" I could hear the weariness in his voice.

"I have to find my niece. She was at home with Kelli and got dragged into the car with us. I didn't have time to drop her off with anyone or call my parents and tell them Kelli was here. A nurse came and got her when we got to the hospital. She was scared in the car. I've got to go find her.

I've got to call our family." I sighed. "I have to track Alonso down for the sake of my sister's sanity."

I could tell Trevon was not happy about the sudden need to disconnect the phone call.

"Kai, you and I…," his exhale was heavy. "Never mind, do what you need to do. Tell Kelli I asked about her and congratulations. When things calm down, Kai, we need to talk."

Chapter 31

"Mr. Campbell, the customers at table five asked to speak to you."

"Thank you, Lacy." I watched the waitress head back in the direction of table five.

Opening night was going better than I ever expected.

Before the doors opened for the afternoon lunch rush, I asked the staff to come in early so we could review company policies, answer questions, and make sure we were all on the same page as to what type of customer service I expected them to bring to our patrons. I even surprised them with a small token of appreciation, Visa gift cards, to give them all a boost in their earnings for tonight. Even the cooks in the kitchen, who didn't receive tips of any kind, were given a token of my appreciation.

The boost in morale had everyone jumping to do their best. Most of my day had been spent walking around the restaurant, greeting customers and defusing small issues to make sure everyone was happy. The work was tiring, and after nearly nine hours of being on my feet, I was exhausted.

I drained a glass of water and then I headed to the table that required my attention.

"Surprise!"

It took a moment for me to realize that the customers at table five were my friends. Sharice stood and gave me a hug, while Andre shook my hand and patted my back.

In the booth beside them, Justin and their son, Junior, bounced in their booster seats.

"What are you guys doing here?" I slipped into the booth and ran a hand over my son's head before kissing his cheek.

"Hey, we had to come support you." Andre looked around the restaurant. "Man, this is great. It's been a while since I was here, and man, can I tell the difference."

"Kelli did this?" Sharice stared at one of the wall sconces illuminating their booth.

"Sure did. She's good, right?"

"Oh yeah. I might have to get her to come do my office at work."

Andre's gaze went around the room. "Are we the only ones here? I know Kelli said she wanted to come through."

"I don't expect to see here anytime soon. She just had her baby."

"Oh, that's right."

Beside Andre, Sharice rolled her eyes. "Leave it to a man to forget details like that." Her attention turned to me. "Where's Kai? I expected her to be here."

I kept my sigh internal. "She's back at work, and tonight is one of her 'on shift' days."

"That's got to suck." Her attention turned to Junior whose enthusiasm for being out of the house was evident.

"You okay, Trevon?"

Apparently my disappointment was obvious on my face.

"Yeah, I'm good. It's been a long day and I'm tired, that's all."

"What time do you get off?"

I consulted my phone. "I've got about an hour and a half left, then I'm turning it over to my assistant manager. I can take Justin off your hands then."

"Hey, whenever you're ready."

"Thanks, I don't know what I'd do without you guys. I've got to head to my office and take care of some paperwork. I'll tell the waitress to have your meal placed on top of the list to keep your wait time down. Oh, and the meal is on me."

"Now, that's what I'm talking about. See, Sharice, it's good to have friends in high places."

They both laughed; I punched his shoulder and told Justin I would see him soon.

In the back, I skirted through the kitchen, delivered my message to Lacy about their meal, and escaped into the small confines of my office, shutting the door behind me.

The door did little to mute the clashing, banging, and sizzling sounds of the kitchen. I sat down in my chair, rested my head on the headrest, and shut my eyes. It was then I realized exactly how tired I was.

I ran a hand over my forehead and contemplated exactly what was left to do before I clocked out for the evening. When I sat up, I went over to the file cabinet in the corner to retrieve this evening's reports and turned back to my desk.

My attention went to a small dent in the wall. The dent made by the desk when I made love to Kai.

What should have been a happy memory was now unexplained. More than two weeks had gone by since that night and we had yet to fully address what happened between us. Every time I brought it up, she found a reason to change the subject or to suddenly be too busy to talk about it. It wasn't as if I had a ton of time on my hands either. With the restaurant's renovation completed, inventory orders, planning for the re-opening, last minute hires, and a myriad of other things that didn't include the annual doctors' appointments needed for Justin, I didn't have time to chase her down.

But I shouldn't have had to.

We were in this relationship together. If there was something wrong, we should be able to make time to talk about it, regardless of what was going on in our lives.

Now that she was back to work, it was even harder to find the time.

Life for either one of us was not going to get easier. We needed to decide how we were going to go forward with our relationship.

And if we weren't, I needed to know.

****

"Come on, Kai, pick up the damn phone!"

"Wat's wong, Daddy?"

I looked down at my son's eyes and saw fear.

Damn.

I ran a hand over my eyes and squeezed them shut. "Sorry, little man. Daddy's just upset. It's okay." I opened my arms. Justin crawled into my lap and snuggled his head against my chest, then stared at the TV.

After a long day, Justin and I retired to the sofa to watch *Thor*, one of his favorite movies.

It was movie night, a time that had included Kai for the last few weeks. Justin looked forward to seeing her as much as I did.

After what happened between us, it seemed as if movie night and Kai being a part of it would never happen again.

Neither would date night, sex night, nor any other night, for that matter.

Kai had been in our lives for months. During that time, my feelings for her were put on the back burner, and it had been impossible to realize exactly how important she was to me. To us.

Opening up and having her reciprocate those feelings gave me hope for our future. A future where I was no longer a single parent. A future with a woman I loved and who loved me back. The opportunity to have a strong female presence in Justin's life. A future that didn't involve me being alone for the rest of my life.

The perfect slice of the American dream.

A wife, a child, a dog, a home.

A job I loved.

Then, like the night we met, sex got involved and what was mutual between us hit a brick wall. Again.

Sex without protection.

Mistakes happened when feelings took over and will and brainpower went out the window. We were both at fault, yet it felt as if her anger was directed more at me then about what happened. What did I do wrong? Was it because I didn't stop to put a condom on?

I would have if I had been able to think. I would have if we had gone back to her place after showing her what my hard work at the restaurant had been about. An innocent stop off after meeting her family turned into mind-blowing passion that I hadn't instigated.

I was willing to be patient. She, on the other hand, wasn't, just like the night we met.

I could have stopped, but why? I wanted her as much as she wanted me. Having the memory of making love to her where I worked ramped up the moment. Reasoning and attention to details such as protection was the last thing on my mind.

So why had the lack of condom made her angry to the point that she was too busy to talk on the phone for extended periods of time? Our last actual conversation had been when, after avoiding my call earlier in the day, she answered by accident. Kelli had just given birth to her baby and Alonso was nowhere to be found. I forced myself to understand she had family issues to deal with and didn't try to force the conversation she obviously didn't want to have.

To make matters worse, she didn't call me back.

After nearly forty-eight hours, I gave in and called. And what did I get? Nothing but a chance to leave a voicemail.

She responded with a text message a few hours later. Everything since then had been text or extremely brief phone calls.

Enough was enough. Not only was she hurting me, she was hurting Justin.

That was unlike Kai. She cared for him so much that I was sure if she hated me, she would not take it out on him.

That hurt more than anything else did because the last thing I wanted was to have his young emotions caught up in my romantic issues. Thus the reason I decided not to go looking for love while raising him.

But Kai had been different. With her, it wasn't a matter of convincing her to accept me and my son. Justin had been the priority on both our parts from the beginning. Everything else after had been a wonderful side effect of our friendship.

I checked my phone again. No response to the text messages, no response to the phone calls.

Guess that meant email was out of the question.

I glanced at the time. Kai was working at the fire station. She told me that her first days back on the job as she got back into the swing of things might make it difficult for her to respond to my messages. Maybe that was the reason she hadn't called back. That I could understand. What I wouldn't tolerate would be her using it as an excuse to avoid talking to me at all. She did enough of that the night I took her home.

Derrick's words came back to me. Maybe Kai and I were better off just being friends.

Who was I kidding? Staying friends with Kai would be impossible. Not that we couldn't be adults and stay out of each other's beds. We'd done it for months. But now that I'd had another taste of her…it would be impossible to give her up.

She, on the other hand, was proving right now that it would not be a problem for her.

We needed to talk. I needed to hear her voice. I wanted to make her laugh again…and…

I just want…her.

How was I supposed to handle this? What was the rule for boyfriends who screwed up and didn't know what they did wrong? Flowers were out of the question because she was a florist for crying out loud.

I couldn't exactly look back at my track record with Trina because…well, that was just, weird. Our relationship had been fine up until the time I willingly cheated on her because I wanted her to break up with me.

Unfaithfulness between Kai and I wasn't the problem.

What I was feeling right now wasn't exactly the type of thing you talked to your boys about. Calling Derrick or Andre was out of the question. What I needed was the next best thing.

I punched a few buttons on my phone and then listened as it rang. "Pick up, pick up."

"Hello?" Ebony's sleepy voice came through the line.

"Hey, sis. You awake?

"Barely. I'm five months pregnant. I was asleep." She yawned. "Is everything okay?"

I cringed with guilt. In my desperation to get my twin sister's advice, I hadn't thought about what she could be doing at this time. "Everything is good, I guess. Justin is fine. I'm…I've got some stuff on my mind and I need to talk. Do you have a few minutes?"

"For you, sure."

"Who's that, baby?" Brian's voice could be heard in the background.

"It's Trevon. Can we get back to this when I get off the phone?"

"Sure. Hey, Tre!" Brian yelled.

"Tell him I said what's up." I listened as Ebony relayed the message. "Okay, hold up before you start talking, I've got to pee!" She sat the phone down, and in the background I could hear a guitar being played.

Brian was a good man and took care of my sister. Now that they were expecting their first child, it was obvious he was excited. So was she.

"Okay, sorry about that. Your niece is wreaking havoc on my bladder."

"Niece?"

"Yes, we found out this morning that we're having a girl!"

"Congratulations, Ebony!" The happiness that radiated through the phone was infectious. "It seems like I interrupted something? I can call back."

"Not really. I was resting, but Brian was playing his guitar for the baby. We read that playing music during pregnancy can encourage creativity in an unborn child. He's been giving my belly music lessons when I go to sleep."

I laughed. "That's love, for sure."

I couldn't help but wonder what crazy dad thing I would have done if Trina and I had been together when she was pregnant.

I was truly happy for my sister. She'd been through a lot over the past three years, but through it all, she found a man who loved her, the job of her dreams, and now she was starting a family.

I imagined what my bi-racial niece would look like. Her father had blond hair and blue eyes so she'd probably have light colored hair and eyes. She, no doubt, would be as beautiful as both my sisters.

If Kai were to have a baby, she'd be beautiful, too.

Wait, if Kai and I had a baby…

"Oh, damn." I would have punched the side of the sofa, but Justin was still lying against me.

Ebony laughed. "I wasn't gone that long."

I rubbed the bridge of my nose, slid Justin off my lap, and headed for the kitchen. On the verge of saying more expletives than in the movie we watched, it was time to remove myself from the living room.

"No, I just realized where I went wrong. Shit!"

"Um, okay, so do we still need to talk?"

"I can't believe I was so insensitive, Eb. She's right, men are jerks."

Ebony burst out laughing. "Brian may agree with you, but that depends. I assume this involves a woman. Who did you piss off?"

I shook my head. "The woman of my dreams, your future sister-in-law."

"Oh, that's deep. What did you do?"

"I asked if she was on birth control."

Ebony laughed. "Before or after you slept with her?"

"After she realized we didn't use anything."

"And that makes you a sucky boyfriend because?"

I sighed, preparing for the fallout to come. "Because…she had miscarriages in the past."

The line went dead.

"Hello?"

"I wouldn't be talking to you either." She sighed. "And you know this as a fact?"

"We talked about this a few weeks ago. She wants to have kids, but after the miscarriages, she's scared to try again and feels useless to a man who wants kids."

"And you had unprotected sex which could lead her to have to live through losing another baby all over again."

That was my issue in a nutshell.

"That's messed up, Tre."

"No wonder she won't talk to me. In her mind, I'm probably writing her off as we speak."

"Are you?"

"What?"

"Writing her off? It wasn't so long ago that you told me having a kid or a relationship was not a priority on your list. And here you are, a single father who seems to be falling for a woman who's not the mother of your child. Now there's the possibility you could have gotten her pregnant. What if history, God forbid, repeats itself? Do you want to watch her go through the pain of losing yet another baby? What if she is hoping the third time is a charm? Are you willing to support her? Chances are she'll have to be on bed rest for a majority of the pregnancy in order to make it to term. What if the baby is premature or ill? Are you ready to handle two kids with life threatening illness, plus maintain a lasting relationship?"

I was speechless to the point my knees went weak. I leaned against the counter. "Is that what she's thinking right now?"

Ebony blew out a breath. "I don't know, but if I were in her shoes, I know I would be."

"What should I do? None of that is how I feel. I want to be with her, regardless of what the future holds. I love her, Eb, I really do."

My sister blew out a breath. "If you are sure she's the one and have faith in your relationship, don't wait around for her to figure things out or else she may make the wrong decision. You need to find her and make her understand that you want to be with her, regardless."

And just like that, a light bulb went off in my head. I knew exactly what to do. "Thanks, Eb, I owe you."

Chapter 32

"Malone, what's taking so long? Light duty doesn't mean you can't handle the kitchen."

I ignored the laughter following the comment and bit back my irritation. Now that I was back on the job, the comments from my co-workers irritated me more than they did before. Had I really gotten that desensitized to the stereotypical male chauvinist?

I slammed a cabinet door. "If you guys hadn't put everything in places that wasn't designated for it to go, I wouldn't be wasting time trying to find a freakin' spatula!"

More laughter.

"You sure you wouldn't rather be at home playing house again?"

Eyes narrowed, my attention went straight to Thomas who lined up another shot at the pool table. "Who says I've been playing house?"

All eyes went to Lopez, who tried his best to zone out on the game playing on TV.

"Lopez…" I ground out.

My response evoked more laughter from the guys.

"Malone, you've got a visitor out front." The dispatcher's voice over the intercom drowned out the men.

Visitor?

I washed my hands and punched Lopez in the arm as I walked by. "That's the last time I tell you anything!" I hissed.

"Sorry." He rubbed his shoulder.

The last thing the men on my squad needed was a reason to make domesticated jokes about my love life. Or lack of.

At this point, I wasn't sure which one was true.

"Loretta, who's here?" I stopped off at the dispatcher's desk and looked around the lobby area of the station. It wasn't very big so there was no way to miss anyone.

She pointed up without looking. "He went outside."

I went to the door and saw Trevon leaning against the hood of his car. His arms were crossed and his gaze was focused on the top floor of the station house. The minute the door clicked shut behind me, his gaze found me and stayed there as I walked towards him, I stopped at the edge of the curb a few feet away.

I slipped both hands into the pockets of my uniform pants. "Where's Justin?"

It had been days since we'd spoken; all of which had been my doing. Still, it was eye opening to realize just how much I missed him. Every part of me wanted to run up and wrap my arms around him.

He huffed. "Now you ask about him?" He looked away for a moment, his jaw clenched, then relaxed. "Asleep in his car seat." His lips tightened. "And that's it? No hello, no hug, nothing?" He stood and walked to the curb and looked me right in the eye.

"Hi." I forced myself to stare back at him.

He sighed, shook his head. Then he looked me over, his eyes traveling from head-to-toe. I could damn near feel the heat of his body even though there was little more than a foot of space between us.

"I've never seen you in uniform before. I have to admit, it's hot. No pun intended."

My brow pulled together. Navy blue Dickey pants, a matching shirt with the fire department's logo, and clunky boots tough enough to kick someone's ass was not sexy on a female.

"Is this some weird type of booty call or—"

"Why are you avoiding me?" Trevon got straight to the point.

What else did I expect? He wasn't exactly one to beat around the bush.

I bit my lip. "Avoiding is a strong word."

"When you don't answer your phone or respond to a text message in nearly two days, its avoidance. I know you're busy, Kai. You're getting back to work is important, I get that. But that doesn't excuse the time you're not working. You can't sleep for twenty-four hours. You make time for those you care about. I know you're pissed at me and it's something we need to work through. But what about Justin? I thought you cared about him. Even if you don't want to talk to me, you can still talk to him. He misses you. Tonight was movie night. He could understand why you weren't there, but not why you didn't call."

My heart ached. "Justin missed me?" And I guessed Trevon didn't. I don't know which one was worse.

But I couldn't be mad. As he just said, I was avoiding him.

"I've been calling you for the past few hours and got nothing but voicemail. I can't keep doing this, Kai. We need to figure out what's going on between us."

I glanced over my shoulder to see if nosy eyes and ears were taking in our conversation. "I've got a lot on my mind."

His brow knit together. "And I don't?"

I fought the urge to roll my eyes. "It's not the same. Work is—"

"I've got work issues, too." He crossed his arms.

"It's not the same. You manage a restaurant. I rescue people."

Trevon unfolded his arms and let his balled fists drop to his side. "Like I don't remember that?" He huffed. "You're barely back on the job, Kai. You're a female returning after a back injury and the way you do your job is important. I get that. But that has nothing to do with our relationship. You act as if nothing we've talked about over the past few months matters anymore. It's as if our decision to be a couple has taken the back seat to everything else in your life. I mean, come on, Kai. We made the decision to be together, had sex, and then…I don't know what the hell happened. So we slipped up and had unprotected sex, I get that, but what did I say? What did I do wrong? We're a couple, Kai, we're supposed to talk about stuff like this. I'm trying here, but you keep blocking me. Are you scared about something?" He took a step towards me.

I crossed my arms and looked away because, damn, my eyes were beginning to water.

"Is it because I said I love you?" His voice softened.

My throat tight, I shook my head.

He reached out and touched my arm. When I didn't pull away, he rested his hand there and stroked. "Is it because we made love?"

I swallowed hard. "No," I whispered.

Because I didn't move, he reached over and gently pulled my face up to meet his. After weeks of avoiding physical contact, the fact I could now feel the inviting heat of his body made me want to melt directly into his arms and hold on forever.

"Is it because you're scared you could have gotten pregnant?"

I closed my eyes and a tear escaped as I nodded.

Trevon let loose a soft exhale. When I opened my eyes again and met his, sorrow was there.

"I'm sorry, Kai. What we did was irresponsible. What I asked you was insensitive. I wasn't trying to blame you or, I don't know, make you feel like anything was your fault." He reached out to wipe my cheek. "Nothing changes the way I feel about you. You know that, right?"

I was about to respond when the house siren went off. The dispatcher's voice went out over the loud speaker giving details of the emergency. Firefighters ran out from behind closed doors, kicking off shoes and stepping into their turnout gear.

I turned and watched as my squad suited up and wiped the tears from my eyes. Years of instinct had me wishing I was going with them, but I was on light duty, which meant I was grounded at the station. The only thing I had to look forward to was going back inside to finish cooking dinner. It was amazing how many calories were used up when fighting a fire. They guys would be hungry when they returned.

But before that happened, I had to have this conversation with Trevon. He was right; we did need to work things out.

"Trevon, I—"

"Malone! Let's go!"

Confused, I turned to look over my shoulder and saw my captain standing at the base of the fire truck, waving his arm, directing me to join them.

"But Captain, I can't—"

"Screw that! Did you not hear the details? This is big! We need all hands on deck. Kiss lover boy and get your ass in your gear and on the truck, now!"

A surge of adrenaline pumped through my veins. I turned to Trevon. "I've got to go." I turned, but he grabbed my arm.

"Go? Kai, you can't."

"Didn't you hear him? A five-alarm fire means all hands on deck. I'm needed for back up. Chances are I will just be there to run the truck pumps. Either way, I gotta go now!" I pulled away and ran up the driveway to where my gear was stored.

I kicked off my regular workboots, and stuffed my feet and legs into the turnout boot/pants/suspender combination that sat ready to be worn at a second's notice. Next came my coat; helmet followed. When I turned to run to the truck, I risked a glance and saw Trevon staring at me with a mixture of awe and fear on his face. Justin was in his arms, no doubt awakened by the sirens.

The last thing I saw as I climbed into the cab of the truck was Trevon mouthing something while holding his hand to the side of his face as if saying 'call me', and Justin's wide eyed wonderment of the lights of the fire truck as we pulled out of the station.

Chapter 33

Watching Kai climb into the fire truck was the hardest thing to do.

I wanted to grab her and make her stay. For as long as we'd known each other, she was always safe, nearby so I could see her, reach out and touch her if I needed to.

Now that she was back on the job, I was scared.

Kai had been a firefighter for over five years. She knew how to do her job. She knew how to survive. The injury she sustained had come from doing her job, from rescuing my family.

How many other near misses had there been? Would she ever tell me?

Would she tell me about anything that happened now?

The truck gone and street clear, I fastened Justin in his seat, then headed for the nearest McDonald's to get him ice cream as promised.

Unable to settle, I found myself flipping through the radio stations haphazardly looking for news. Anything that had music playing, I skipped past. She said the fire was huge, all hands on deck. I took it to mean every fire truck in the county would be there. So would the news stations. In today's society, news hit the airwaves and social networking sites in seconds.

I scrolled through my Facebook app on my phone while sitting in what felt like the longest drive-thru line known to man.

Still nothing.

The minute we got home, I settled Justin at the kitchen table and turned on the TV to check the news stations. No luck. It was past the time for the evening edition and too early for a late night update.

My temples felt tight and ached from worry. Damn. What kind of boyfriend or husband would I be, taking on the role of a woman in a relationship who worried about her man who held a dangerous job? There was nothing for me to do but wait until she called.

Our conversation wasn't over and she was about to tell me something important, I could feel it. She would call as soon as she could. Now all I had to do was wait.

****

The ring and vibration of my cell phone woke me from a fitful sleep. As I came aware of my surroundings, I realized infomercials were playing on TV. What time was it?

The phone stilled once I reached for it. Seconds later the voicemail alert sounded. I wiped my eyes and yawned. The time on the phone read one A.M.

The missed call log showed Kelli's number. I sat up with a start, my heart pounding. Why was Kelli calling me at this time of the morning and not Kai?

The last time I got a call this early, Justin was in the hospital, and Trina was hours away from death.

And Kai had been injured.

I was off the sofa, pacing the floor as I waited for Kelli to answer my call. "Pick up, damn it!"

"Hello?"

"What's wrong? Is she hurt?"

"Calm down, Trevon. She's going to be okay, but she is in the hospital. The doctor's keeping her overnight under observation."

I stopped in my tracks and felt the earth spin beneath my feet. I made it over to the sofa and collapsed. My heart beat so fast it felt as if it would fly out of my chest.

"What happened, Kelli? I just saw her a few hours ago!"

"It was a huge fire. She had to go in."

My head was heavy and my temples pounding. I put my head in my hands and forced myself to breathe. "How in the hell did that happen, Kelli? She wasn't even supposed to be on that damn truck!"

"All the Captain told me was that she got hurt and was sent to the hospital. That's all I know. I would be there, but Alonso is not home. I just had the baby so I can't take him out yet. She needs you, Trevon. Can you—"

I jumped up from the sofa and made my way to Justin's room. "Where is she?" Kelli gave me the details. "I'm on my way."

****

My nerves were shot to hell by the time I arrived at the hospital. Kelli had informed me that another relative was with Kai. I called him the minute I arrived in the parking lot and asked him to meet me in the foyer of the hospital. Visiting hours had ended hours ago. In order for me to see Kai, he would have to walk me in since he was staying the night with her. What was taking so damn long?

I paced the lobby of the hospital with Justin in my arms somewhere between being asleep and consciousness.

"Trevon?"

I turned to find Ricky, Kai's cousin, step off the elevator. "How is she?"

Ricky held his hands up. "Take a deep breath for me and sit down for a second, honey. You look like you're about to pass out over here."

"But—"

"But nothing. Sit down." He pointed to the waiting area.

Obviously, I would only get answers if I complied, so I sat. Besides, he didn't appear to be worried, so it couldn't be that bad.

I settled in a seat and changed the position of Justin's head on my shoulders. "What happened, Ricky?"

"There was a warehouse fire in an abandoned building where people were squatting. Apparently, some folks were trapped. Kai had to suit up and go in search of people who were trapped in a lower part of the building. The ceiling collapsed and she got hit in the head by falling debris. Her helmet saved her. She lost consciousness for a few minutes, though. They got her out and she seems to be okay." He paused and studied me. "The question is, are you okay? I swear you just changed several shades and now your face is pale."

I inhaled, not realizing I'd been holding my breath. Somewhere between the words big fire, trapped, falling debris, and unconsciousness, all functions that kept me alive ceased.

"I need to see her." My voice was heavy and thick. "Please."

"Sure, sweetie. Follow me."

I stood with Justin in my arms and followed him to the elevator. It seemed to take hours.

"Kai just got settled into a room. They're going to take her for a CT scan or MRI, one or the other; to be sure she has no brain or spinal cord damage." He chuckled. "But if you ask me, she's fine. Just as stubborn as ever."

We got off the elevator, walked down a few doors, and paused. There were a few guys in fireman uniforms standing outside her door.

"Oh yeah, some of the guys have been hanging out to keep an eye on her."

I studied them as they watched me walk closer. One guy stepped away from the group and came over with an outstretched palm.

"Hey, you must be the man." He chuckled when my eyebrows rose.

"Excuse me?"

"Sorry, I meant Kai's man. My name is Lopez. I watch her back at work." He cringed. "That didn't come out right. I mean we started at the station around the same time. We look out for each other."

Irritation flooded me. "Then why the hell did you let her go in? She was supposed to be on light duty, not fighting a fire. Not yet."

I felt Ricky's hand on my shoulder and Justin squirm in my arms.

Lopez put his hands up in defense. "Hey, man, you and I both know once Malone…Kai, decides to do something, you can't stop her. She heard people screaming and all the other ladders…firemen were in other parts of the building. She did her job, man; it's what we do, what she does." He shook his head and looked down, putting his hands on his hips. "I just wish I could have been there to have her back. I was in another part of the building and she was alone. If it wasn't for the alarm on her suit to tell the captain she wasn't moving, who knows what would have happened?"

I felt my knees go weak.

"I can take him if you want." Ricky held out his arms for Justin.

"Thanks." I shifted Justin's weight into Ricky's arms. He barely made a peep.

"We'll be in the waiting room down the hall. Take as long as you need. I'm not going anywhere."

I nodded then waited for him to leave before taking another deep breath and facing Lopez. "How bad was it?"

He ran a finger across his brow and blew out a breath. "She had a close call. Kai was doing something that should have been easy, which is the only reason why she was allowed to go in. The main part of the fire was upstairs, on the second floor. Kai was on the entry level. What we didn't know is that the fire had spread to the back side of the building where the room already had a damaged floor. It didn't take much for the fire to spread there and for weakened floor beams to fall. One caught her on the back of the helmet and knocked her unconscious. Another firefighter and I went in and got her out."

I could see it all happening in slow motion in my mind, like a bad movie with a horrible ending.

"How long was she out?"

"She came to when the EMT's used smelling salts. Her helmet took the brunt of the force, though, so she should be okay. We just left the room; she's awake, waiting for you." Lopez reached out and I shook his hand again. "From what I've heard, you're a good guy. Take care of her, okay?"

"It's the only thing I want to do."

The remaining firefighters nodded in my direction before walking down the hall.

My attention went to the door leading into Kai's room. After hearing the tale of what happened to her, it took a lot for me to steel myself. I held back the tears that threatened to fall. After wondering how close I'd come to losing her tonight, having the facts didn't make seeing her any easier.

After what she went through, seeing me worried wouldn't help her. My woman was strong. She needed her man to be strong, too.

I said a quick prayer of thanks that she was alive and took a deep breath before opening the door. The room was semi-dark. Kai lay in bed, eyes closed. The top knot hair style she'd worn earlier was gone. The long dark strands were in disarray on a white pillow. There were a few cuts and bruises on her face that had been cleaned and shined from antibacterial cream. A white sheet was pulled up and tucked beneath her breast.

I cleared my throat. "When I said call me, this isn't the call I expected."

Kai's eyes flew open. "Trevon…I'm so sorry!"

Then she burst into tears.

Chapter 34

"Kai, don't cry." Trevon stood beside my bed and pulled my hands from my face. "I'm here, baby, I'm here." He choked back what sounded like a sob.

I couldn't tell if he was crying because my eyes were blurred with tears of my own. "I'm so sorry," I managed again.

"For what?" He ran a thumb across my forehead, lightly grazing the knot on my head while examining my face.

I sniffed. "For not calling all this time…for being angry at you…for nearly dying on you."

Trevon closed his eyes and his jaw tightened. So did his grip on my hand. "It's okay, it's okay."

I shook my head. "No, it's not. I didn't answer your questions earlier. All I could think about when I was trapped in that building was how much I loved you and that if I died, you would never know how sorry I was for the way I acted and that I love you so much."

Trevon stared at me with deep worry lines on his forehead. "I thought you were knocked unconscious."

"Not at first. I felt when that beam hit me, felt it when I hit the ground. I was awake for a few minutes and all I could do was think of you and Justin…how upset you were when you came to see me and—"

"Kai, you don't have to do this."

I squeezed his hand. "Yes, I do. I didn't before because I was scared. But you need to know, right now."

His eyes closed, he lowered his head to our joined fingers and kissed the back of my hand. "I'm listening."

I grabbed onto our connected fingers with the hand riddled with an IV, and held on for dear life. "I didn't avoid you because you love me. I love you so much it scares me. I've been hurt before, so sometimes I can't help but think that our relationship is nothing but a dream."

"It's not, baby, believe me, it's not. I'm here. This is you, this is me. This is us." He kissed my hand again.

"Making love to you was perfect. I wanted you that night more than I wanted anyone in my life. But I screwed up. I put us both in a situation that was unfair to either of us."

His brow creased. "We're both grown and consenting adults, Kai. You didn't make me do anything I didn't want to do, believe me."

"True, but I was the one who initiated sex in your office. I rushed things because I was impatient. But just like our first time, I wanted what I wanted. I didn't think about using a condom or the fact I wasn't on birth control. I put myself in this situation, not you."

Trevon stared down at me. "That's what I don't understand, Kai. What situation?"

My stomach tightened. "I could be pregnant."

He shrugged. "And what? You think that scares me?"

I moved my head slowly, because my head ached. "Honestly, I don't know, but it scares me." More tears welled up in my eyes. "I've had two failed pregnancies before. It hurt me so bad, Trevon. After everything that happened with Malik, I figured maybe it was for the best because I wasn't supposed to be with him. It hurt, but I handled it. But with you, it's different. I want to make you happy. I want you to be happy with me. I want to have a baby with you, and I'm scared to death that if I ever got pregnant and had a miscarriage, I wouldn't be able to recover…that you would be disappointed and not want to be with me anymore."

He looked at me as if I'd gone crazy. "Kai, baby, I am happy with you! And I'm not him, so let that be the last time you make that statement!"

I cringed. That was the first time Trevon had ever spoken to me in anger.

"Maybe not now but, what about years from now?" I succumbed to tears again, losing the fight to keep them in. "You want more kids. Justin needs siblings. If I can't have your baby then—"

"Then we'll adopt, or not, I don't know. Frankly, I don't care! What I want foremost is *you*. Baby now, baby never…*I. Don't. Care.*" He slid a finger under my chin, lifted it. "Look at me."

I wiped tears with my free hand and turned what had to be red swollen eyes in his direction.

"If you're pregnant, we'll work through doing whatever it takes to protect you and our baby. If things go wrong, then," he lifted my chin again when I pulled away. "We'll make it through. You won't be alone. I'll be here, always. You can call me Walmart."

"Ha!" His comment made me smile through tears.

"That's what I want to see. That smile." He leaned forward and kissed me, red nose, snot, and all.

"Stop it, I look horrible!" My hands went back to my face.

He pulled them away. "You're beautiful. You're always beautiful to me."

I didn't protest when he leaned in to kiss me again, and instead, wrapped my arms around him as much as I could, nearly pulling him down into the bed with me.

Trevon did what he could to slide his arms around me as well. Feeling him against me, even though the limited contact wasn't nearly as much as I wanted, I reveled in what I almost lost.

A knock on the door announced a visitor. "Excuse me for the interruption. Ms. Malone, I'm Debra, a Nurse Practitioner. How are you holding up?"

Trevon kissed me once more, then moved to the far side of the bed to give the nurse space, but kept our fingers joined.

I lounged back in the bed. "My head hurts so bad it's hard to think. When can I get some aspirin?"

Nurse Debra checked my pulse and jotted down notes after reading the machines I was hooked up to. "I may be able to get you some in a few minutes. The doctor wanted you to have the MRI first so he could get a true reading as to what's going on, but it seems to be delayed. Instead we're going to go ahead with the CT."

"What are the tests for?" Trevon asked.

"The CT is going to focus on her head to check for any bleeding or swelling on her brain since she was knocked unconscious. Those helmets you guys wear are built to withstand heat and protect your brain. From what I saw of your helmet, you're one lucky gal."

"And the MRI?" Worry grew on Trevon's face.

"That was going to be a full body scan to check for any spinal cord damage from the fall and weight of the beam."

Trevon groaned.

I hadn't told him the full story about what happened because I wasn't fully aware of it, either. But since Lopez had exited my room shortly before Trevon arrived, I had no doubt if he had a moment to speak to him, he would have answered any question he was asked.

Nurse Debra referred to the chart. "It appears you already had existing back trauma."

"From a previous fire," Trevon supplied, squeezing my hand. "She's pretty tough."

"I'd say." The nurse studied the chart, then looked at me, Trevon, and back to the chart.

"What?" My nerves were already on edge. "What's wrong with me?"

"Nothing at all. It seems congratulations are in order." The nurse smiled. "We run a pregnancy test when we draw blood before doing x-rays; it's standard procedure if you're childbearing age. According to this chart, you're pregnant."

I felt the blood drain from my face. "Oh no…"

"Kai, it's going to be okay. Look at me, baby, look at me." Trevon squeezed my hand, but my attention stayed on the nurse who seemed confused by our reaction to the news.

"Um…okay." She held my medical file to her chest.

"This can't be happening." My throat was thick as tears started to come.

"Ms. Malone, what's wrong?" Nurse Debra looked from me to Trevon.

He responded as the nurse's eyes grew wide. "She's been pregnant before and lost the baby, both times."

"Oh dear, I'm sorry. I had no idea. Do you know what happened?" She walked closer to the bed and rested a hand on my leg.

I closed my eyes for a moment in an effort to find my voice. Our fingers were still linked, so I held on for strength. "Once the embryo settled in my Fallopian tube. I had to have surgery to remove it. The next one didn't implant in my womb, and the miscarriage was natural." My heart went to the pit of my stomach.

I was pregnant with Trevon's baby…

What should have been happy news was my worst nightmares come true.

"Do you know how far along you were at those times?" The nurse made notes on my file.

"About a month, maybe more? I got cramps and was in pain, even bled a little. That's how I ended up at the doctor's office and found out. I was worried about the bleeding because it wasn't time for my period." I shut my eyes at the memory.

It was hard to tell which was worse: the loss of the baby or the disappointment in myself because of my inability to carry a baby.

I risked a peek at Trevon. His expression was of love and concern.

"Ms. Malone, do you have any idea when you could have conceived?"

"It would have been three weeks ago," Trevon supplied.

The nurse scribbled on the chart and made more notations. "Okay. Have you experienced any pain or symptoms like before?"

I thought long and hard. "I've been tired…nauseous sometimes. I did bleed a little like my period was light. I didn't think about it because I've been stressed out for the past week due to work."

Trevon squeezed my hand. When I glanced his way, I saw disappointment, not because I was pregnant, but because I hadn't shared any of this information with him. I mouthed an apology, then focused on the nurse.

Her eyebrows went up. "Really? Hmm…interesting. Let's do this. I'm going to inform the attending physician of what's going on. We'll get the OB/GYN on duty to come down and examine you, okay?"

I nodded, unable to think of the results of the exam.

"Do me a favor; don't stress. You've been through enough. I'll be back soon." She patted my leg again then left the room.

The minute the door shut, I closed my eyes to find strength before facing Trevon, whose eyes were on me.

"Why didn't you tell me how you were feeling, Kai?" Trevon turned and sat on the edge of my bed. The worry in his eyes was overwhelming. He seemed to be more concerned about my wellbeing, while I was racked with guilt for getting knocked up.

"There was nothing to tell. I figured it was stress from going back to work. I've been away for months."

He didn't seem to buy it, but instead of responding, he stayed quiet as if deep in thought.

Oh God, here it comes. I closed my eyes and prepped for the inevitable.

"Kai…"

I took a deep breath and exhaled slowly. When I opened my eyes, Trevon's expression was beyond serious.

"Yes?"

"Marry me."

I stopped breathing for a moment as my mind went blank.

"What did you say?"

"I said, 'marry me'. I'd get down on one knee, but your bed is up too high." He smiled a little, but the seriousness of his words was still on his face.

My heart raced. "Why?"

He shook his head ever so slightly. "What do you mean, "why"? What woman gets a marriage proposal and questions her lover's intentions?" He chuckled. "Only you. God I love you."

I tried to sit up, but the pain in my head and back was too severe. "Trevon, we just found out I'm pregnant. We both know the chances of me losing this baby are beyond enormous."

He stroked my cheek. "Stop being negative; let the past be the past. I have no idea what's going to happen next. The only thing I do know is regardless, I'm not going to stop loving you. I'm not going to be mad either. Sad, yes, but I'm here and I'm not going anywhere. Whatever happens, we'll deal with it. You, me, and Justin. He loves you, too. So like I said, will you marry me?"

For once, I was speechless.

With everything going on in my life, the last thing I expected was to get a marriage proposal.

In a hospital bed.

Banged up, with blood shot eyes and a nose swollen to the size of a plum.

Pregnant with no idea as to what the outcome would be.

Yet, this man proposed because he loves me.

How could I ask for more?

Sometimes, true love was nothing like the stories found in fairy tales.

I reached for his free hand and looked him in the eye. "Yes, Trevon, I will marry you."

Epilogue

"Trevon, I'm okay, I swear." Kai eased down on the bed and fluffed the pillows behind her back.

I set her hospital bag in my closet…our closet, then went over to take off her shoes. "Remember what the doctor said. Take it easy. Between the pregnancy and concussion, you need to get plenty of fluids and rest."

Justin jumped on the bed next to Kai. I winced and was about to tell him to keep away from her, but Kai shot me a look of warning, then placed a pillow in front of her belly. "Come here, sweetie." Justin grabbed her face, planted a big kiss on her cheek, then settled in her arms. She reciprocated the affection. "I've missed you, too."

Satisfied that he would be still, I focused on her again. "Do you need anything?"

Kai bit her lip in thought. "Some juice would be good."

"Juice, juice, juice!" Justin broke free from her grip and began bouncing on the bed again.

Kai grabbed him and pulled him down. "Justin, I need you to do me a really big favor, okay?" He nodded. "I'm not feeling very well so I need you to be really still so I don't get sick again, okay?"

"Kay!" He flopped down one last time and laid his head on the pillow in front of her belly.

Kai smiled and ran a finger over his head.

I sighed in relief. "Your wish is my command."

As I left the bedroom, I heard the television click on and Kai asking Justin what he would like to watch.

In the kitchen and alone, I leaned against the counter and recalled the events of the past days.

Once again, my life had changed.

This time for the better.

I had custody of my son.

The woman of my dreams agreed to marry me.

And she was pregnant.

For forty-eight hours I watched Kai go through a variety of emotions, everything from ecstatic to fearful, hopeful to expecting the worst. All I could do was be strong for her.

My efforts paid off. By the time we left the hospital we had pictures of an ultrasound, visual confirmation that the fetus had indeed implanted in her womb. The OB/GYN who visited Kai in the hospital did wonders to calm Kai's fears. The bleeding she experienced was evidence that the embryo had implanted in her womb and started to grow. As long as Kai kept routine appointments, avoided stressful situations, and took her daily vitamins, the chances of her carrying to term were good.

I pulled out my wallet and unfolded the picture given to us. The grainy black and white image showed a small white shape the size of my thumbnail in a sea of black.

Our baby.

I rubbed my chest and blinked back the wetness of my eyes.

Our baby had a chance.

Now that I was alone in the kitchen, I was ready to admit I was scared.

The idea of having another child wasn't the issue. The opportunity to have a baby with the woman I loved and enjoy the experience was more than I could ever ask for. Months ago, the idea of having this type of opportunity was the beyond my wildest dreams. I looked forward to it, embraced it even. Every corny thing a father could do for the mother of his child as he watched her belly grow was what I wanted more than I could ever explain. The happiness

Andre experienced, what my brother-in-law Brian was living now, was finally mine to grasp and hold on to.

It was the fear that this opportunity could end in disaster that scared me.

While everything looked good now, we weren't out of the woods just. With Kai being thirty-five, the doctor said she would have to be monitored for a variety of health issues that could affect her and the baby. It was the standard procedure for women who had 'late in life' pregnancies. I thought the term was absurd. Fortunately, between my job and her county health benefits, she would be covered.

Once the pregnancy had been confirmed, the first thing Kai had to do was determine how her job would handle her pregnancy. Having female firefighters was still a bit new in the county and she had no idea what the policy would be to handle the situation. It was obvious she wouldn't be allowed to fulfill her regular job duties, so finding out what the alternative was to quitting was key.

While I wished she would retire, I refused to ask her to give up something she loved. If she decided to quit working at the fire department and take on motherhood fulltime, I would support her. If she wanted to remain on the job, I'd support that as well.

After all, her being on the job was the reason Justin was still alive.

Regardless of what happened, one thing Kai was emphatic about was that our baby was her priority. Anything she needed to do in order to have a successful pregnancy, she would do.

I don't know if I could have loved her any more than I did at this moment.

"Daddy, Daddy, Daddy! Juice!" Justin's voice floated down the hall.

I wiped my eyes, gently folded the picture, and slid it back into my wallet. We wanted to tell our families the good news, but decided to wait until she made it through the first trimester. She wouldn't be showing until then. Not even Justin would know.

"Coming!" I grabbed a glass for Kai, Justin's sippy cup, and filled them both with ice-cold apple juice from the refrigerator.

For good measure, I grabbed a can of fruit cocktail out of the cabinet and emptied it into a bowl. Andre mentioned once how much his wife, Sharice, ate while pregnant. I made a mental note to get a list of Kai's favorite foods and anything she might crave. My refrigerator needed to be filled.

"Here you go; two glasses of juice, and a side of fruit."

"I got cup, Daddy." Justin burst into laughter.

"You know what, you sure do." I tickled his belly and kissed him on the forehead.

Kai accepted her glass and eyed the bowl; seems like I hit the mark. She drank, then scooped a spoonful of fruit into her mouth as she studied my bedroom. Our bedroom.

"You know, you've got the perfect set up here."

I settled on the opposite side of the bed. "What do you mean?"

"A three bedroom house with a fenced in yard. Justin has his room. The…," she looked at him as he drank his drink. "…new addition will have a room." She beamed. "The fenced in yard is perfect for Sugar. She's going to lose her mind not having to be on a leash and able to run around all the time."

I smiled. "It's exactly what I wanted when I bought the place; a family to fill it up with."

Kai reached over Justin's head and clasped my hand. "I'm glad you chose me to be a part of it."

I squeezed her hand. "We chose each other. Remember that."

Finished with his cup, Justin handed it to me, slid off the bed, then ran down the hall to his bedroom to play. The sound of toys being dumped out of his toy box was music to my ears. Kai smiled as well.

I took advantage of the space left vacant by Justin and got comfortable. "Now, here's a question. What kind of wedding do you want?" I stretched my arm out, and motioned for her to lie against me.

Kai slid over, nestled her head just below my chin and ran a hand over my chest. "Hmm…wedding. I still can't believe this, you know. I used to want a big wedding, I'm talking grandiose stuff. Now I want simple. We can have family and friends over and make it private. Hey," she poked me in the ribs. "What if we did a gazebo in the back yard?"

I thought about it. "Private, personal. Perfect. If it's what you want, we'll make it happen." I kissed her forehead.

"It's exactly what I want. But I have to meet your parents and sisters first."

"You've met my parents."

She shook her head. "That was a lifetime ago and the circumstances were different. Then, I was the firefighter who saved their grandson's life. Now I'm going to be their daughter-in-law and step-mother to Justin."

I reached over and rubbed her belly. "Don't forget, the mother of their next grandchild."

Her hand went over mine as she smiled. "True."

"I say we wait a few weeks to see how your feeling. If the doctor says it's okay, we'll drive up to North Carolina for the weekend. We can stay with them, they can visit with Justin, and you'll get to meet LaShana and her family. We'll have to Skype with Ebony, though. Since both of you are pregnant, neither one of you need to be in a plane or in a car for an extended period of time."

Kai linked her fingers with mine. "Sounds good to me. So, what date?"

I looked down at her in surprise. "You're asking me? It thought that would be your decision."

She smiled. "It's ours. It looks as though I'm going to be out of work for a while. You on the other hand, have a business to run. I can't see there being time for the General Manager to take off and go on a honey moon just yet."

"True. We'll work it out. Personally, I can wait for the honeymoon. I want to keep you close to home and the doctors. I'm more concerned about getting you moved in and buying your ring."

Kai held up her naked ring finger. I pulled it to my lips and kissed it.

"I'll have that remedied by this weekend. I want you to go with me and pick out what you want. I'm not good at these things."

She shook her head and smiled. "You were supposed to have a ring when you proposed, you know. It's tradition."

"Can I help it that it was unplanned? Don't get me wrong, making you a part of my life has always been my goal. If I had the opportunity, I would have done it differently and had the ring."

"I know, and I still think it was perfect. I love spontaneity. Now I will forever remember the day you asked me to marry you as the day we found out I was pregnant."

I angled my head to look at her. "Do you wish we did things a bit differently? You know, be engaged or at least married before getting pregnant?"

"No. That would be like wishing we'd met and you didn't have a son. I've learned that finding happiness isn't about having the perfect set of circumstances. The way we met, fell in love...you and I being together was meant to be. I've always thought of having you and Justin in my life as a chance to have something I thought could never be. And now, not only do I have you, I've got a bonus!" She held her stomach.

"I feel the same way." I cleared my throat. "Can I tell you something without you taking it the wrong way?"

"Um…sure. What's on your mind?" She twisted in my arms so she could look up at me.

I waited for her to settle. "Before all of this…crazy happened, I thought making things work with Justin's mother was the right thing to do, for him…for her. I thought it would have been the right thing for me. Not a day has gone by since she died that I didn't wonder what would have happened if she had lived. I would have kept trying to make things work between us, but I don't honestly think I would have been happy. A part of my heart would always be wondering what could have happened with us."

The expression on Kai's face was a mixture of sadness and something else I couldn't determine. "And now?"

"Now I know it wouldn't have worked, no matter how hard I tried. Somehow, I would have ended up finding you again."

"Wow, aren't you full of yourself?" Kai laughed after poking me in the chest. "Who says I would have taken you?"

I shrugged. "I'm not full of myself, just confident enough to know that you felt the same way I did. It wouldn't have taken much to convince you to fall in love with me." I leaned down and kissed my future wife. "It didn't take much at all, did it?"

Kai ran a hand over my cheek and wrapped her arm across my chest, settling in. "No, it didn't". She sighed and we lay in silence for a few minutes until she spoke again. "Two months. That's how long I give us to get my things moved in, our jobs squared away, and for us to get married. Deal?"

I pulled her hand from my waist and kissed the bare finger. "Deal."

"But there is one thing I need you do to first."

"What's that?"

She turned in my arms and looked up at me. "Go to my apartment and get our dog."

I smiled.

Yes, life indeed would be perfect, no matter what happened next.

The End

COMING 2016 ~ ALONE

Prologue

"Derrick, welcome back. You know I love to see my regulars. What can I get you to drink?"

The sexy bartender had on a layer of extra clothes in comparison to her workmates.

"The regular, Samantha." I dug into my back pocket for my wallet as she winked and walked away, making a show of swaying hips.

The lights and music in the club I frequented was loud and made it damn near impossible to think. Just what I needed, to be numb…to take an hour or two and forget the hell that was my life.

She returned with four shot glasses. I slid a few twenties across the counter to cover my drinks and gave her a generous tip. "Keep 'em coming, love."

She accepted the payment, slipped the tip into a well-endowed cleavage, and winked. "Sure thing."

I downed two shots, back to back, and coughed. The mahogany liquid felt like silk running down the back of my throat. I closed my eyes and let the effects wash through me, waiting for it to reach every part of my body.

The remaining shots were consumed to speed up the process. The minute I put the glasses down, I signaled the bartender and pointed to the empties. She nodded and walked over with the whisky bottle in hand and topped me off. She winked. I drank, then closed my eyes again.

No way would I be driving home tonight. Thus the reason why I'd taken a cab.

It's funny how life can kick you in the nuts, take away everything you've worked for, and leave you damn near destitute.

It's one thing when you're the one at fault.

It's something completely different when it happened by someone else's hand.

I love my family, but my brother had gone from one to look up to, to the bane of my family's existence, damn near taking everything we had worked for.

And for what?

A drug habit that drained our family's construction business dry from constantly putting him into rehab.

Now, due to bad decisions and contracts he'd done under the table without my or our father's knowledge, the company had been forced to file bankruptcy.

I loosened the tie around my neck. After spending hours with our attorney to see if there was any way for us to get out of this mess, my father and I parted ways. He went home to explain to my mother the depth of her oldest son's deceit, while I, on the other hand, decided to take up residence on a bar stool in a strip club and get drunk.

It was either that or find my brother and kill him.

The last five years of my life were devoted to our business. Our father, well really, stepfather, taught each of us the ins and outs of the construction business based on our strengths. The goal was for him to retire and spend much needed time with my mother, who was dealing with Lupus.

Shaun and I had been handed the reins two years ago. I took it and ran with it. Shaun caved under the pressure and left not only the business, but his wife and two beautiful daughters. Apparently, his drug of choice to escape the pressure went from weed to crack. A huge leap from a manageable drug to a killer.

I should know. I experimented with weed when I was in college and a few years beyond. But it was just a recreational thing, not habitual.

Bad decisions were made; the repercussions affected me and my family.

I had a lot of shit to make up for, and I did. Thanks to Shaun, I was about to start over.

Again.

"Hey, baby. Is my girl on stage boring you?"

I opened my eyes and found a pair of perfect breasts covered by the barest material known to man. My eyes traveled down to the small square between her thighs, and down a set of shapely legs that ended in a pair of heels that had to be twelve inches. Then I found her face.

"Honestly, I'm not in the mood to pay her any attention."

She smiled at the comment, tilting her head in a seductive angle and licking her lips. "What about me?" A hand went to my thigh, ran up and down, then squeezed somewhere near the area of my groin.

She was about that money, that was for sure, and I had to admit, she had my attention.

"What do you have in mind?"

Her eyes lit up. I could have sworn I saw dollar signs in her eyes and heard a cash register ding in her head. Or between her thighs. Was there a difference?

"For starters, you can get a lap dance for five, but if you really want a show…," she leaned forward, intentionally resting her boobs on my arm and whispered some very suggestive deals in my ear.

I chuckled. The rational part of my mind said to say no, that I should swallow my drinks and catch a cab home. No amount of money spent tonight would ease the pain of what I was feeling.

The irrational and rather horny part said to hell with reason. This was my last night in Charlotte before moving to Georgia and starting over. Who gave a damn about what I did tonight?

Not my parents. Not me; and certainly not the hoe that had just licked my ear.

"Why the hell not? You only live once."

Her smile was wicked as she took my hand and led me to the back of the club.

Chapter 1

"Georgia traffic sucks."

"Derrick, I warned you, didn't I? You'd think your last trip down here would have taught you to leave early if you want to get on the south side of Atlanta on a Friday night." Trevon laughed.

"Yeah, well, I was staying on that side of town at the time since that's where the job was. Now I'm working above downtown Atlanta. I go where the work is."

"You don't have to explain it to me. Do what works for you, man. Anyway, dinner should be ready by the time you arrive. I guess Kai will be able to wait. These days, she's eating everything in sight! But I'm happy, man, because she's happy. The baby is growing and life is good."

"I'm happy for you. Look, I'm gonna get off the phone because I just passed a cop who was lookin' at me as if I was texting. I should be there in twenty minutes."

"See you when you get here."

I hung up the phone and sat it in the cup holder, just as the cop rolled up beside me.

I glanced his way, did a head nod, and focused my attention back on the road. My papers were in order, my license straight. Unless he just wanted to pull me over for some imaginary infraction, there was nothing for him to do but continue to drive in the bumper-to-bumper traffic.

It's hard to believe I gave up life in North Carolina and moved down here. This wasn't my first trip to Atlanta, but live here? I couldn't help but feel as if my life was about to go through some major changes.

And to make matters worse, I wasn't comfortable with my new work situation.

Five years of being part owner of a lucrative construction company owned by my stepfather had given me a taste of control. Not over my employees, but over my time. I did the work I wanted and set my own schedule. My stepdad, Charles, ran the company, secured jobs and did the foot work to keep it going. My brother, Shaun, and I, ran different divisions. I was in charge of the projects as they started from the ground up; while he was in charge of interior finishing and the finer details. Our mother handled the three P's: payroll, permits, and paperwork.

Until she was diagnosed with Lupus.

From there, everything spiraled out of control. Her health took the front seat to everything. Charles retired early to see that she got the medical attention and support at home she needed. I stepped up to fill Charles's shoes, and Shaun…well, that's when shit fell apart.

Putting thoughts about a past that could not be changed aside, I checked my GPS again and found I was now minutes away from my boy's house. It had been months since I last visited Trevon. Other than the time I spent completing a renovation on the restaurant he worked for and the overnight trip back to stand as Best Man at his wedding, it had been six months.

I pulled up to his house, parked in the drive, and surveyed my surroundings. He had a nice home in the suburbs with a manicured lawn with a fenced in yard, cars in the driveway, and a dog. The one story home seemed to be perfect for what he had going on in his life.

I stepped out of my truck, grabbed the package I'd brought with me, and heard children's laughter and a barking dog, all of which seemed to be coming from his back yard.

I walked up the stone walkway and rang the doorbell. My attention went to the basketball goal in the driveway. It had been a long time since I had played. Maybe I could talk Trevon into a game of one-on-one after dinner.

"Well, well, look at what the cat dragged in."

I turned, expecting to see Trevon's wife, Kai, but instead faced her sister. The first time we came face-to-face had been during the renovations. A delay in the work schedule had her fuming. She searched me out and jumped down my throat, demanding my crew be finished so she could keep to her interior decorating schedule before she had her baby. She'd been heavy with child and bore a pregnancy glow. She'd had the baby by the time I came back for the wedding.

But today…

"Kelli, you look…" Unable to help myself, my gaze traveled the length of her body. All the baby weight was gone and damn, she was fine.

She wore a pair of ripped jeans, a t-shirt, and her feet were bare. Long jet-black hair rested on her shoulders and cat-shaped eyes drew my attention.

"I look what?" A hand went to her hip as a thin eyebrow arched.

She may have had her baby, but she still had the attitude.

Before I could respond, a little girl, the spitting image of Kelli, ran to the doorway and tugged on her shirt. "Mommy, Aunty said the timer went off on the stove."

Kelli ran a hand over the little girl's head. "Okay, tell her I'll be there in a second and that Uncle Tre's friend is here."

The little girl looked at me. Her eyes widened as her head went back to take in my full height.

Kelli clicked her teeth. "What do you say, Christina?"

The little girl snapped back to attention. "Hello." She grinned, than ran off to deliver her messages.

Kelli's attention came back to me. "You were saying?"

I cleared my throat. "You look nice. The last time I saw you, you were—"

"As big as a house, you can say it." She stepped aside and directed me to come in.

I wasn't taking the bait. "I was going to say pregnant."

She laughed; the musical quality struck a chord inside of me. She breezed past and walked down the hallway. I followed, unable to take my eyes off her waist and hips as they swayed. I'm pretty sure she wasn't trying to be sexy, but in those fitted jeans…

I ran a thumb over my brow and forced myself to look away and remember she was a married woman. As much as I appreciated a woman's anatomy, there was at least one line I didn't cross. Married women were completely off limits, even if they were the ones to seek me out.

The smell of cooked food grew stronger as we neared the kitchen and my stomach growled. It was the perfect distraction.

"Hungry?" Kelli glanced over her shoulder.

Damn, those eyes…

"Is it obvious?"

She laughed again. "Well, dinner will be ready in about thirty minutes. Kai and I are putting the last touches on everything. She wanted to make it all, but I forced her to stay seated. She's too far along to be up and moving around too much. Her doctor wants her on bed rest, but has allowed her to move around as long as she's at home."

Before I could respond, we entered the kitchen and there was Kai, her face round and beaming.

"Derrick!" She went to get up, but I moved to her side and put a hand on her shoulder.

"If you're supposed to be resting and got up to hug me, Tre would have my neck." I leaned down and hugged her. "These are for you." I handed her the box that was in my hand.

She didn't hesitate to peel off the thin wrapper. "Chocolate covered strawberries?" Her eyes grew wide. "Did Trevon tell you about my crazed obsession with these?"

"Yep."

"You have earned an even warmer spot in my heart."

A snort came from the opposite side of the kitchen. I glanced at Kelli whose back was turned. Again, my eyes slid to the eye-catching logo stitched on the back pockets of her jeans.

"So where is that husband of yours?" I forced my attention back to my hostess.

"He's in the backyard with the kids."

"Kids?"

"Justin, of course, and my niece and nephew."

The mention of Kelli's kids was enough to keep me from looking her way again.

"Oh, yeah. Well, do you mind if…," I pointed towards the backdoor.

"You're family, Derrick, make yourself at home." Kai shooed me in the direction of the backyard. "We'll let you know when dinner is ready."

I headed to the back door and did my best to avoid eye contact with her sister.

The transition from inside to outside was a slap in the face. From the mouthwatering aroma of a home cooked meal, to the smell of new leaves and budding flowers on the trees and bushes. Spring was in the air, which meant opportunities of various kinds were about to begin, which was why spring was my favorite time of the year.

I spied Trevon on the far side of the yard throwing a ball back and forth between himself, his son, and niece. A little distance away, a little boy sat in the grass, one finger in his mouth watching the activity as if sitting at a tennis match. He was too young to participate, but that didn't keep him from reaching out and clapping his hands every time the ball was thrown in the air.

I was about to call out when a white blur darted across the yard and stopped in front of me, teeth bared, growling.

"Hold up, I'm a good guy." I stopped in my tracks, but stood my ground as the pit bull sniffed everything her short legs could reach.

"Sugar, friend!" Trevon jogged over to where we stood, reached down, and rubbed the dog's back. After a few seconds, she backed off and settled next to him, but her eyes were on me.

"Damn, that little thing packs a punch." I laughed and reached out to clasp hands with my best friend.

"Yo, D, you made it." He stood back and looked at me. "Look at you, same as always. I invited you over for a home cooked meal and you come dressed like you're headed out to the club."

I chuckled and looked down at my attire. Yeah, I was cleaned up, a pair of jeans and a fresh shirt and matching Timberlands. "Hey, you never know when you're gonna roll up and meet a fine woman. You only get one time to make a first impression."

"True, but unless you have plans to go out later, there's no one to impress around here." His attention went to the kids as the ball hit him in the back. "Hey, grown people talking! Come here you!" He ran after Christina and Justin who let out a squeal of laughter and ran across the yard, zigzagging to keep from being caught.

I laughed, but remained still since I was being guarded by the furry white bodyguard.

Trevon caught up with the kids, swooped them up, and tucked one under each arm before heading my way.

"Justin, do you remember Uncle Derrick?"

My god-nephew giggled as he squirmed in his father's grasp. "Yes!"

"And this little angel in disguise is Christina, Kelli's daughter."

"I know him already!" she laughed. With her being bigger than her cousin, she managed to squirm out of Trevon's grasp and ran towards the infant sitting in the grass.

"What's his name?" I watched as Christina helped her brother stand on wobbly legs.

"Carlos." His attention went back to Christina as he sat Justin on his feet. "Be careful with him."

I looked over in time to see Christina supporting the baby under his arms as he tried to take a step.

"How old is he?"

"Seven months, I think."

Seven months? Had it been that long since I last saw Kelli when she was pregnant with him? Man, time flew.

I studied the yard. "Where is their father? He didn't come for dinner?"

Trevon let out a false laugh. "The hell if I know. He's probably at home with his new wife, I'm sorry, girlfriend…that's if he isn't cheating on her."

My head whipped around. "Say what?"

Trevon grabbed the ball he had tossed back and forth with the kids and sent it flying across the yard. Sugar ran for it. "Alonso left Kelli and the kids high and dry, right after she had Carlos." He shook his head. "It's a shame what he's put her through."

My eyes widened. "She's divorced?"

"Almost. The paperwork's been filed, but they're having issues about custody and housing. It's a shame because she did so much to help him get where he is in his career. And what does he do, leave her to foot the bill, literally, and goes to start a whole new life. She's lost nearly everything."

"Damn." My attention went to the kitchen window; Kelli was looking my way. Our eyes met for a moment, then she walked away.

"The worst part of it is, he moved out and left her the house, but he didn't pay the mortgage. He let it go into foreclosure. Kelli didn't make enough to keep it. Now they live with us while she gets back on her feet."

My brow creased as I shook my head.

"Hey guys, it's time to eat!"

Kelli stood in the doorway, wiping her hands on a towel. Once again, our eyes met, but this time, she turned away before our gazes truly connected.

****

"This has got to be the best meatloaf I've ever had…well, not as good as my mom's, but it's a close second." I forked another helping and savored the juices that pooled on my tongue.

"Thanks." Kelli didn't look my way, but instead she spooned some type of mashed baby food into Carlos's open mouth.

"If there's one thing Kelli's good at, it's cooking," Kai said, then reached across the table to get what had to be her third serving.

Damn, she could eat. Then again, I guess that's what a baby would do to a woman's body. I kept my shudder internal. As beautiful as Kai was, the whole pregnant woman thing was something I just couldn't understand.

Across the table, Trevon watched her with love in his eyes. I chuckled. It had to be true love to watch an attractive woman go from sex goddess to baby maker.

My gaze went back and forth between the two of them. Did they still have sex? If so, how?

I shuddered, forcing the unexpected and unwanted image from my head.

Across the table, Carlos sputtered, sending baby food flying onto Kelli. Justin and Christina laughed; Kelli sighed, frustration on her face as she looked down at her shirt. A sickly combination of yellow and green decorated her rainbow colored top and stood out like a sore thumb.

"So, how long are you going to be in town?" Kai asked around a mouthful of food.

"It depends on the job. Right now, my plan is to get in and see how this company works. I can't lie; it's been years since I worked under someone. I'm used to being the Foreman who reported to only one man, my father. Now, I'm the new guy in the company, and I'm black. The construction industry has several levels. Most work goes to Hispanics because they are willing to work for pennies. Somewhere in the mix are the Blacks…if you've got the skills. Above all that, it's nothing but the Good Ol' Boys. Company's owned by families who promote from within. Whether or not they have the skills means nothing."

"What about companies owned by African-Americans, like your family had?" Trevon reached for a second helping of mashed potatoes.

"We," I gestured in-between us, "can't seem to work with one another without stabbing each other in the back. The first job I took before leaving home was with a black owned company, one similar to my family's." I shook my head. "I didn't last a week."

"Couldn't get the job done on time?" The smartass comment came from Kelli's side of the table.

My eyes narrowed. Nearly a year had gone by since our first knock down drag out argument about the scheduling changes that had to be made for the job I did for Trevon. Man, this woman didn't know how to let go.

"Oh, I know how to do my job, never doubt that. But when you're better than the boss's son…"

"Back stabbing begins," Trevon said around a fork full of food.

"Exactly."

"So, where are you staying?" Done eating, Kai sat back from the table and rubbed her belly.

"For now, at an extended stay hotel. If things work out, I'll look for an apartment and make the move to Georgia permanent."

"Extended stay hotel?" Kai shook her head in disapproval. "That's a waste of money. If you need a place to stay, you can stay here." She looked over at Trevon who nodded.

"It's not a bad idea, but where? Kelli's got the spare bedroom and the other's for the baby."

"He can have the baby's room. I mean we haven't decorated it yet and I've got two months left before the baby's even born. Besides, our bundle of joy will be sleeping in a bassinet in our room for the first couple of months. Derrick is family. In my family, you help one another." She looked over at Kelli, whose face had turned a few shades red. "Did I mention the benefits?"

My brow went up. "Benefits?"

"Home cooked food and friendship. Can't go wrong with that." Kai grinned.

I risked a glance in Kai's direction. While the offer was tempting, the last thing I wanted to do was infringe on my best friend and his wife as they prepared to welcome their first child into the world. As it was, the house already had its fill of unexpected guests, Kelli and her two kids.

Kelli.

The idea of seeing her on a day-to-day basis was tempting, especially since she was now single.

Laughter erupted from the end of the table where Justin and Christina sat. The giggle fest sent little Carlos into a fit of excitement. He banged the table with his hands and spit more food onto her shirt. She groaned again.

Then again, Kelli was a mother. No matter how much I found her to be attractive, a relationship with someone who had kids was not my speed, especially young ones.

“Thanks for the invitation. I’ll kick it up the road for now, but if things change, I might take you up on that offer.”

About the Author

M.J. Kane stumbled into writing. An avid reader, this stay at home mom never lost the overactive imagination of an only child. As an adult she made up stories, though never shared them, to keep herself entertained. It wasn't until surviving a traumatic medical incident in 2006 that she found a reason to let the characters inhabiting her imagination free. Upon the suggestion of her husband, she commandeered his laptop and allowed the characters to take life. It was that, or look over her shoulder for men caring a purple straitjacket. And the rest, as they say, is history.

No longer a television addict, if M.J. isn't reading a book by one of her favorite authors, she's battling with her creative muse to balance writing and being a wife and mother. She resides in the suburbs of Atlanta, Georgia with her high school sweetheart, four wonderful children, and two pit bulls. MJ can often be found hanging out at the local library where she is director of a local writer's group, or online connecting with readers and other authors. Other activities she enjoys include: creating custom floral arrangements, assisting her children in their creative pursuits of music and art, and supporting her husband's music production business, 3D Sounds.

Also by M.J. Kane
Available at
http://www.5princebooks.com/mjkane.html
A Heart Not Easily Broken
Jaded
Lonely Heart

Also available from 5 Prince Publishing
www.5princebooks.com
~~~

A Secret to Keep *Railyn Stone*
The Three Wives of Adam Monroe *Bernadette Marie*
How to find Happiness *Lindsay Harper*
The Dacque Chronicles *Doug Simpson*
Redemption Series *Melynda Price*
An Everlasting Heart Series *Sara Barnard*
Fatal Obsession *Christina OW*
The Doom of Undal *Katrina Sisowath*
The Escape Clause *Bernadette Marie*
Permanent Spring Showers *Scott Southard*
Reasons to Stay *Lisa Hobman*
Reasons to Leave *Lisa Hobman*
The Lost *Bernadette Marie*
Betrayed by the Ocean *Christine Steendam*
Love Finds its Way *Wilhelmina Stolen*
The Paper Masque *Jessica Dall*
The Silver Unicorn *Wayne Orr*
Lessons From a Two Year Old *Pete Abela*
Christmas Presence *Lisa J Hobman*
The Christmas Tree Guy *Railyn Stone*
The Calling *Jim Hanley*
The Merger *Bernadette Marie*
Braving the Darkness *Melynda Price*
How to Have a Happy Marriage *Lindsay Harper*
The Three Mrs. Monroes- Vivian *Bernadette Marie*
A Gift For Chloe- *Susan Lohrer*
The Three Mrs. Monroes- Penelope *Bernadette Marie*
Bridge of Hope *Lisa Hobman*
The Painted Room *Pete Abela*
The Three Mrs. Monroes- Amelia *Bernadette Marie*
Lilac Lane *Ann Swann*
~~~

CPSIA information can be obtained at www.ICGtesting.com
Printed in the USA
BVOW05s0440270715

410491BV00003B/4/P

9 781631 121203